Beneath the Grove

Maddie Castle

Book 7

L.T. Ryan

with
C.R. Gray

For information contact:

contact@ltryan.com

https://LTRyan.com

https://www.instagram.com/ltryanauthor/

https://www.facebook.com/LTRyanAuthor

The Maddie Castle Series

The Handler

Tracking Justice

Hunting Grounds

Vanished Trails

Smoldering Lies

Field of Bones

Beneath the Grove

Disappearing Act

Want a free copy of the Maddie Castle prequel novella? Sign up for my newsletter and download a copy today:

https://liquidmind.media/maddie-castle-newsletter-signup-1/

Chapter 1

It wouldn't happen again.

Phoenix wouldn't *let* it happen again.

The pink hand-knitted cardigan offered him no protection from tonight's fierce breeze, despite the fire that'd been burning in his chest all afternoon. Ever since he'd caught sight of her on the porch with Bronwyn, that fire ignited and burned hotter.

Every second he watched them through the window, the blaze intensified. Jasmine stood before the one at the corner on the second story, staring at the mountains in the distance. Her long hair floated around her bare body like a curtain.

That wrinkly old man stood behind her. He wore the same paisley printed robe he'd had for years. The warmest of smiles rested across his lips, eyes shut in bliss.

Until now, Phoenix had only taken a few glances through the window. He hadn't wanted to see what had gone on in that bed. Once it was over, when the noises stopped, that's when he fixed his gaze on that pane of glass, letting it linger there for at least a hundred cricket chirps.

He could've sat inside his tent. Probably would've been a better move. Less chance of someone seeing him spy.

Maybe he wanted to get caught. Maybe Phoenix wanted to fight him. Maybe he wanted to spit in that bastard's face.

He certainly couldn't sleep. He had tried this afternoon after his high had worn off, but those flames were like a forest fire, engulfing him faster and faster. If there'd been a sheet of drywall nearby, he would've pounded a fist through it.

Not because that would have helped anything. Just because that's what he always saw angry men do.

Jasmine and Bronwyn shared one more kiss at the window. When she spun around, Phoenix saw more of her than he wanted to. Only then did he look away for a moment. As he looked back up, the light clicked off.

Thank Gods. It would work. The plan he'd been mustering all afternoon would work.

A few heartbeats later, the front door of the farmhouse creaked open. Wearing one of the kimonos she always wore at this hour, Jasmine walked through its threshold and down the steps.

Every night, when she was done with Bronwyn—or rather when Bronwyn was done with her—Jasmine came outside, walked around the house, sat at the old wooden bench by the cellar door, smoked a joint, and stared at the moon. She would sit there for at least half an hour. That would be enough time.

When she made it there, settling in her usual spot, Phoenix stood. Dew-dampened grass caught on the ankles of his flowing drop-crotch pants as he trekked around the house. The dampness annoyed him, but he'd gotten used to it. He had lived outdoors for more years than he remembered now.

But she didn't have to.

Peeking his head around the corner, Phoenix gave a smile. "Boo."

"I saw you." Jasmine laughed, then grimaced at the crimson slice on her lip. "What are you still doing up?"

"Pondering life's greatest questions." Hands perched on his hips, Phoenix tilted his head back to absorb the rays of the moon. "Are ticks really a necessary part of the ecosystem, or should we find a way to eradicate them?"

She held the joint out to him. "Did you get bit again?"

"Pretty sure I didn't get the head out either." Accepting the joint, he leaned against the house. "How's your night going?"

She spared him a glance, and Phoenix braced for that to be all he received. But she looked up at the stars and said, "Very nice."

"And your morning?" He gestured to the wrist she kept close to her body, covered by the kimono.

Jasmine shot him a look and turned back to the sky.

Maybe not the best way to address it. But what would be?

He sat beside her on the bench, ignoring the moisture creeping through his pants to his ass. "Are you okay?"

"I'm fine." Yet, she wouldn't look at him.

"No." He held the joint before her. Only then did their eyes meet. No wonder she had looked away. Those pretty blues were full of tears. "You're not."

"Don't." She held the burning herbs to her lips. "Just don't, Phoenix."

"I care about him." Phoenix lowered his voice, leaning closer to his friend. "I care about Ophelia, and I care about you. Out of the three, I care about you the most."

"That's stupid." Jasmine's puff of smoke blurred her face. "They matter more than I do."

His heart dropped into his stomach. Was he too late? Lily had said the same thing. That she was here for a purpose, and hers was smaller than Bronwyn's.

She hadn't listened either.

Phoenix grabbed Jasmine's face and forced her to look at him. A tear escaped as soon as their eyes met, and he thumbed it away. "Never say that again."

"There's a bigger picture, Phoenix." She swatted him away. "We're in it, but the project is the sun, and we're just stars."

"Bullshit." Phoenix kept his voice quiet, but not soft. "There's no way you believe that."

A moment of silence. "I believe that we're working toward a larger goal—"

"And that makes *this* okay?" Phoenix touched her wrist, barely more than a tap. She jolted and swallowed down a yelp. "No. We both know it doesn't."

"You just say that because you don't understand yet—"

"And I'm never going to." The fire had moved from Phoenix's chest into his eyes. "Whatever he's working on, there's a reason he hasn't shown it to me. Because he knows no matter what it is, if these are the means, they don't justify the end."

Jasmine's lip quivered, and she looked away.

Phoenix took her hand, the one that wasn't injured, and closed his palms around it. The action wasn't romantic. Jasmine knew that as well as he did. After all, she didn't have the parts he required.

It was meant to be kind, soothing, and it seemed to do its job. The tears came down heavier, but she squeezed his hand back. Hardly above a whisper, Phoenix said, "You have to go."

She frowned. "Even if I wanted to, my car's boxed in, and he has the keys—"

"I've already figured it out." He stayed quieter than the crickets in the distance. He knew he had to. "But we have to go, right now."

Jasmine's frown deepened. "Are you coming with me?"

No. He couldn't.

Phoenix had faced worse than Bronwyn. His father made that man look like a God. Of all people, Phoenix could handle him.

But could Ophelia? Could Starlight and Raven? All the girls here, the ones who would come next. Could they handle that son of a bitch without Phoenix?

No. Even while he was here, he couldn't stop that bastard. Not every time. But enough. His presence here may not have been a cure all, but it lessened the harm. That made it worthwhile for him to stay.

And Phoenix wasn't like Jasmine anyway. She had somewhere to go. He didn't.

"You've got so many people who want you home." Phoenix frowned. "Your brother. Your ex. Your mom. You've got a degree, and job possibilities, and a whole life waiting on you."

"So that's a no?" Jasmine asked.

"Not a forever no." He gave a half smile. "It's just different for me. I'm not in the same danger here that you are."

"I'm not in danger—"

"Then what the hell was that?" He pointed to her wrist, then her lip. "If that's not danger, what is it?"

She frowned at him, then looked back up at the stars.

"A lot of us would kill for what you have," Phoenix whispered. "So many people out there, in the real world, care about you. They'd bend over backwards for you. Most of us don't have that. Eventually, I'll get out of here, but I've got time to kill. The more time you spend here, the worse it's going to get for you."

"I'm well aware of the privilege I had." She shot him a look. "But that doesn't matter anymore. It doesn't matter *here*. We have a mission—"

"Of course it matters."

What Phoenix meant was that her privilege mattered more to Bronwyn than she could understand.

Of all the girls here, he'd always picked ones like Jasmine. Starlight and Raven had come from backgrounds similar to Pheonix's. Messy. Chaotic. They were low hanging fruit. Easily, he could scoop them up and they could be the new light of his world, and him, theirs.

But he didn't pick low hanging fruit. He chose women like Jasmine. Strong. Opinionated. Smart.

As much as he loved the other girls here, most of them couldn't be described that way. Not because they were incapable of becoming strong or opinionated or smart, but because life hadn't granted them the opportunities to.

Phoenix had his theories. He suspected Bronwyn got off on knocking girls like Jasmine down a few notches. Like part of his sick, twisted game was to humiliate and defile the women most likely to take him down.

But he couldn't say that out loud. That would just make Jasmine defensive. Instead, he rebutted her other point. "How you feel matters. Your safety matters. *You* matter."

Another tear dripped over the edge of her eye.

"If this mission is as important as you believe it is, as he's told you it is," Phoenix whispered, holding her hand tighter, "then the gods will let it come to fruition. Regardless of whether you're here."

A hard swallow bobbed her throat. "It's not much better on the outside, you know. My family looks perfect, but it's not. At least here, I feel better."

"Because here, you have support. It's not because of him, and we both know it." Phoenix glanced up at the second-story window. Nothing shone through the darkness. "You can find that outside. Support, I mean. Your brother, he always supported you, didn't he?"

Nibbling her bottom lip, she shrugged. "I guess, yeah. But my mom, and my fiancé—"

"Tell them both to go to hell." Phoenix huffed. "Screw them. Don't go back to that piece of shit, and cut your mom off if you have to. But if you left right now, and you showed at your brother's door, he'd let you in, wouldn't he?"

"Yeah." Jasmine rubbed her shoulder against her face, wiping up her tears. "But I don't want to cut my mom off. Not really. I wish she cared more than she does, but I do miss her."

"Then show up at her door." Or her brother's, or the door of an old friend from high school. Phoenix didn't care. It didn't matter where she went. It only mattered that she left Willow Grove.

Because some never did.

Jasmine let out a dry laugh. "I don't know if she'd open it."

"But your brother would."

Taking one last hit off the joint, she tilted her head back and looked at the stars. As she exhaled, she tossed the butt to the soil. "Yeah. He would."

"Then you've got something waiting for you." He squeezed her hand. "If you stay, it's gonna happen again. And it will be worse."

She frowned at him. "He was just upset. He promised—"

"I've seen this before." Phoenix was all but begging now. "You're the seventh one, just since I've been here. And I have no idea where the others went. One day they were here, and then they were gone."

"What?" Jasmine's brows scrunched down. "What do you mean?"

"Every few months, maybe once a year, a new girl shows, and Bronwyn likes her. Right before you came, it was Lily. She was around your age, kinda looked like you. Really smart. Had some degree in chemistry." Chills erupted over Pheonix's arms, and he shuddered at the memory. "She hid the bruises at first. Like the girls before her did. Then I was walking one night, and I heard her screaming, and I heard him yelling, and—" A sharp breath cut him off. "I got in the middle of it, but she told me to go. And then, the next day, she was gone. Just *gone*, Jasmine. But I watched that parking lot all night, and her car never left. Neither did any others."

For a few heartbeats, Jasmine's face stayed screwed up in confusion. Then she frowned. "You think he killed her?"

Why that was a stretch to her imagination after he'd broken her arm this afternoon, Phoenix would never understand. "I think he uses girls like you. One day, you matter to him. One day, you're the savior of this mission he's on. And the next, you're gone. You're a vague memory that we're not allowed to talk about, not even allowed to remember."

A greenish tinge touched Jasmine's cheeks. "You're not screwing with me?"

"No." Phoenix's voice trembled. "No, I'm not. I'm just trying to help you before it's too late."

A long moment of silence passed. They stared into one another's eyes, and Phoenix prayed. He prayed and prayed and prayed. He wasn't even sure who he was praying to.

Phoenix wasn't like the others here. Maybe he believed in something bigger than himself. Maybe he believed in nothing at all.

But on the chance that the others were right, he prayed to any god who would listen.

Please. Help me get her out of here.

"You have keys?" Jasmine whispered.

Phoenix's heart skipped with excitement. Relief loosened his shoulders. "And a full tank of gas."

Her hand quivered in his. But she nodded. "Okay. I'll go."

Chapter 2

Was there a word in the English dictionary for this?

Half a dozen feet ahead on the long lead, Tempest pressed her nose to the ground. Butt perched high in the air, her tail wagged like the blade of a windmill. A bright pink flower swayed in the breeze beneath her. Atop its bud, a blue and black butterfly slowly raised and lowered its wings.

She tilted her head to the left, then the right, jaws chomping periodically. Not with aggression. The little creature bewildered Tempest for whatever reason. If a stinkbug buzzed through our living room, or a fly banged repeatedly off the window, she'd run back and forth through the house chasing it. The butterfly, however, only enchanted her.

Maybe that's what this was. Enchantment.

Enchantment tied up with something else. I didn't know what it was, only that it thickened the back of my throat.

On a trail almost identical to this one, just as the summer heat calmed to a warm breeze, two years ago nearly to the day, Bear had done the same thing. He hated the flies and stinkbugs, but butterflies fascinated him. When one sat still for long enough, and he could observe it, that was all he did. He observed, cocking his head to the left and right, chomping his jaws, trying to engage the little creature in play.

Bear and Tempest were siblings from separate litters. Their similarities were abundant. Everything from their shiny black coat, to their warm brown eyes, to the way they carried themselves. Most of the time, I would look at her and think of him, and my heart would warm. Moments like this, though, when they were all too similar, when Tempest was a damn near indiscernible imposter, I just wished he were here too.

He was the kind of dog that I could've let off leash on this trail. Tempest had her long lead, and that was as much as she would get. It was easy to imagine her tailing right behind him, though. Would the two of them bicker about who got to sit closest to the butterfly? Bear had been such a gentleman, he would've given it up for his little sister.

If he were still around, those confidence-building techniques I had done with her for the last year would've been half as valuable. Just his presence would have improved her behavior. Like all things, dogs learned by example. Bear would have been the greatest example.

But he was gone.

That tightness in my chest only grew, remembering that one day, I wouldn't have Tempest either.

So many things in life were that way. Supposed we had to be grateful for the things we had while we had them. Just as Tempest smiled ear to ear as the butterfly took flight from the flower bud. It fluttered a foot off the ground, and then another, and I braced for Tempest to run the length of her lead to chase it.

She sat instead. With that same enchantment in her eyes, she panted and watched as it floated away.

Maybe I could learn a thing or two from her example.

My phone dinged in my pocket. When I fished it out, an unfamiliar number flashed across the screen. Not uncommon in my line of work.

Beneath the Grove

The message read, *Hey, Maddie. It's Daisy. I hope it's okay that Grace gave me your number. (Finally got my own phone again, thank god!) We're on our way to their place now. I was hoping we could hang out tonight if you're not busy? No worries if you are!*

Daisy and I had spoken a dozen times since we'd gotten her out of captivity. I'd rushed home after finding out she was safe, but her recovery in the hospital hadn't been a quick one.

I couldn't call the two of us friends yet. But I liked her, and it seemed that she liked me. Considering we'd be neighbors for the fore-seeable future, and that she mattered so much to Grace and Bentley, I wanted to get to know her better.

She also had a blunt but friendly nature that I appreciated.

I texted back, *Of course it's okay! And nope, not busy. Just come over whenever.*

"Come on, Tempy." Clapping my hands together, I gestured up the trail. "We don't have much daylight left."

She hopped up on all fours and galloped onward.

This trail was a few miles long, spanning through the woods behind the trailer park. Because of its proximity to home, it had been my favorite place to walk lately. Especially at this time a year. The soil underfoot was damp from early autumn rainfall. All the greenery left and right of us was still in full bloom, albeit thinner than it had been a week ago.

Jogging wasn't the easiest on my knee, but getting home by dark was ideal. Going uphill was less painful overall. My heavy breaths disagreed, but the incline was smoother than walking the flat or downhill roads of the trailer park. Something in the upward motion allowed me to stretch out those joints in a way that I couldn't on other trails. Soil also made for a softer impact than gravel or concrete.

There was the added bonus, of course, that I didn't have to interact with any of my neighbors when I walked back here.

Halfway up the hill, struggling to keep up with Tempest, my phone rang in my walking belt. Over the pounding of my heart in my ears, I was surprised I heard it. As I slowed my pace, I eyed an old log off to the left.

"Wait, Tempy." I fished for my phone and sat on the old moss-covered wood. "Mommy needs a break."

Pants as heavy as mine, she plopped down before the log.

The area code that flashed across the screen was familiar, but not the number. I slid the green bar. "Hello?"

"Hi, um, yes." A woman's voice. "Is this Maddie Castle?"

"It sure is." I stretched the phone away from my face so she wouldn't hear each gasping breath. "Sorry, I'm walking my dog. Can I ask who's calling?"

"Yeah, of course. I'm sorry. I probably should've texted, or sent an email, I just—" She took in a deep breath as well. If I didn't know better, I would've thought she was on a run too. "That's not what you asked. Sorry. My name's Debbie. Debbie Armstrong."

"Nice to meet you, Debbie." Water bottle from my belt in hand, I popped open the collapsible water dish I kept clipped to me for Tempest. "Are you calling for an investigation consult?"

"I am, yes." Another deep breath, this one more relaxed than the last. "I'm sorry. The guy who gave me your number. He didn't explain how all this goes. I looked for a website, but I couldn't find one, and he had given me your number, so I just thought it would be okay to call, and—"

"It's a hundred percent okay that you called." Chuckling, I held the bowl of water out for Tempest. She slurped it all up, no care for the splashes that landed on my feet. "Who gave you my number?"

"Ethan Lambert, I think? I could have gotten it wrong, if I'm being honest." Papers rustled in the background. "He said you guys used to work together?"

Yeah, I remembered Lambert. We'd been in the police academy together. He wasn't my favorite person in the Pittsburgh PD, but I didn't have any negative feelings about him either. He always seemed like a nice enough guy. "Lambert, yeah."

"He's married to my cousin's daughter," Debbie explained. "And

I already talked to everyone I could get on the phone at the police department. But everybody keeps saying there's nothing they can do. And I know they're probably right, but I can't do nothing. I've been doing nothing for too long, and I have to do something. I have to—Oh my God, I'm sorry. Tell me to shut up. I'm a rambler. I try not to be, but when I'm nervous, I ramble, and I don't know how to stop."

"I can relate." Shaking the leftover drops out of the water bowl, I collapsed it and clicked it back to my belt. "Let's start at the beginning then. What do you want me to investigate, ma'am?"

"A business, I guess?" Some more papers rustled in the background. "Maybe? I don't even know if I would call them a business. It's about my daughter, though. She's connected to them, and—" Another sharp breath. "She started working with these people, and now she's lost. She's just... lost."

"She's missing?"

"No. Not physically. I know where she is. But she's not there anymore." I could practically hear the woman rubbing her temples and massaging her eyes. "Mentally, she's not right, and she hasn't been since she started working with these people."

Cocking my head, I searched for a follow-up question. I couldn't think of any. "I'm sorry, ma'am, I'm not sure I understand."

"Of course you don't. Because this sounds like gibberish. I'm sorry." A long pause. "My daughter Jasmine graduated from Columbia two years ago. She has a whole life ahead of her. But something happened earlier this year. I don't know how she got in touch with these people. I don't know what they've done to her, but it's like they put a spell on her or something. And I know how crazy that sounds. But I can't wrap my head around how much she's changed. She's an entirely different person. And not in a 'young adult finding themselves' kind of way. She's different. She's not right. When she calls me—which is rare anymore—it's like somebody's holding a gun to her head and telling her what to say."

Still confused, I asked the only question I could think of. "Do you think someone is? Holding a gun to her head?"

"I don't know. Maybe. I don't know much of anything, and that's what's so strange. She and I have been close her whole life. When she was a teenager, she went through a bit of the usual angst, but that got better when she went to college. She texted me all day, throughout the day. She called me almost every night. Her brother, he decided to go to college in New York too. The two of them hung out every weekend. She had a nice boyfriend, and they decided that they were going to move back here after she graduated. They did. He asked for my permission to marry her, and he proposed, and they were so happy. Everything was perfect. And then she took this job, and she called off the engagement, she got rid of her phone, sold all her belongings, and moved to this farm in the middle of nowhere. Now, I'm lucky if I hear from her once a month. And the last time she called, something just... wasn't right."

Far from my usual case. But it had my brows rising and the gears in my mind turning. Those were my favorite kinds of cases.

"What do you mean by that?" I clicked the phone onto speaker and started jotting notes down in a separate app. "That something wasn't right? Aside from the obvious that everything changed for her. What about this specific call made you want to reach out?"

"I'm a family medicine doctor," Debbie said. "It's not that I have a lot of experience in psychology, but I did have to do a psych rotation to get my doctorate. Jasmine has said a couple of things over the last few months that were concerning, but it was the way that she said it this time. Like she was a robot or something. Like someone in deep psychosis."

"Does Jasmine have a history of psychotic episodes?"

"No, not at all. When her dad died, she did a little bit of grief counseling. For a few months, she was on antidepressants, but who isn't these days?" Debbie asked. "She only needed them for a year or so, and then she weaned herself down. Under the supervision of her primary care, of course. That was her freshman year, so, five years ago now? It looked like when she graduated, she was gonna have a perfectly normal, happy life. Then, after this last year, everything just changed. And that last call, I guess she did say something. Something that made me think I had to ask for help."

"What's that?"

"That the end was coming." Debbie's voice was quieter, puzzled. "And that maybe we would see each other again then."

"The end," I repeated, "as in, end of the world? Or end of her life?"

A long moment of silence. "I don't know. She hung up before I could ask any more questions."

Suffice it to say, my interest was piqued. "Well, I understand why the cops told you they couldn't help. But I might be able to at least find out more information about these people she's working with. Can you send me the name of the business, your daughter's full name, and links to her social media accounts? I'll start going through everything, looking for information, but I'd also like to meet in person. When are you free?"

"Anytime you are." Debbie's sigh of relief echoed through the speaker. "I'll move things around. Thank you. Thank you so much."

Chapter 3

The text from Debbie came in a moment or two later. For the rest of my walk, I flipped through the links in her message, occasionally looking up from the screen to make sure I didn't walk into a tree. Social media wouldn't load, so I focused on the business Jasmine worked for.

Willow Grove

A Simpler Life

I typed it into a Google search and clicked on the first result. The website resembled the Etsy page of a twenty-something-year-old trying to make a career out of their passion for crafting. Not to say that it was poorly done. All the photos were professional grade, their quality crisp and lighting full of depth. Navigating the site itself was seamless. But the products advertised were handmade, cheesy, and gimmicky.

They sold all kinds of things, from handcrafted soap and essential oils marketed as locally sourced and organic, to handmade pottery and ceramics, even some decor and furniture pieces. One of their best sellers was a massive dream catcher. I rolled my eyes at that.

There was nothing wrong with a dream catcher on its own, nor handcrafted soap or essential oils. But the founders featured on the

About section of the website were a middle-aged white couple. Didn't seem like their place to mass produce and profit off an item so sacred to Native Americans.

I went back to their products, scrolling past the white sage to a listing for healing crystals. Apparently, wearing rose quartz would heal my chronic pain. And the fermented sauerkraut—handmade on their farm—would do far more than help my gut health. Because the gut was the root of all problems, if I healed my gut, it would reduce inflammation and heal any and all pain all over my body.

People like these pissed me off. Of course, natural medicine had a place. Obviously, sauerkraut was healthy for most people. It was true that some rocks had therapeutic effects. Lithium, for instance, was an antipsychotic sourced from the element lithium itself.

But that was just it. Natural medicines that worked became regular medicine.

Each product on Willow Grove's site came with a carefully worded tagline. Beside the sauerkraut was, "The corporations don't, but we care about your feedback. Email us with any questions or concerns about your order, and we'll get back to you in no time!"

People like me, who've lived with pain every day for years, had tried Western medicine. We wound up either zombified and addicted or in the same state we'd been in before walking into the doctor's office. In pain. It made sense that people who paid hundreds or thousands of dollars a month for healthcare would seek out alternative healing when doctors offered no help and didn't care about the constant pain we suffered.

But Willow Grove didn't either. They just knew how to act like they did. These assholes did the same thing as the corporations, with a few ambiguous niceties. They offered a miracle cure in the form of polished rocks and fermented cabbage, sold at the reasonable price of $59.99, only to profit from the placebo effect. They were predators who preyed on the wounded.

I resented people like this as much as I resented the pharmaceutical and insurance companies. At least we all knew the corporations were slimy bastards. People like this pretended they weren't.

I hated a money hungry asshole in a suit as much as I hated a money hungry asshole in mandala-covered harem pants.

So immersed in the products shown on the website, I stumbled over a rock. Once I recovered, I headed back to that *About* page.

The middle-aged couple was attractive enough, but just their photo had me cringing. The man wore a flowy white shirt with a v-neck, exposing a chest of graying black hair. It matched the thinning hair on his head, pulled back in a man bun. Vividly colored harem pants flowed around his legs. The woman wore a similar style shirt, though hers was green. Her skirt was floor length, a similar pattern to his, but rainbow colored. It was her hair that had me groaning. The graying strands were teased into tight locs. A middle-aged white lady with dreads—what more needed to be said?

The headline read, ***Our Story.***

Ophelia and Bronwyn started out just like everyone else. They grew up in the suburbs outside of Philly, fell in love in high school, and headed into the workforce in their twenties. Ophelia was a travel agent, and Bronwyn was an insurance agent with a big company. Once they had their little box that looked just like everyone else's, they decided it was time to have a family.

But after years of trying, seven angel babies, and thousands of fertility treatments, they started to rethink everything. What was the purpose in all this? Why were the suburbs their goal? When would the hustle and bustle end? As much as they wanted a family, what was the purpose if they never got to see one another anyway?

Between the long hours, the poison they fueled their bodies with, all the drugs the doctors pumped into Ophelia, as worn down as they were by the hustle and bustle of modern living, they couldn't find the meaning in the lives they were leading. What they wanted was more time together. The most fun they had in their life was in one another's company. Their weekend hiking trips in the Appalachian Mountains were the only time they felt fulfilled.

Beneath the Grove

One day, as they were driving home from their weekly hike, a sign caught their eye. Five-hundred acres for sale, only a handful of miles from their favorite place in all the world.

After nearly a decade of questioning their entire lives, they decided it was time for a change. They sold their home, bought the land, and Willow Grove was born.

Twenty years later, they haven't looked back.

Is the hustle and bustle of modern living tearing at your soul like it was Ophelia's and Bronwyn's? Fill out the form below. Let's get in touch.

Below the contact form they'd embedded a slideshow with pictures that resembled paradise. Rolling farmland, framed by rich green trees. Home-cooked meals on an old wooden table, illuminated only by candlelight. A twinkling lake with a boardwalk and gazebo situated in the middle of the water. Parties around campfires. Live music performed on patches of grass behind a barn.

Idyllic, to say the least. Sentiments almost everyone in the modern world could agree with. The hustle and bustle of modern living was exhausting. More times than I could count, I had critiqued the cookie-cutter homes in the suburbs. There was no denying how much I enjoyed making my own schedule and living on my own terms.

If this was how they recruited people to join their community—which I was now prepared to call a commune—it was easy to understand. The idea would attract any modern person, fed up with society's insistence that stress was a badge of honor and "the grind" was the key to respect.

But if Debbie hadn't heard from Jasmine and wouldn't be hearing from her until "the end," I didn't have many options if I wanted answers.

I scrolled back up and filled out the form.

It had been a while since I had done any undercover work, but the prospect of it this time had my heart drumming.

Just as I pressed submit, now only a dozen yards from my front door, a familiar voice called, "Hey, Maddie."

Bentley sat on the stairs. A sad smile stretched across his lips. He held a small bouquet of carnations and roses.

It had been almost three weeks since we'd been in the same room, and nearly a month since we'd had a conversation. The last detailed one had been in my car, the day we brought Daisy home from her captor's torture.

I'd learned he was secretly conveying details of the case to my father. The same man who'd abandoned me and served over twenty years in prison for manslaughter. Why did he kill that guy? Still had no idea.

But I did know he had killed Salvatore Deangelo, rather than letting the FBI catch the guy and put him in prison, only to give him the death penalty themselves. Now, why would my father have done that? I hoped his reasons were because that monster Deangelo had tortured and murdered over a hundred innocent young women over the last thirty years.

But I didn't know his reasoning. I *couldn't* know.

We'd only just rekindled our relationship. I barely knew the man. Until a month ago, I'd hoped we could make up for the decades we'd lost. Maybe we could be the normal happy family I'd always dreamed of. He hadn't gotten to be my father, but maybe one day, he could make up for that as a wonderful grandpa to the family I hoped to have eventually. Bentley and I had been together for a while—wasn't that what we were working toward?

The dream was just that. A dream.

Because not only had my father killed a man, but Bentley had helped him do it. Then hid it from me.

This wasn't the happy, normal family I'd dreamed of.

"Nope." I held Tempy's leash tighter when she pulled to get to Bentley. "I'm not doing this."

"I know you're upset—"

"If you were about to follow that up with a 'but,' you can shove it." I snapped for Tempest to return to my side. Her ears collapsed to her crown, but she did so. "You're blocking my door. Please move."

Frowning deeply, he laid the flowers on the stoop and stood. "You said we'd fight about it when we got home."

"If we fight about it right now, I'm gonna say some shit I'll regret." I brushed past him. At the foot of the steps, not so much as paying him a glance, I tugged Tempest's leash when she stopped before him. He crouched to pet her, but I said, "Come, Tempest."

Her ears flattened again, as if to say, *But I haven't seen him in forever, Mom. I missed him.*

Guilt pinched my chest, but I pushed that away.

"Really, Maddie?" Bentley grunted. "You're not even gonna let me pet her?"

"I have to work." Only a glance. "Sorry my life doesn't revolve around you."

"This is stupid and you know it."

So was conspiring to kill a man with my dad. "Oh, me having my own life, and my own job, and my own thoughts and feelings is stupid?"

Shoulders slumped, Bentley released a slow, careful exhale. "Alright. You want space right now, and I can respect that. But whenever you're ready to talk, I'm here, Maddie."

"Don't hold your breath," I said under my own.

"Daisy and Grace will be back soon though," he said behind me. "They went shopping, but they were asking about you. I didn't know what to say."

"They can come over whenever they want." A glare over my shoulder. "They didn't lie to me. You did."

"I didn't lie."

"A lie by omission is still a lie." He opened his mouth to rebut, but I spoke before he could. "We're not doing this right now. I have a case to work on. You need to fix up that guest room for Daisy. Give me the space you just said I could have, Bentley."

Clapping his mouth shut, he raised his arms in surrender.

Which loosened my tight jaw but stabbed something deep in my heart.

Maybe I was better off alone, because I hated navigating all these stupid feelings.

* * *

"WHAT ARE THE NAMES AGAIN?" DYLAN'S VOICE VIBRATED through the speakerphone.

"Ophelia and Bronwyn," I said, squinting at the about page displayed on my laptop. "Probably bullshit though."

"Yeah, since it sounds like something George R. R. Martin would've named his main characters," Dylan said. "That's all you've got? Ophelia and Bronwyn?"

"And the website I just sent you. The business is called Willow Grove. There should be a way to look up who owns it, right?"

"Right," he agreed. "But I don't understand. What are you looking for?"

Chewing my bottom lip, I swiped back and forth from the product listings to that *About* section on the website. Music played quietly from a speaker in my kitchen. A couple of lamps glowed on either end of my sofa. Tempest was curled up beside me, resting her chin on the edge of my keyboard.

"I don't know, man." Neck tense from staring at these webpages for so long, I kneaded my fingers over the back of it, wiggling out the knots. "The way Jasmine's mom talked about it just has me thinking something's up."

"From what I can see, they're new age hippies," Dylan said. "Who, yes, appropriate other cultures and sell nonsense health supplements, but that's a far cry from your usual serial killer cases. All their labels clearly state that none of their supplements are FDA tested. Morally ambiguous, sure, but everything here looks legal."

"I'm sure everything they sell is perfectly safe." For a reason I couldn't put into words, I just kept staring at that about page and chewing my lip. "New age hippies, sure, but doesn't something here look off?"

"All hippies look off to me, new age or otherwise."

"It's the wording they use." I read that closing paragraph again. "It's like their proselytizing."

"They very well could be, but there's nothing illegal about that either."

"I'm not saying they *are* doing anything illegal." Lightning flashed through the windows, followed by a thundering roar. As if mother nature herself had to argue my last statement. "I just—Can you find me their legal names? And the names of anyone you can tie to this place, this Willow Grove."

"You know I can," Dylan said. "I'll send you the invoice when I'm done."

"Don't know what I ever did without you."

"Probably wasted a lot of time." As I chuckled, he said, "Talk to you later," and ended the call.

Never was one for decorum.

Another flash of lightning brightened the windows. Tempest tensed. I pulled her in a little tighter and ran my fingers over her scalp. Bear never liked storms either. Unlike his sister, he always darted under my bed and stayed there until it passed. At least Tempy wanted to cuddle when she was scared.

Holding her closer, I reached down for a kiss. As I breathed in her scent, my phone buzzed with a text from Debbie.

Hey, Maddie. I can't get into Jasmine's Facebook to accept your friend request, but if you want to take a closer look at her posts, here's the login for my account. She and I are friends. I think you'll be able to see everything she's put on there from here.

That certainly made my job easier.

Hey, Debbie. Thanks so much. This will be a huge help. Are you able to meet tomorrow at noon?

Just as I finished logging into Facebook from Debbie's account, her reply arrived.

Yes, I can. My son and Jasmine's fiancé will be here as well. Here's my address and thank you!

I heart reacted to the message and turned back to the computer. In moments, my stomach was turning.

Debbie had left out a lot, to put it mildly.

Jasmine had begun her descent into the holistic lifestyle well before the start of this year. From what I could gather, it'd started in her senior year of high school, shortly after her father died.

Judging by all the pancreatic cancer awareness posts she shared, I had to assume that'd been how he'd passed. The photos told me the two of them had been close. He was in his late forties, early fifties, and always smiling. Until he got sick, anyway. Jasmine had written a long post about how he had gone to the doctor only two months before he died, and they told him everything was fine. Tacked onto that, she said they painted him as a hypochondriac. Shortly after, he was hospitalized, and his white blood cell count was through the roof.

That was it. Her turning point, when she'd stopped trusting medicine, despite having a doctor for a mother, and began a slow descent into a thousand other conspiracy theories.

One was that big pharma did have a cure for cancer, but kept it hidden so they could continue to profit on people's treatments. Another stated that the government sprayed chemicals into the environment to control the minds of the masses.

She also believed that essential oils could cure anything, whether it be a common cold or heart failure. For the last two years, leading up to when she joined Willow Grove, she shared daily photos of detox drinks she made that 'rid her body of toxins.' Weekly, she did a coffee enema—which, yes, she recorded and posted on the Internet for millions of strangers to see.

In another post, she and her mother argued about sunscreen. Jasmine insisted it was poison, that sunlight was a necessity for overall wellness. Debbie agreed. It produced vitamin D, boosted endorphins, and released all kinds of happy chemicals from the brain. But UV rays also caused skin cancer. Debbie made clear that was a fact, not an opinion, citing family friends who'd died from it. And even if that was true, zinc was the active ingredient in sunscreen, and an active ingredient in one of those detox drinks she had each morning. Why was a lotion with that ingredient any different?

Still, Jasmine argued. In her mind, skin cancer was a risk, but it was grossly exaggerated. Debbie asked why, and Jasmine explained that it was the government and big pharma's way of keeping people from the best medicine on earth. Nature itself.

Eventually, Debbie stopped arguing.

That's where it started, but not where it ended.

Somewhere along the way, she moved past a valid, rightful distrust of medicine into deeper, esoteric conspiracies. She believed in something called 5D consciousness, which meant that humanity was evolving to vibrate at a different frequency, one full of love and peace and awareness, that could only be reached through meditation and giving yourself over to the goddess. Which goddess, I didn't know. Because that's how these theories worked.

It was what separated a religion from a cult. There was no structure, heritage, or culture here. It started with a general distrust of society that shot Jasmine's common sense down a rabbit hole I feared she would never crawl out of.

But as Dylan said, there was nothing illegal here. People were allowed to hold their beliefs, no matter how ludicrous they seemed to the rest of us. Individual liberties allowed us to harm ourselves within reason.

Was it really Willow Grove that had brainwashed Jasmine? Or had they simply latched on to the brainwash she'd already embraced?

I jumped when another clap of thunder pelted the sky, and *knock, knock, knock!* sounded at my door.

Chapter 4

Two familiar faces greeted me on the other side of the door. A pair of big blue eyes, a warm smile, all while juggling a cooing baby on her hip and a bag of takeout in her free hand.

Daisy looked a hell of a lot better than she had last time we saw one another.

I offered to hold the bag of takeout and got Tempest into her cage before inviting Daisy inside. Tempest may or may not have been well behaved around a baby. I didn't know. She wasn't around babies often. So safe was better than sorry.

After the usual greetings, Daisy and I sat on my sofa. I started the conversation with, "How was your drive?"

"Longer than I expected," Daisy said, situating Bella comfortably on her lap. "Not nearly as long as all that rehab and physical therapy though, so I'm not complaining."

"They did have you admitted for a while, huh?" I lifted my legs onto the sofa and crisscrossed them beneath me. "I figured they would release you in a couple of days."

"They probably could've." Once she got the plastic bag of Chinese food open, she held up two paper wrapped utensils. "Chop sticks or fork?"

"Fork, preferably," I said. "But you didn't have to do this. I already ate, and—"

"You saved mine and my daughter's life. Least I can do is get you dinner." Daisy waved the fork in my face. "Eat. Please. I insist."

"Shouldn't you be saving your money?"

"I'm saving plenty, believe me. Grace started this crowdfunding thing for me, they raised a bunch of money, and I also got some direct offers from publishers about my story. I can afford to get you some damn Chinese." She tossed the fork into my lap. "I'm actually going to be super offended if you don't eat."

Raising my hands in surrender, my mouth watered at the smell of General Tso's wafting from her lap. "Fine. Fair enough. Thank you."

For that, I finally got a smile. She passed me a white container of fried rice and a plastic takeout bowl. "But, yeah, I think they were keeping me in the hospital so they could make sure I was safe while they're looking for Delu—Deangelo." She rolled her eyes. "Don't think I'm ever going to get used to saying that."

"You know how in movies, when someone catches someone else lying, they say, 'if that's even your real name?'" I asked. A dry, humorless laugh escaped Daisy, and I joined in. "Just wild that he lied about that too."

"Yeah, well." Adjusting the baby in her lap to make room for the buffet, Daisy ran her tongue along her teeth. "Safe to say that was the least awful thing he ever did."

"To put it mildly." There wasn't much else to follow that up with, so I took a bite of rice. "So, you got some offers from publishers?"

This time, her smile was genuine. "Big ones, yeah. I guess the story went viral. A bunch of true crime podcasters are making series about it. Which is kind of annoying? But it's like you said. Someone's gonna profit off what I went through. Why shouldn't I?"

"Can't argue with you there."

"They think it'll be easy to market, and it's already with an editor. I think they want me to expand on some things, edit some things out, and also add interviews and perceptions of law enforcement. So I might be asking you for a few quotes, if you don't mind."

"Not at all. Anything you need, let me know." Heart warm, I glanced at the cooing baby in her arms. "I'm just glad it worked out. It would've worked out better if it never happened, but it did, and you lived to tell the tale."

"Barely. But thank you for not losing hope. Grace told me that you were the one who found the poem, and that you convinced Bentley to okay the investigation, and—" Biting her lip, she raised her shoulders. "I'm really grateful. That's all."

"I just did what the cops should've. There's nothing to thank me for." Before she could offer a dozen more compliments, I chimed back in. "Where is she, anyway? Grace, I mean. I thought she'd be glued to your other hip."

"Oh, she has been." Daisy laughed, offering Bella a little spoonful of rice. As the baby gnawed on it, Daisy shook her head. "I don't mind though. I missed her like crazy. More than she could ever comprehend. It is crazy though. She was a little kid when I left, and now, she's a whole ass adult."

Between chews, I covered my mouth and said, "She sure thinks she is."

"We were all like that though." Daisy shrugged. "At least the worst she does is bully her dad. He doesn't deserve it, but it's better than drugs."

"It's a privilege she feels safe enough to do so." I swallowed down a bite of rice mixed with chicken and fragrant sauce. It was entirely worth the second dinner. "I never could've talked to my mom the way she talks to him. And I think that says something about parenting. If your kid feels safe enough to fight with you, to question you, to argue with you, I think you're doing something right."

"Yeah, I would've run away before I talked to my mom like she talks to him." Daisy wiped some slobber from her daughter's cheek. "Not looking forward to the days when you act like your Aunt Grace does, little missy."

"You've got plenty of time."

"Goes quick though. Feels like only yesterday when the line turned pink." She paused, shaking her head. "Anyway. Grace is helping Bentley set up the dresser we just got. The doctor didn't want me lifting anything with my back injury, not for a little while longer, and I mentioned wanting to talk to you, so Bentley suggested I come over. Grace said when they're done, she's gonna come over. She said something about kitchen sink cookies, if that's okay?"

"Of course he did," I said under my breath. "Yeah, that sounds good. I'd cut off a limb for one of those cookies."

Squinting, Daisy cocked her head to the side. "Of course he did what?"

"What?"

"You said, 'of course he did.'"

"No, I was saying, 'of course I'd be down for some cookies.'"

"Are you trying to gaslight me right now?" A half smile teased the corners of her lips. "Because I feel like you're trying to gaslight me into forgetting you said something about Bentley that you didn't mean to say out loud."

"Gaslight is a strong word." But yes, that's what I was trying to do. "I didn't realize I said anything else. That's all."

"Gonna go out on a limb then and say that you also didn't realize you hauled ass back home as soon as I was safe in the hospital?"

"I had a case." Which wasn't a lie.

"Was it a high-profile case?"

"Sorry." Scooping some rice between my lips, I shrugged. "Confidential."

"I call bullshit. There was no case."

"Call bullshit all you want, but it's the truth."

And it was. The day Daisy made it to the hospital, I got a call from a woman in Pittsburgh. She wanted to prove that her husband was having an affair so that she wouldn't get screwed in her divorce. Sure enough, he was having an affair, and I made sure she got *everything* in that divorce.

Daisy traced her tongue along her teeth, studying me. Eventually, she raised her hands in surrender. "Fine. Maybe you had a case."

"I did have a case."

"But that's not why you left."

No, it wasn't. I'd left Bentley, Grace, Daisy, and Bella in Lancaster because my work was done, and I hadn't wanted to be around Bentley. I was angry. There'd been dozens of cops around, even the FBI, and if I'd stayed, they would've picked up on my tension. They would've known I was upset about something. Maybe they'd glance at my phone when I left the room, and then they would learn the truth.

Not only had I revealed details of a high profile, ongoing investigation to my boyfriend, but he'd conspired to commit murder with my felon father.

To protect us all, I had to leave. The case was just an easy out.

But the confidence Daisy spoke with had my heart hammering.

"No?" Doing my best to remain stone-faced, I took a sip of my soda. "Why did I leave then?"

"Because you and Bentley got into a fight."

Good. The vague response was good. If she knew what me and Bentley were fighting about, she would've said it. She was just an emotionally attuned young woman who could snap two obvious puzzle pieces together.

That considered, I could play along.

"Something like that," I said. "My therapist says that I have a fearful avoidant attachment style. When I'm upset, I put up walls. That's all it was."

"Yeah?"

"Yep." Another bite of chicken. "This is really good. Where'd you get it?"

"I'm again going to have to call bullshit." Bella fussed in her lap. Daisy dug around in the diaper bag on the floor for her bottle. Once she had it properly positioned, she frowned at me. "Grace filled me in on you guys. You grew up together. You were best friends all your childhood. You reconnected a couple of decades later, fell in love, saw each other every day. Something small wouldn't have kept you apart for this long."

"You're right. Something small wouldn't. My career and you coming back from the dead did." I gave a teasing smile. "Everything went a little crazy for a while. That's all."

"So that's what it's about?" She squinted me over. "Me?"

"What?" My heart sunk, and my shoulders slumped with it. "No. God, no. It's not you. It has nothing to do with you."

"Well, the two of you were doing just fine before you came looking for me, so basic deduction skills tell me that I'm, at the very least, the common denominator. So if I said anything, or did anything, or if just the stress of the situation caused a rift between you guys, I'm sor—"

"Don't apologize to me." My mouth curved downward and I shook my head. "You didn't do anything wrong. None of this was your fault. What happened to you, what's going on with me and Bentley, it's not about you, Daisy. I'm so happy that you're back. For months, I wasn't sure if you were even alive, and in this line of work, there aren't always happy endings. I can't put into words how grateful I am that yours is. Please. Don't think that this has anything to do with you."

For a few heartbeats, she just studied me. Likely trying to figure out if I was being honest or only kind to stroke her ego. Apparently deciding the former was more likely, she just frowned back. "Then what is it?"

I couldn't stop the sigh that billowed from my nostrils.

"I'm sorry," she said. "I'm not trying to pry. It's just, ever since my sister died, Bentley's been miserable. He pretends not to be, but we know he is. And Grace said that changed with you. Not that you changed him, but just—I don't know. You make him happy. But he hasn't been happy. Since I've been back, it's just that same face he always wears. Like a mask. And Grace knows it has something to do with you, but she isn't sure what, and if it does have something to do with me, or if there's anything I can do to help, it's the least I can give you both."

As heartwarming as the sentiment was, it didn't change the fact. I couldn't promise that Bentley and I would be fine, because I wasn't sure if we would. I wasn't sure how I felt about our relationship now. All I could tell her was the truth.

"He kept something from me," I said. "Something big. And he has a history of doing that. When I first found out that you were missing, it was because I found an expunged case on his record. At first, I thought that maybe he had been involved with you—"

"Ew." She wrinkled her nose. "He was married to my sister. He's literally like a dad—"

"Yeah, of course. I know that now. But I didn't then. He'd never mentioned you, not once, until I gave him no choice. Then there was this other thing that happened, where he was keeping something big from me, and I just—" I took in a sharp breath. "It's not easy for me to be vulnerable. But when I am, like I've been with him, and that's not reciprocated, it hurts. And that's how I feel right now about the two of us. I'm hurt, and I need time to think about things. It's not about what happened to you, or the way things went down in Lancaster, or anything like that. I just need time right now."

Daisy stayed silent, studying me for a few heartbeats. She chewed on the side of her lip and nodded. "I can understand that. If you need time, he has to understand."

"Thank you. I appreciate that." And I did. I just hoped that Bentley understood my perspective when Daisy, inevitably, relayed everything I had just said.

"But don't you think you could at least get coffee and talk things through?" Her tone was soft, delicate. We were just getting to know one another, but she did fascinate me. Her demeanor was somehow a cross between abrasive and meek. "I mean, you don't have to work through everything, but maybe just communicate a little bit so he doesn't feel like he's being abandoned either?"

No. Like I said earlier, the conversation would only lead to me saying something I'd regret. I wasn't sure how I felt, or what I wanted, or where we would go from here. This wasn't a small disagreement. This was big. There were two roads before me, and I had to decide which one I wanted to walk.

"I wish I could commit to that," I said. "But I just started working on a really weird case. I think I'll have to go undercover to get any more information, so that's gonna keep my schedule packed for the foreseeable future."

"Really?" Now that Bella was sleeping in her arms, Daisy cozied up into the corner of the sofa and rested the warm plastic bowl atop the baby's side. Taking a bite, she cocked her head to the side. "How weird is it?"

"I'm not sure yet. It's this business called Willow Grove." Now that I had read more on it, I understood why Debbie had such a hard time describing what it was. "But I think it's more than that. I don't know for sure yet, but they invite people to join them. Like, live with them on their farm up in the mountains."

"As in, a hippie commune?"

"Honestly? I'm leaning more toward hippie cult," I said. "But I've never worked on a case like this before. It's all new territory. These are the same kind of people that think that 5G is poisoning us, so I don't know if I'll have my phone for a few days. Maybe a week. If they ever get back to me, anyway. If they don't, I'm gonna have to break and enter. Either way. I'm going to get started on this tomorrow, so I don't want to commit to anything else right now."

"I think I've heard of that place actually," Daisy murmured, cocking her head to the side as she swallowed a bite of rice. "They sell organic and holistic stuff, right?"

"Alongside pottery and home decor and crystals they claim will heal all ailments." I rolled my eyes. "Where did you hear about them?"

"Deangelo," she said, nodding slowly. "He ordered some stuff off the website a couple of times. He was all into that wellness culture shit. Not in the normal, wanting to be healthy way, but in a weird, obsessive kind away."

It wasn't all that serendipitous. Businesses like Willow Grove thrived in online wellness circles. That was probably how they managed to sell so many products.

And how they found recruits for their cult.

If that was what they were. Maybe they were less extreme than Jasmine was. But they claimed rose quartz would magically heal the pain of my knee replacement, so forgive me if I was a bit judgmental.

"Yeah, it's weird. This girl's mom called me." I leaned back on the sofa as well, shifting so I faced her better. "I guess she joined the community earlier this year? But I don't know. From what I can tell, she's been deep into the conspiracy theories for a few years. I don't know if there's anything I can do, but I'm going to at least try to get an understanding of how this place works."

"Damn, really?" Laughing, Daisy shrugged. "I'm not gonna lie, I indulge in the occasional conspiracy theory too."

"I think everybody does, to some extent. But I think pondering Marilyn Monroe's death is different than selling off all your assets and moving to a farm in the middle of nowhere."

"Yeah, that's valid," Daisy said. "I guess I'd be—"

"Knock knock!" The front door swung open, and in walked Grace in a pair of sweats and a baggie T-shirt, carrying bags from the local grocery store that nearly toppled her over. But her smile? I hadn't seen it so big in as long as I'd known her. "I got popcorn, everything I need for cookies, and face masks. What do we wanna do first?"

Laughing, I started her way and grabbed a few of the bags from her arms. "Hello to you, too."

Her grin reminded me all too much of her father. "Well, I haven't seen you in, like, a month. No point in wasting time. Let's get this girls' night started."

Chapter 5

After Grace made the cookies, the four of us sat around for a while eating them and watching trashy reality TV. Grace brought up the tension between Bentley and me. I diverted the conversation. While Daisy and I didn't know each other well yet, she was an adult. Discussing, even vaguely, what was going on between me and Bentley was different than discussing it with Grace.

No matter what happened between me and Bentley, I hoped Grace and I could still have the relationship we did now. For my own benefit, sure, but for hers too. She was a good kid, and she needed a decent feminine role model to look up to.

Was I a decent role model? It was hard to say lately.

By 10:30, Grace was passed out, Daisy's eyes were bloodshot, and I couldn't stop yawning. Daisy headed out, wishing me good luck on my case, and I tossed a blanket over Grace. When I woke up at 8:30, a text from her on my phone said, *Your couch sucks. I went home. But I left you a few cookies!*

Chuckling, I thanked her. After the usual morning routine, I mapped out the route to Debbie Armstrong's home. It was a three-hour drive, one I wasn't opposed to. It was mostly highways, meaning

I could shift my car into cruise control, and my knee wouldn't be aching by the time I arrived.

As Tempest and I loaded into the car, I shot Debbie a text.

Hey, setting out now. GPS says I'll get to you around 1, but it'll be closer to 3 with stops.

I was twenty minutes into my drive when she texted back, *Looking forward to it! Would you prefer to meet somewhere in town? That might be closer for you.*

Where Jasmine lived growing up contributed to the woman she'd become. I wanted to see the Armstrongs' home and autopsy the place.

When I arrived, I was glad I'd declined Debbie's offer to meet elsewhere.

Jasmine's childhood home embodied the childhood I had always dreamed of.

It was on the edge of a suburb, with only a few neighbors down the street, but enough individuality to separate it from the boring cookie-cutter homes. At least an acre framed the pretty farmhouse sitting on the hilltop.

Mulch beds filled with flowers and vines climbed the white siding and wraparound porch. A cozy porch swing swayed in the cool, autumn breeze. Paired with the dozing golden retriever on the front lawn, the blue sky above provided just the right ambience. The perfect combination of comfort and class. I stepped from the car, the image in front of me a perfect shot for Better Homes & Gardens.

When Debbie walked outside to greet us, shaking a bag of treats for the dog, the picture all snapped into place. She was in her mid-fifties with a medium build, the right natural shade of salt-and-pepper hair, half tied at the back of her head. Along with her friendly smile, Debbie wore a pair of stretch fit mom jeans, a white button up, and an apron speckled with white powder.

The living, breathing, personification of the American dream.

She showed me inside, offering a spot on an old but maintained floral sofa, not much different than my own aside from the lack of cigarette burn holes. Debbie moved Rufus, the golden retriever, to a crate in the corner of the hardwood floor where he sat panting and whining and wagging his tail at Tempest periodically. Logs crackled in the fireplace behind the velvet armchairs across from me. Its cozy and inviting smell mixed with the apple crumble laid out on the table only further illustrating the conclusion I'd already come to.

If this was how Jasmine had grown up, she'd lived the perfect life. So why had she wanted to leave it?

That thought kept circling through my mind as Debbie introduced me to Jasmine's brother, Matt, and her fiancé, Chase. Matt was in his early twenties, with mousy brown hair, a handsome but average face, and a medium build. Chase wasn't much different, aside from his blonde hair and slightly larger stature. They looked exactly as I would've imagined them.

The average American family.

How could Jasmine have gone from all this normalcy to where she was now?

"Please, help yourself." Debbie gestured to the pastry. "I've got some lemonade, or coffee, or tea, if you want something to drink. Oh, and a bowl. Honey," she said, gesturing to Matt, "go get a bowl of water for her dog."

"I grabbed a burger on my way here, but I'm sure Tempy will appreciate the drink." I gave Tempest's head a scratch. "Thank you, though."

"Of course." Smiling, Debbie pulled off her apron and sat in one of the armchairs. "I just appreciate this so much. It's such a strange situation, and no one seems to be able to help, so just the fact that you've come so far to meet with me, it means a lot."

"It's definitely strange." While I dug around in my purse for my recorder, I glanced around the room. "As long as it's okay with everyone, I'm gonna record this meeting. It's just easier for me to refer back to."

"Yeah, that's fine," Debbie agreed.

"We just ask that it remains private," Chase said. "Not that we think you'd share this information publicly or anything. It's just that, with the way Jasmine's been acting, we're worried about a lot of things."

"We hope she comes back to reality at some point." Debbie swallowed hard. "It would be really unfortunate if she damaged her reputation more than she already has."

Concerned with appearances. Very American dream.

That wasn't to say that I didn't see their point. If my kid was obsessed with esoteric conspiracies and essentially disappeared from the life I'd spent time creating for her, I'd want to keep that quiet too. Problem was, Jasmine had already published all her opinions online. Good chance those were going to come back to haunt her someday regardless.

"Sure." I clicked record. "This conversation will remain private."

"Great," Chase said. "So, where do we begin?"

"To start, I want to get a feel for Jasmine." Propping my elbows on my knees, I gave the formal sitting room another once over. "Looks like she grew up in a well-kempt home with a nice, normal family. That makes understanding how she wound up where she is kinda hard. But I don't want to get into that just yet. I'm curious about her career."

"Her career?" Debbie asked. "Can I ask why that's so important?"

"On the phone, you said she graduated top of her class. That tells me that at some point, she was really focused on building a life like the one she grew up in. Maybe if I understand those dreams, I can understand why she gave up on them."

"I wouldn't say she did." Matt's voice carried as he came down the hall behind me. Careful to keep it from leaking over the brim, he set the bowl of water before Tempest. As she gulped the liquid down, he sat on the opposite side of the sofa, facing me. "Willow Grove offered her a job. One she liked better than the corporate office she was at for the last year."

"Corporate girl, huh?"

"That's what she always said she wanted," Chase said. "Work Monday to Friday, nine to five, with evenings and weekends off. It's what we both wanted."

"Maybe when she started college, that was what she wanted." Tracing his tongue along his teeth, Matt raised a shoulder. "Maybe even when she got the job. The money was good, and she was lucky to land something like that right out of school. But she hated it. That's how she found Willow Grove. She was job hunting, and she came across the website, and they roped her in with the promise that it'd be different."

"What did she hate about her corporate job?" I asked.

Chase said, "She didn't hate it—"

"If you really believe that, you were never paying attention." Matt shot him a look. For a heartbeat or two, the only sound in the room was Rufus panting in the corner. Matt returned his gaze to mine. "The hours were fine at first. But she had some drama with a couple other girls in her office. Her boss complained that she listened to music on shift, then that she scrolled on her phone when she had a free minute, and then there was a huge ongoing issue for months about the coffee machine, that she was taking too much from it. Stupid shit, right? But it all piled up. It wasn't the biggest deal, but from what she told me, yeah, the place seemed kind of toxic. Her breaking point was last fall."

"What happened?"

"She'd been complaining about some back problems for a while." He crossed his arms and leaned back in his seat. "There was pain going down her leg. Mom told her it was probably sciatica, that she needed to go to a doctor. But she wouldn't. Not until she was carrying in groceries one day, and she felt a pop."

"Finally let me take her to a doctor," Chase said. "Only because she couldn't walk. Like, at all. The pain was excruciating. Turns out she had a herniated disk."

"She had to do physical therapy for six weeks, and it helped while she did the exercises, but the pain came right back." Matt chewed on his lower lip. "Then she would go to work, and she would have to sit at a desk, and sitting just made it worse. Walking helped. So she asked her boss if she could get a treadmill desk, and they said no. Something about it being a safety hazard. But she couldn't do it anymore. She was hurting. A lot. Doctors told her there was nothing they could do, that no one was going to do surgery on someone so young unless it was life-threatening. So she started looking for other options. A job she could do that would give her a little more freedom to focus on her health. She was still willing to put in her forty hours, she was just asking for accommodations."

So it hadn't been her dad's diagnosis and later death that radicalized her so far from conventional medicine. At least, not entirely.

Her own diagnosis had played a part. Living with chronic pain myself, it was easy enough to understand. For a while, they had given me pills that helped. Until they didn't. Physical therapy did, for a while. Until it didn't.

The freedom of working for myself, building my schedule and cases around my disability, was the only way I could work. I understood why she would want to do the same.

"And she just happened upon Willow Grove?" I asked.

"I don't know if she was looking for job listings or what, but yeah," Matt said. "They were looking for a business director. That's what she has a degree in. Small business management."

"She had talked about opening up her own business one day." Chase rubbed down the bridge of his nose. "She was really into yoga. Right before she accepted the position at Willow Grove, she asked about getting a loan to start a studio of her own. In hindsight, I should've said yes."

She *asked*?

Obviously, partners would discuss major life decisions together. But Chase phrased that as though she had asked him for permission. Permission he had denied.

That told me a little something about Jasmine too.

And Matt. He glanced at Chase, tightened his jaw, and took another gulp from his energy drink.

Debbie, though, stayed exactly the same. No change in expression. No rebuttal.

She found it normal.

"So she takes the job right away?" I asked.

"She takes a *meeting* right away," Matt said. "Drives up there, stays for a weekend, and comes back with this changed attitude. She was optimistic about the place. Said that they were willing to let her work from home most days. Hours were flexible, unlimited paid time off, and that the environment was just really relaxing. That she actually might *want* to spend time there."

"Probably a nice contrast to the strict corporate world," I said.

"Especially considering the pain she was living with," Matt agreed.

"But I was concerned about all the logistics," Chase said, face screwed up in confusion. "How is unlimited paid time off even an option? What was the salary? What about a 401(k) and health insurance? But she got defensive when I brought all that up. Said it was none of my business."

I agreed with Jasmine. It wasn't.

"You felt that it was?" I asked.

Chase's brows fell deep into his blue eyes. "We're engaged. We're planning a life together. So, yeah. The career she chose mattered to me."

"Were," Matt said.

"What?" Chase asked.

Matt took another gulp from his energy drink. "You *were* engaged. You *were* planning a life together. She broke it off."

Chase scoffed. "She had some mental breakdown, but that doesn't mean that we're–"

"Maybe she did." Raising his shoulders, Matt shot Chase a look. "If you want to wait around for her, go ahead. But you're not together anymore."

Chase huffed and leaned back in his seat.

There was so much tension in the air, you could pop it with a pin.

To maneuver around it, I cleared my throat. "Degree in small business management. Got it. Now, this might seem unrelated, but was religion ever a big part of your lifestyle?"

"I'm an atheist," Debbie said. "So was Jasmine's father. We always taught our kids about science and history and other things that can be proven. Which is why it was hard for me when she started believing the things she does."

"Was that your experience too, Matt?" I asked.

"Mostly, yeah. Still is." Dangling the energy drink between his thumb and forefinger, he rocked it back and forth. "When Dad died, I experimented with Catholicism. Wasn't for me. I think that's when Jasmine took up the spiritual philosophy. She just couldn't wrap her mind around the fact that he was gone. Really gone. Believing in something cosmic made coping with it easier."

Understandable. Many people found religion after the death of a loved one.

I turned to Chase. "Did you guys share that faith? Or was it a point of contention between you?"

An almost unnoticeable eye roll. "I'm more agnostic. I believe in something, but not the way Jasmine does."

"No one believes the way Jasmine does," Matt said. "Except for that place. They believe a little bit of everything. She knew that when she started there. It's probably how she fell for all that shit so quickly. Because we all told her she was crazy, and they didn't."

There was a certain edge to his voice there. Shame, maybe? In his position, I imagined I would've felt that way.

"I never told her she was crazy." Debbie's hazel eyes were like knives aimed at her son. "A few times, I said that her beliefs were irrational, but I never—"

"Bullshit, Mom."

"Don't talk to me like that."

"Then don't lie to the woman you're paying—what? Two-hundred bucks an hour?" He glanced at me, and I only scratched the side of my head. He turned back to his mother. "Look, we feel the same way. Willow Grove is a cult. It's a weird, hippie, wellness cult, and there's something going on. But don't act like you're not partially to blame for Jasmine falling into that rabbit hole. You are. We all are, and—"

"Watch your mouth, Matthew," Debbie snapped.

Releasing something between a scoff and a laugh, Matt rubbed a hand down his face. "Whatever. I don't want to hear you bitch when she calls me instead of you."

Before Debbie could rebut, I chimed in with, "You two are still in contact?"

"Not daily, but semi-regularly."

"She doesn't seem herself to you either?"

Another deep exhale, this one calmer than the last. "No. Not at all. Tried to convince her to check herself in for help, but she won't do it."

"What seems out of the ordinary?"

"Honestly?" He shrugged. "She's high."

"She doesn't do drugs," Debbie insisted.

"She hates pharmaceuticals," Chase snapped.

Matt let out an ironic laugh and rubbed his eyes between his thumb and forefinger. "Sure. She's never touched a drug in her life, Mom."

"My daughter isn't an addict." Debbie's eyes were wide, brows raised. "That's not what this is."

Now I understood what I was dealing with. A mother in denial.

"God forbid," Matt said, pressing a hand to his chest in mock awe. "It's one thing if she has a mental disorder. That, you can explain away. But how could you tell your friends that your daughter's a junkie?"

"I don't appreciate that word—"

"Neither do I." Doing my best to calm the tension, I raised my hands at my sides. "But the verbiage matters a lot less than the grand scheme."

"You know what the grand scheme is?" Matt propped his elbows on his knees, leaning closer my way. "Jasmine hasn't been normal since Dad died. She did everything right, everything she was supposed to, and life slapped her in the face for it. The nine to five destroyed her body. When she went to her fiancé and mother for help, for advice, they basically told her to get over it—"

"I never—" Tears filled Debbie's eyes.

"That's not what—"

"Mom said Jasmine has three herniated discs," Matt told me, "and she lives with them. Chase told Jasmine she had to be grateful for the career she had, no matter what it cost. Then someone told her that her pain was valid. They offered her solutions. A job that wouldn't kill her, a lifestyle that was compatible with her body, a community that believed the same thing she did. And probably drugs." He targeted a look at his mother, who covered her quivering mouth with a hand. "As much as I want her to come home, I don't blame her for staying where she is. If there is something going on there, I hope you can get to the bottom of it." He stood. "I'm not gonna sit here and act like we're perfect and Jasmine is the problem. This family *isn't* perfect. Perfect moms don't side with their kid's asshole ex. But if you need any information from me, you can find me online through Jasmine's accounts. Thanks for coming, and I hope you have a good day."

Matt gulped the rest of his energy drink and walked out of the room.

A heartbeat later, the door slammed shut.

Debbie jumped.

Chase leaned back in his seat and sighed.

I pressed my lips together.

Not an American dream after all.

Chapter 6

Debbie and Chase asked me if I had any other questions. If I thought about it long enough, sure. I could come up with a few.

But they wouldn't tell me the truth.

Debbie was too concerned with what people would think if they knew Jasmine was on drugs. Chase hadn't gripped the fact that Jasmine had ended their relationship. Not to mention the fact that he seemed like a controlling asshole. Which must have contributed to why Jasmine had left.

Matt gave me more information at that meeting than anyone else, and now he was gone.

For now, I had enough. I understood why she had joined the commune.

I thanked them for their time and headed out the door without another word. As Tempest and I loaded into my car, my phone rang with another call from Sam. I pressed ignore.

Ten years ago, if you told me I'd ignore a call from my father, I wouldn't have believed you. Back then and throughout my childhood, I craved a relationship with him, with any adult aside from my mom, the way I craved sunlight in the dead of winter. I still did. Or had, anyway. We hadn't known each other long, but what I did know of him, I loved.

Until he murdered somebody and lied about it.

Now, I didn't know. I didn't know what I thought or how I felt or what a future with him in it looked like. And I didn't have the capacity to figure it out right now.

Listening to the voicemail he left once I settled into my seat didn't make me any more certain.

"Hey, Maddie." His voice was soft, strained. Sadness tinged the edge of it. "I know you're upset. I get it. You got every right to be. In your position, I would be too. I don't blame you. Not one bit. But I guess I just—Hell, I don't know."

A long pause, followed by a deep breath. "I was trying to help. That doesn't change anything. I know that. But I knew you were tied up in red tape, and I know how much that girl means to Bentley. The whole situation, I know how much it meant to you. And I wouldn't have been able to forgive myself if I did nothing, you know? But I guess that doesn't matter.

"You're allowed to feel however you need to feel. What I feel doesn't matter, because I'm the one in the wrong. I know I'm the one in the wrong. The whole situation was just wrong. But you and me, we were just starting to build our relationship, and I really hope that wasn't for nothing. I really hope we can still have that.

"If you just need space right now, that's okay. If you never want to talk to me again, well, it would hurt, but that's okay too. I guess I'm just wondering where your head's at, because mine's all over the place, and I can't really talk about everything like this. I mean, I would, but—Shit, you know what I mean. Could we just get together for breakfast or something? On me? Or maybe I could pop by and make you dinner? I don't know. Just, please, give me a call back. Or a text. Something to let me know you're alive and you don't completely hate me. Alright. I love you, kid. Bye."

Hate him? No. I didn't hate him. It was a hard thing to hate a parent. Even after everything my mom did, I still didn't hate her.

But I still didn't know how I felt about Sam, or where my head was at.

After I shifted the car into drive and clicked on the GPS, I replayed the memory, hearing his voice through Bentley's phone, relived the hole it'd punched through my chest, and I hated the way that felt. Driving through the mountainous terrain usually required a lot of mental focus, but autopilot took over today. Blue skies watched over me, early autumn leaves brightened the green landscape, and two yellow lines guided my path forward.

Nothing conscious turned through my mind. A ball of something sat in the center of my chest. It was heavy and tight and it burned. All the way into my eyes, it burned.

I turned back to Jasmine. She was easier to focus on.

Matt believed she was on drugs. What kind? And why?

Stimulants or hallucinogens incited grandiose delusions more than most drugs. Modern hippies used both. Not that I liked to stereotype, but I'd yet to meet a white person with dreads who hadn't taken mushrooms at some point or another.

Mushrooms had a short life in the body though. When I was a kid, and we all took them, we expected the effects to wear off in a few hours. Then spend a few more on the toilet.

Hallucinations on those types of drugs involved watching the walls breathe and marveling at how bright the stars were. Usually, that was the extent of it. Most users took it only on occasion. Unless they microdosed daily, which helped with anxiety and depression, but doses so small didn't cause delusions. If microdosing, Jasmine wouldn't have seemed high to her brother.

Life altering delusions about the end of times were more often associated with acid or methamphetamines. But Chase was right about one thing. Jasmine hated pharmaceuticals. She didn't even trust sunscreen. Could I really believe she was smoking meth or snorting Adderall?

Just as I turned off the highway, an unfamiliar number flashed across the screen on my dashboard. Matt, maybe? With some more context about his sister, something he didn't want to mention in front of his mom?

I clicked the green button. "Hello?"

"Hi, yes." Not Matt. A woman. Her voice reminded me of the swaying trees out the window. Soft and slow, so quiet that I had to turn the volume up ten notches. "Is this Madison?"

"I usually go by Maddie, but yes." Just ahead, roughly a quarter mile on the foliage surrounded, overgrown street, was a shoulder. We'd been on the road for an hour now. Tempest needed a break. "Can I ask who this is?"

"Yes, of course." Her voice was hardly above a whisper. "My name's Ophelia. I'm the owner and director of Willow Grove. You reached out on our website?"

Now the voice made sense. A jolt of electricity ran through me.

"Oh, right. Right, I'm sorry." Slowing to glide off the pavement and onto the shoulder, I checked my mirrors. "I'm driving at the moment. Can you hold on for one second?"

"Of course," she said. "Take your time, Miss Kramer."

I knitted my brows together and then remembered. Almost forgot I'd given her a fake name.

Like the old woman in Hansel and Gretel. That's who Ophelia reminded me of.

Once my wheels settled into the gravel, I shifted the car into park, disconnected my phone from the Bluetooth, stepped out, grabbed Tempest's leash, and snapped for her to join me in the grass. She pranced around, sniffing a dozen yards or so from the road. Safe, away from traffic. There wasn't much of it back here anyway. Since I'd turned off the highway, I hadn't driven past a single car.

Leaning against my passenger door, I held the phone to my ear. "Sorry about that. I was already pulling off the road to let my dog do her business, so figured it was best to chat with you out here."

"A dog, you said?" Strange. Her voice was so strange. Mature, a bit raspy, but so delicate. Almost childlike. "What kind?"

Odd question, but I'd entertain it. "German Shepherd."

"Aw, how sweet. We have a few of them around here. They're mostly mixed breeds, but sweet as can be." A quiet chuckle, nearly a giggle. "What's her coloring like?"

My life revolved around Tempest. I loved her more than anything. But why the hell did her coat matter? Fingers crossed I wasn't walking into a Cruella de Vil situation.

"Uh, she's black." Something rustled in the bushes. Tempest's head shot up to follow it. A snap caught her attention. I gave her a look, the kind that said, *Don't worry about it.* She went back to sniffing the grass that came halfway up her legs. "Head to toe, all black."

"Beautiful, I bet. Like a valiant steed. I'd love to meet her."

"Yeah?" A bug whizzed past my face, and I swatted it away. "She can be a bit temperamental. Especially with people she doesn't know."

"I'm sure she'll be fine. I've yet to meet an animal who doesn't like me." So many giggles. "Any who. About the form you submitted. You said you were looking for information?"

Knee aching from the long drive, I rubbed a hand down my thigh. "A friend of mine bought a few things from your website. I've got chronic pain from an old injury, and she said that your remedies helped a lot. I started doing a little bit of digging, and I wound up on the about section of your website. Yours and Bronwyn's stories were so impactful. They really touched me." The words tasted like vinegar on my tongue. "It said something about reaching out at the end, and it just felt like a calling. So I figured, what the hell? Why not reach out?"

"That means the world to us here at Willow Grove," she said. "Friends recommending our work here. Tell her how grateful I am, would you?"

"Yeah, sure thing."

"I'm so sorry to hear about the pain you're in too," Ophelia said, sounding less like the old woman from Hansel and Gretel and more like a sweet grandma. "That's just so awful. A lot of our folks here live with that sort of thing. We have all sorts of products we're testing out at the Grove. Menthol creams, eucalyptus—they seem to be making a difference. We haven't put them up for sale yet, still perfecting our recipes, but they might be a big help to you."

Menthol was the active ingredient in most topical anesthetics. I imagined they would help. Icy Hot usually did for a while. "I'd love to try them out."

"Of course, sweetie. If you make a trip up, you're welcome to whatever you like," she said.

Was this how she did it? The warm, nurturing tone would invite anyone. Especially people worse off than I was. If Bentley had stumbled upon Willow Grove when he'd been in the trenches, trying to get out of Ohio and away from the drug dealers he'd once been indebted to, would this have worked on him? Maybe. Probably not.

But I could understand why this had worked on Jasmine.

Ophelia just sounded so inviting, so warm. It was like Matt had said. No one in her life validated Jasmine's experience, her pain. Debbie and Chase made her out to be a lunatic, told her she needed to get a grip and stick with it.

But Ophelia cared. She cared about my dog. She cared about my pain. If I were in a vulnerable place and had no support elsewhere, hearing these simple phrases would mean everything to me.

"Do you have any idea what the pain is coming from?" Ophelia asked. "Or is it one of those things the doctors could never find an answer for?"

I gave her a fake name for a reason. No way in hell would I tell her I'd been a cop. "I took a nasty fall on a hike. Needed a knee replacement, but it still flares up. Most days, I'm in a flareup."

She gasped. "Oh my, you poor thing. At your age especially. What are you? Thirty?"

Was she asking to relate? Or to research me? Vague answer would have to do. "About that, yeah."

"Geez, that's gotta be tough. Around my age, everybody has a knee replacement. And everybody pays for it. Each and every day, they pay for it. I tell you, medicine these days. Don't know if it helps or hurts more."

It was either a knee replacement or figuring out how to walk with a shattered one. Something that literally could not be done. The pain sucked. I wouldn't argue that for a second. But if my options were a painful knee, or never taking a step again, I picked the pain.

"At the moment, it's hurting more than helping." I lied. It hurt, but it wasn't unbearable. Just the dull throb I'd grown accustomed to.

But I needed to be the type of person she could convince. The type she would invite to the Grove. If I showed my nihilistic views on alternative healing, she'd end the call.

"I'm so sorry, sweetheart," she said. "Do you have anyone around who helps? A husband or something like that?"

"It's just me and my dog at home. My boyfriend, he does what he can, but—" A half laugh escaped me. Damn, the magic of this woman. Here I was, about to fall into her open arms. "We're going through something right now. I'm not sure what our future looks like. I'm trying to do things independently. Trying to break away from a lot of systems that have been ingrained into me, you know? That's what was so interesting about your website."

"Oh no, that's such a shame. I love young love, but sometimes things just don't work." Silence snuck in for a moment. "Any who. What was it that you liked about our website?"

"All that stuff about the hustle and bustle of modern living." As if I weren't watching Tempest frolic through knee-high grass, chasing some flying critter or another. Dragonfly? No, maybe a bumblebee. Looked small. "I'm a dog trainer. I was working with this agency for a while, and they were great. Really good people. But all the rigidity of the schedule. The lack of freedom just really keeps me from doing my best. Especially with my chronic pain. Sometimes I just need to relax more than other people. Often, I need to pause and do some yoga or physical therapy." Only a few of those sentences were lies. "So I don't know. It seems like you went through the same thing. Was it advice you were offering with that contact form?"

"Advice, of course. But healing too, if that makes sense? Here at the Grove, that's our primary focus. Healing. The life everyone leads now, just existing in it all, you need to heal from. Shame that is. But that's what the Grove is really about. Community, helping one another, healing together. Where are you located, Maddie?"

"I'm about an hour out of Pittsburgh usually, but I was visiting a friend upstate. Why do you ask?"

"Well, we're coming up on the weekend. If you don't have work tomorrow and Sunday, why don't you take a trip up here? Just visit for a while, spend some time with us all. See if you feel more rejuvenated by the time you head home. If you want to head home, anyway."

My hackles raised. Who invited a total stranger to their home? But if I didn't know better, if I wasn't investigating Jasmine's case, the giggle Ophelia let out would've been comforting. Inviting. We were strangers, but she opened a door to more. To join her community, something that everyone in the modern world craved, even if we denied it.

"We do have a lot of dogs around here," she said. "They all need a bit of training. Maybe I could give you some work for a while, if you'd like."

"I can't say I'm ready to quit my job just yet," I said. "But are you sure? I can come visit?"

"Of course! We're like a big campground, you know? This time of year's beautiful here at the Grove."

"Maybe that would be nice," I said. "I'll have to run to my house and get some clothes, but—"

"We've got plenty of things you can wear here. It's encouraged, actually. Not to say we have a dress code at the Grove, but we prioritize comfort. With all of our outdoor activities, it just makes sense. Please, give it a try. Leave everything behind for a little while, come relax, get to know us, and let us get to know you."

So long as they didn't insist I wear harem pants, fine. "That sounds pretty cool actually. A nice little adventure."

"Never done something spontaneous and fun before?"

Alarms rang in the back of my mind. Ophelia latched on to the bland normalcy of life. This was her pitch. The same one she had given Jasmine.

Drop everything. Do something you've never done before. Be wild for a while. Come visit us, you'll love it here. You'll never want to go home.

At a moment's notice, I dropped everything I was doing to be there for my clients, to search for answers they needed. This didn't appeal to me. But I understood how it could to someone who found their life mundane.

"Nothing this spontaneous, no," I said.

"Well, that changes today, Maddie. Who knows? Maybe you'll look back in a year and think, *Wow. This was the day my life really began.*"

Doubtful.

Chapter 7

THE GPS SAID FORTY-FIVE MINUTES TO WILLOW GROVE. THAT only took me to the entrance. From there, I still had what felt like a never-ending drive on a gravel, tree-canopied road. I tried speeding up, but a thousand potholes cratered the ground. If I went too fast, I would blow out a tire. A crisp fifteen miles per hour would have to do.

The further the gravel road stretched, the more hairs raised on the back of my neck. Normally, I loved an autumn drive through the mountains. Was there anything more beautiful than trees of a thousand colors, painted by nature herself? Back home, we still had so much greenery. Here, fall was in full swing. Everyone called it spooky season these days. I never felt that.

Not until now.

Aside from the crunch of gravel under my tires, silence enveloped the open windows. The wind nipped at my skin with a ferocity we had yet to face in the lower elevation. I passed a squirrel and a handful of chipmunks, but not a single person.

If I screamed, would anyone hear me?

Ring, ring, ring!

I jumped.

Dylan's name flashed across my screen.

Shaking off the startle, I pressed the green button. "Got anything new for me?"

"I wouldn't have called if I didn't."

"Right. Silly me."

"Ophelia's real name is Beatrice Anderson. Bronwyn's is Calvin. The story on their website matches what I found. Beatrice worked as a travel consultant, and Calvin was a car insurance agent. They did write off lots of medical debt in the year before they switched careers."

"The fertility treatments," I murmured, pressing on my brakes as an opossum started across the road. Every opossum I'd ever encountered before turned and hissed at me. Scary looking, but harmless. This one glanced at my car and kept walking. Not a run, but a slow trot. Must've known that the humans around here were more friends than foe. "Good to know that checks out. Anything else stand out to you?"

"Yes. They make a lot of money." Keys clacked in the background. "They reported just under a million in net income last year."

"Holy shit." I scoffed. "What the hell for? Just sales from their website?"

"As well as cash sales, yes. That's less than five percent of their income though. Mostly, it's online retail."

"A million net, all from sauerkraut and rocks," I said under my breath.

"Another strange thing. Calvin is the owner of Willow Grove. Beatrice is his dependent. She doesn't own any of the business."

"Can't say that's very new age hippie of them."

"If I were in her position, I would hope there was a nice prenup in place." Dylan's voice muffled for a moment. "Especially strange because the deed to their old home was in both of their names, even though it seems like she inherited it from her parents. She took the extra effort to make sure that he owned what was theirs as a couple, but this setup gives him all the power."

"Also all the responsibility if something goes wrong." The opossum finally got to the other end of the road, and I pressed the gas. "Are you looking at their tax records?"

"Not at the moment, but I could dig them out. Why?"

"I'm curious about their expenditures and write-offs," I said. "If they have a million net, what did they gross?"

"I'm not sure. What are you thinking?"

"Jasmine's brother thinks she's on drugs." Hammered to a tree on my right, a wooden sign hung. It read, *A Simpler Life one mile ahead.* "Maybe they're dealing."

"Maybe. Neither of them have criminal records that suggest it though."

"I just can't see sauerkraut and crystals making that much money."

It almost sounded like Dylan chuckled. Almost. A breathy harrumph was the closest he got. "That does seem unlikely."

"What the hell would they even be selling? Weed makes sense, it's natural and all that shit. But weed doesn't make as much on the street as it used to. It's legal now. Everyone has a medical card."

"That's true. I'm sure some people still buy it on the streets, but the market is surely smaller than it once was."

"Doesn't explain Jasmine's delusions either," I murmured. "Sure, some people have bad reactions, but these are mass, grandiose delusions."

"It's still possible. I knew several people in college who had some type of drug induced psychosis from marijuana."

"To this extent though? Selling your home, leaving your partner, cutting off your family?"

"Not to that level, no."

The hair rising on my neck and the goosebumps lifting over my arms was proof of something wrong in my book. In moments like this, I had to lean into my instincts.

"Well, thanks for your help," I said. "I'm at the Grove now.

Taking a tour over the weekend. I don't know how good service is going to be, so I'll get back to your invoice on Monday, if that's okay?"

"That will be fine, yes. Be careful. And good luck."

"Thanks."

Had the feeling I was going to need it.

* * *

NOT JUST DOGS. CATS TOO. THERE WERE DOGS AND CATS everywhere.

As soon as the barn came into view, so did the dogs and cats.

Emaciated dogs and cats.

The moment I saw them, I pulled off the gravel into the grass, stopped the car, and got out. Tempest stayed inside while I looked around, blinking hard at them all.

Six dogs and twelve cats, just in my immediate line of sight.

They looked at me, and I looked at them, and I forced myself to smile, but my heart collapsed into my stomach. The water in my eyes burned like flames.

Bringing myself down to a knee, the good one, I stretched out my hand for the nearest dog. Some type of lab mix judging by the shape of his head and his floppy black ears. His tail wagged as he stepped closer, but his eyes were wide and heavy. The bones beneath his short black fur protruded like weeds beneath landscaping fabric. There wasn't enough to keep them inside. Like one wrong move would rip the skin apart.

"Hey, pretty boy," I said, wiggling my fingers. "Come here."

His tail still wagged, and he took a slow step in.

A white cat with a swollen stomach ran between us.

He jolted backward.

What the hell had these people done to him?

"It's okay, it's okay." Voice soft and melodic, I grabbed a few treats from the satchel I always kept on my hip. In the car behind me,

Tempest whined. She could have some in a bit. This poor guy was my priority at the moment. "Are you hungry? Do you want a treat?"

He sprinted to me. I didn't even have time to process it. He gobbled them all up, leaving slimy drool in the palm of my hand.

"You are, huh? You're hungry." Scratching up his head, I grabbed a handful more from the satchel. He ravaged them, and I petted him, fighting the lurch that ached my stomach.

Skin and bones. He was no more than skin and bones.

"Another newcomer!" a man said. He looked exactly like I imagined everyone here would. A loose, flowing tunic style shirt and vibrant, loose pants. His curly hair reached his shoulders, framing his thin, angled face. He may have had a bit more meat on him than the dog, but not much. His smile was warm though. Kind, too. "You must be the dog trainer Ophelia was talking about."

Bringing myself upright was harder than running through water. This animal needed me, and I was ready to do anything I could for him. The fact that anyone could see a defenseless creature in this condition and do nothing had my heart throbbing. But I had a case to solve. I had to put on a show.

I had to smile. I had to ignore the urge to grit my teeth. "What gave it away?"

Laughing, the guy came closer. He pointed at the dog, now nestled closely by my legs. "Dude likes you. That's rare. He's such a skittish little guy."

"Dude? Is that his name?"

"Yeah." A playful snort. "That was all me. Dude, Bro, Brah, and Man. That's what I named all the pups from his litter. Maybe kinda confusing, but I was really messed up, and it seemed like a good idea." He leaned back, posture smooth. Too smooth. Like he didn't have full control of his limbs. When he leaned in front of me to scratch Dude's head, I got a whiff of his breath. Weed and whiskey, if I had to guess. "Isn't that right, Dude?"

Dude wagged his tail some more, jumped onto his hind legs, and landed with his paws on the man's chest. He licked his face all over, inciting laughs and stumbles. A stumble that almost landed on me.

"Anyway, I'm Phoenix." He held out his hand. "Nice to meet you."

"Maddie." Given his attire, I half expected his hand to be sweaty and limp. Nope. He gave a firm shake with thin, calloused fingers. "Phoenix. That's a cool name."

"I thought so too," he said. "My parents don't. Robert. That's what they named me. Rob never really fit. Lots of people here call themselves new things, so Phoenix. Rebirth. Rising from the ashes, you know?"

"Yeah, I'm familiar with the myth." Damn it. This was gonna be hard. Throughout my adolescence, Phoenix and I would've been the best of friends. A little ridiculous, a little quirky, sure. But charming in a simple, silly way. "I vibe with it. And respect it. That's cool. Literally making a name for yourself."

Laughing, he nodded. "Yeah, I think so too. But anyway. Ophelia asked me to show you around. She's in a session with someone right now, but you'll see her later." He walked around my car. "Mind if I hop in? I'll show you where to park."

"No. Not a problem." I started back to my car. "My dog can be kind of a bitch sometimes though. Let me introduce you before you get in."

Phoenix peered into the pink Subaru. "No way! A German Shepherd?"

"Yep." Joining him on the passenger side, I grabbed the door handle for Tempest. When I opened it, she stayed seated. Leash in hand, I commanded her to join us outside. She hopped, sat, and waited for the next one. "Say hi, Tempy."

Her eyes flicked to Phoenix, then back to me.

"I had a German Shepherd growing up. Looked just like her, actually." Squatting down, he offered a hand. "Can I pet her?"

"If she'll let you."

She wiggled her nose, smelling his open palm, and met his gaze.

"I think she likes me." Phoenix reached out to scratch her head. Tempest didn't protest, just sat there panting. "If we didn't already have so many dogs around here, I'd get a German Shepherd. I love how attentive they are, you know? They love to work, and they listen, and they sure as shit keep you busy."

Had to agree. Tempest did seem to like him. She only sat there, enjoying the pets, glancing at me periodically. Which was great, because the last thing I needed was her biting off his head when we got in the car.

Plus, Tempy was my litmus test. If she was alright with Phoenix, I could be.

"You're not kidding." I gestured into the car for Tempest. She hopped right back inside. "Where did you say I should park?"

"We'll go down that road back there." He hooked a thumb and gestured behind him. "You think I'm good to get in now?"

"Yeah, she's cool with you." I shut the rear door and headed around the car for the driver's side. Phoenix hopped into the passenger seat. Once I was in, turning the car over, I said, "Why is that, anyway?"

"Huh?"

"All the dogs around here." Car in drive, I started slowly toward the dirt road he pointed at on my left. "And cats. How did they get here?"

"Oh, right. Mind if I smoke this in here?" He pulled a joint from behind his ear. I shook my head in answer. "Ophelia and Bronwyn got a couple strays at some point or another. Some of the people here, we brought pets too. I think there were already stray cats hanging around? And, you know. Animals do what animals do."

"Right," I murmured, nodding slowly. "What do they eat?"

"We put food out every day." His tone softened, quivering a bit. "I know they look skinny, but they eat. Trust me, I put out so much food for them."

"I believe you," I said. Which was the truth. But it didn't change how badly my heart ached in my chest.

Beneath the Grove

Did I understand why Ophelia took in strays? Of course. I was an animal lover too.

But there was a right and wrong way to do it.

When I first moved back to the trailer park, there were more than a dozen stray cats running around. Many of my neighbors left food in bowls for them. They made cute little boxes out of plastic crates and Styrofoam to keep them warm in the winter. It came from a place of love, a place of kindness. I wouldn't hold that against them.

Still, as a cop, I had learned that it was illegal to feed strays. Not because the government was evil and wanted all stray animals to die, but because letting them live like that was cruel.

In the wild, when resources were scarce, animals stopped reproducing. They knew that if there was no food, their young wouldn't survive, and they wouldn't bring more life into a hostile environment. A stray cat who didn't have access to food, but had a litter of kittens, would take care of that single litter and wouldn't become pregnant again until she had access to necessities.

When humans intervened, supplying each breakfast and dinner, they'd start to reproduce again. Then, those kittens would go into heat at a few months old and procreate as well. Even with their siblings and parents.

The incest offspring would have genetic abnormalities. One kitten who was born this way shortly after I moved into the trailer park had skeletal issues. It left her back in a constant arch. The width of her hips was so small, even feces couldn't pass through it. She wound up with mega colon at only six weeks old, and I watched the light leave her eyes as she succumbed to constipation.

Yes, something as simple as constipation.

She would've never been born, and she would've never suffered that painful death, if the people around the trailer park hadn't thought the kindest thing to do was to feed her mother.

After that, I contacted a rescue who helped me trap, spay or neuter, and release those same cats back into the trailer park to live out the rest of their life. Many of them still walked around. Quite a few died of diseases they should've never gotten.

While I understood the intent of Ophelia and the people here, the impact mattered more. They were not helping these animals. They were damning them to painful, miserable lives.

"I know how they look," Phoenix said. He pointed out the window for me to hang a right past an old, red barn. I followed his direction, slowly, to avoid blowing out a tire. "But I do feed them. It's just so expensive to get this many animals to a vet, you know?"

"Ophelia and Bronwyn couldn't help with that?"

They made a million dollars last year.

"I think they tried to a couple times, but... I don't know." He did his best to blow the pot smoke out the window, but the skunk smell still filled my nose. "Ophelia mentioned you had a knee replacement?"

Nice subject change. "I did. Why do you ask?"

"It's a half mile walk back to camp from the parking lot." Now on another tree covered road, the farmhouse and barn I'd seen all the animals at disappeared in my rearview. "Maybe we should have someone else drive your car down here."

"No, that's alright. I can handle half a mile."

"Alright, good. It's that little road up here on your left." He pointed to a break in the brush a few dozen yards ahead. "Do you want to hit this?"

"I'm good. Gives me anxiety." That wasn't true. There was a time in my life that I adored weed. Back then, I also had a Backstreet Boys poster hanging in my bedroom. Now, sobriety was most important to me. "Thanks though."

"Damn, that sucks. It'd probably really help your knee too."

"Probably." Swinging to the left, I squinted ahead.

And my stomach dropped.

Behind the bushes of that dirt road was a field. Parking lot was a fitting description. If I had to guess, these dimensions matched the dimensions of a parking lot for my local Walmart or a concert venue in the city. It was damn near full. Older cars, newer cars, lined up over the rolling hill with anticipation. As if they were each waiting for their owner to return to them.

A downed tree lay on top of one car in the far right corner. Crushed and forgotten.

Its owner, evidently, hadn't reported that to their insurance company.

Around that barn and farmhouse, I'd seen a few tents. A few dozen people, maybe. But not enough to answer for all these cars.

Chapter 8

Since Sam killed Deangelo, I kept a go bag in the trunk. Why? I couldn't tell you. In case I needed to run to Mexico? In case Deangelo's partner reappeared and I had to chase a lead? I didn't know. Paranoid, maybe. But who did preparation ever hurt?

It wasn't enough to last the weekend. Just an extra change of clothes, some cash, a Ziploc full of food for Tempest, a mini bag of toiletries, and a dozen rounds for the gun I always kept on my hip. When I stepped from the car with Phoenix, the weight of it tugged at my jeans. My baggie hoodie disguised it. I was careful to keep it that way as I strapped the backpack around my chest.

"Ophelia said you didn't have time to grab your things," Phoenix said, gesturing at my gear.

"Yeah, it's not exactly what I would've packed, but I always keep this back here." Tightening the straps with one hand, I adjusted my hands-free leash for Tempest with the other. "Just a couple things. Shampoo, conditioner, an extra hoodie."

"I gotcha. I always carried an extra bag in my trunk too." He squinted into the field, then pointed a few rows down. "I think it's still back there."

"How long has it been here?" I snapped the hatch into place, then followed his lead back onto the dirt road. "Or rather, how long have *you* been here?"

"Geez, I don't know." His lips flapped together in a trill, eyes scanning the sky overhead as if a jet would fly by and write out the number for him. "What year is it again?"

I chuckled. He didn't. He looked at me, eyes vacant, brow cocked.

Holy shit. He really didn't know what year it was.

"2023," I said. "October 2023."

"No shit." That, he laughed at. "Almost six years then. Damn, I guess I'm old enough to drink now."

Hopefully he didn't see me flinch.

I hadn't put a number on it, but I would've said Phoenix was in his mid-to-late twenties. But that could've been the hollowing of his cheeks, the dark circles beneath his eyes, and the thinness of his stature.

If he were an addict, that made sense. Addiction did a number on someone's physical appearance, regardless of what their birth certificate said.

"Wow," I murmured, still trying to come to grips with it myself. Tempest was on her long lead, almost at the length of the ten feet. "What made you take the leap? To come and live here, I mean."

His shoulders rose and fell with a deep breath. "I was seventeen, and things weren't great at home. They got a lot worse after I came out. A friend of mine was into all that witchy stuff. It wasn't really my thing, but I figured I'd give it a try. I was searching online for crystals, found the website for Willow Grove, and the about section. I filled out the contact form, and the rest is history."

My stomach spun. What led him here was bad enough. The fact that he'd only been a baby himself when he'd arrived made it that much worse. "I'm sorry."

Bloodshot eyes on mine, he cocked his head to the side. "What for?"

"Going through that. Your family treating you the way they did."

I frowned, tugging on Tempest's leash when she slowed to sniff something in the bushes. "My family wasn't great growing up either."

"You weren't the one who did it. You don't need to apologize." A crooked grin brought some life to those thin, hollowed cheeks. "But then, you get it. It sucks when you're a kid, and you're stuck with people you hate and who hate you. Then this magical thing happens. Adulthood. It always pissed me off when I was a kid and adults would bitch about all the responsibility they had. I was like, shit, I'll take all the responsibility in the world if it means that I can get the hell away from these people."

I laughed because I understood. My heart ached because I understood.

They preyed on the vulnerable. Willow Grove opened its doors to people who needed community and purpose. On its own, that would be a beautiful thing.

But this kid barely had more skin on his bones than the emaciated dogs.

Tempest's ears perked at something in the woods on our right. I tugged her in closer, and she joined me at my side. "I remember thinking the same thing."

"Your family was pretty messed up too, huh?" Pheonix lit another joint from behind his other ear. "Who was worse? Mom or Dad?"

"Whew." I blew out a deep breath. "I'm not sure if there's a good way to answer that."

"Equally bad?"

"My dad left when I was little. So, I thought he was just a dead-beat most of my life? But he showed up a few months ago, and it was a lot more complicated than that. He'd tried to get custody of me, but my mom kept winning in court. Eventually, he probably would've won, but he ended up in prison. Killed a guy." Pressing my lips together, I snorted. "Yet I still think he was the better of the two."

Phoenix took a long drag off his joint, blue eyes wide in disbelief. "You're not kidding?"

"I wish I were."

"Shit, that's wild," Phoenix said under his breath, waving his hand to waft the smoke away. "Your mom a killer too?"

"Just of my will to live." He laughed, and I joined in. My gaze fell to the ground where the dirt road turned to gravel. "She was a violent person. Neglectful too, but that wasn't as bad as the violence. I was in and out of foster care for a while."

"Sounds a lot like my parents." Phoenix swept his hair behind his shoulders, exposing a tattoo just below his ear. I wasn't close enough to make out what it was. "It was bad. Really bad. Yet, when my mom died a couple of years ago, it still crushed me."

"Same with mine," I said. "I think it was more about mourning what could've been than what was, you know?"

"Damn. That's beautiful," he said. "I couldn't think of a better way to phrase it."

"Don't quote me. Pretty sure I got that from my therapist."

Chuckling, he tilted his head to look ahead at the small incline up the hill. All that weed had made his eyes so squinty, they were hardly open. Still, they landed on the opening of foliage where I'd met Dude, where he still lay, waiting patiently for us. "So what about your dad? Are you guys good now?"

"We were." How the hell was I going to answer this question? "I don't know. I found out he was lying to me. About something big. Life-changing big. And I don't know if I can forgive him. I don't know if he is who I thought he was."

"But he's good to you?" Phoenix glanced my way, holding the smoke in his lungs. "He's never hurt you or anything? Aside from leaving, and whatever all that was about?"

It took a long time, too long, for me to say, "Yeah. He's good to me."

"But it was that bad? What he lied to you about?"

In my book, murder was beyond bad. Couldn't say that, though.

The fact that he made me an accessory to murder wasn't even

what I was so upset about. The same went for Bentley. It wasn't about what they did, but...

"I don't know." The gravel underfoot poked through the soles of my tennis shoes, my feet aching with each step. "Maybe I can forgive that? All my life, I'd wanted a relationship with him. I'd wanted to know him. And now he's around. He comes and makes me breakfast at my house. We have dinner all the time. Because I connected with him, I found out that I'm not an only child. I have a brother, and he's great. He's a little quirky, and kinda weird, but I love it?" Phoenix laughed, and so did I. "When Sam first came back, I didn't trust him. Then I got to know him, and the only thing I was upset about was all the time we'd lost out on, because he's great. We talk about life and politics and the universe and the meaning of it all, and I feel like I belong when I'm with him. Like the apple really didn't fall far from the tree. Never really felt that anywhere else. But I just—"

"Don't lose that." His face tightened, eyes on mine. "Connections like that, they're damn near impossible to come by. Especially with your blood. And I know what they say. You can't choose your family. But if you could, and he was still someone you would choose, don't lose that over something you can forgive. Forgive them, because what's this life without the people you love?"

When he phrased it like that, my throat tightened. If I were desperate for love and affection, Phoenix would be right. Letting Sam back in would be the right call.

But I wasn't desperate for love and affection. I'd gotten on by myself just fine for years. I did it when I left Mom, when I left Ox, and I would do it again if I left Bentley and Sam.

My dog walked beside me, and that was all I needed. How could I be lonely when she was right there, always at my heels?

"Looks like you've got a poetic streak to you too," I said, nudging Phoenix's elbow.

"Hey, I'm just saying. If I had family around who gave a damn, I sure as shit wouldn't be here." He glanced around the wooded path. "It's dark as hell around here sometimes."

There we go. "Yeah? The way Ophelia and Bronwyn talk about it, I thought this place was a utopia."

"It is in some ways." A swallow bobbed Phoenix's throat. "But it's rough sometimes, too. People come, and they become your friends. You're so sure that you're gonna be in this together, forever. Then they leave, and you never hear from them again."

If they left, why are their cars still here?

"And all the work can be hard. Like you said about the animals too, that's something that eats at me. It's worth it at the end of the day, but I'm just saying that if I had a dad who came over and made me dinner and talked to me about life and the universe and what it all means, I wouldn't be h—"

"Phoenix!" A woman's voice came from straight ahead. With the setting sun in the distance, it was hard to make out how she looked. But when she continued, I recognized her voice. "Thank the Gods. I was wondering when Maddie would show. I'm so glad you began her tour. Come on, this way. We're starting the fire."

"Coming!" Phoenix said, breaking into a jog. "We can talk more tomorrow once you're settled in. I think we still need to set up your tent."

"Right. Sure." My knee didn't appreciate the speed we picked up to, but Tempest sure did. She broke into a run, heading for the woman at the break in the foliage ahead. "But fire?"

"Nightly ritual," he said, winded. "If you like s'mores, you'll have a good time."

* * *

ONCE WE MADE IT TO THE ACREAGE AROUND THE FARMHOUSE and barn, Dude greeted us again. Greeted Tempest too, immediately falling to his back, belly up for her.

She may not have been the biggest fan of people, but she did like other dogs. Especially submissive ones.

Dude stayed at Tempest's flank as Phoenix led us past the farmhouse. In the setting sun, it was hard to get a good view of my surroundings. There were a couple tents near the farmhouse and barn, but not the kind people usually camped in.

Rather than thick, plasticky canvas sewn together, thin sheets swayed in the wind. Some were aged beige, others paisley print, a few featuring superheroes. None of them were in the best condition though. Splotches of green grass littered the bases, and patches of brown muck and dirt covered the rest.

People living here didn't even get a real tent?

Unhoused people lived in better conditions.

Evening dew moistened my feet through my shoes as Phoenix led me around the big farmhouse to the thing this place was named after. A Weeping Willow, a hundred or so yards from the house, bigger than I had ever seen. It stood three stories high, limp branches hanging to the knee-high grass and wildflowers below.

The smell of the campfire hit me first. It burned bright a few dozen yards before the Willow. Logs for seats stretched around it in a half-moon, facing the woman who started it all. Ophelia.

Or Beatrice.

She didn't look as she had in the photo on her website. There, aside from her questionable, eccentric style, she'd looked like an average woman. Somewhere between a size twelve to eighteen, with full cheeks, a well-endowed chest, and pronounced curves through her midsection.

Now, her cheeks hollowed into the cavern of her mouth. Because of the thinness in her face, her eyes were bigger, almost protruding. In the floor length gown, I couldn't make out her figure in much detail, but she would swim in a size twelve now.

To her right, a young woman sat on a stump with a guitar in her lap. When Ophelia caught sight of us, she said something to the younger woman, and she started strumming. Each flick was quiet, almost haunting.

That didn't change when I stepped closer and got a better look at her.

I could only tell she was a woman because of the dress that hung on her lanky frame. Her face was just as thin, just as sharp, as Phoenix's. I couldn't make out her features from the distance, but the lack of weight she carried was evident even from here.

The same applied to the few dozen people sitting on logs, facing Ophelia. Even the children sitting on their mothers' and fathers' laps. They were all different races, different ages, but wore almost identical clothing. Every man sat in a pair of loose, flowing pants. I was the only woman who wore jeans. The rest had a floor-length skirt. Ophelia included.

The necklines on the men's shirts exposed chest hairs, but every woman's reached her collarbone.

Modesty? Hardly what I expected from a bunch of hippies. I'd imagined them all as nudists.

Once Phoenix and I sat in the back on the last log, Tempest at my side and Dude at his, Ophelia pressed her hands together in a prayer against her chest. "Everyone, please pause and close your eyes. Ground yourself in this moment." She spoke above the guitar, but with her soft tone, I found myself tilting my ear in her direction to hear better. "Listen to the wind. Feel the air on your skin. Smell the burning wood and taste your last meal on your tongue."

I can do all of that with my eyes open, thanks.

Ophelia followed her own advice though. While everyone sat with their hands pressed together before their chest, breathing deeply, she did the same. Kept her eyes closed throughout it too.

I scanned the crowd in search of Jasmine. But so many people had long dark hair here. Men and women alike were underweight. There wasn't enough to distinguish them all from the back of their heads.

"One more deep breath," Ophelia said. "In deeply..." A collective inhale. "Out long and slow." A collective exhale. Ophelia smiled and lowered her hands to her sides, palms open, facing the crowd. "Very good, everyone."

She said something else, but I could hardly hear her back here.

"Soon, we'll begin our affirmations and meditation. But we've got two newcomers today, one who's in the crowd back there." She pointed to me, then scanned her surroundings. "And another who I believe is on a tour. We'll speak with him in a bit. For now, Maddie, would you please stand?"

A cringe worked its way up my spine. But I did as she asked, forcing a smile. Dozens of eyes landed on me. I searched again for Jasmine, but I either missed her, or she wasn't here. No sign of Bronwyn either.

"Excellent," Ophelia said. "Would you like to introduce yourself to everyone? Or are you shy? Would you like me to?"

"Uh," I said, looking around. "The latter."

"How sweet. We could always use another quiet one around here." Giggling, she shimmied her shoulders. "Everyone, this is Maddie Kramer. She is a dog trainer back home. She, unfortunately, lives with chronic pain." Throughout the crowd, sympathetic *awws* sounded, and frowns turned my way. "The rigidity of a nine to five is exhausting her. She came to us looking for pain relief, and when she reached out, I knew we could help. She's only staying for the week-end. For now, at least." Another one of those little snickers. On the phone, it had sounded creepy. Here, it was sweet. Even when the others joined in. "So try to make her feel at home. Say hello if you get a chance."

A few folks waved, and I waved back.

"You don't have to stay for the meditation and affirmations unless you'd like to," Ophelia said. "That may mean you'll miss out on the snacks, but dinner will be served in an hour or two, and you can eat then. Or you can stay." Smiling wider, she opened her arms at her sides. "We are a welcoming bunch."

Any opportunity to understand this place better was one I'd take. "That sounds nice. Thank you."

"What's ours is yours. When we're finished here, we'll set up your tent, and—Oh, there you are!" Ophelia looked behind me. "This is our other new guest. Everyone, say hello to Bentley."

My head spun around so fast, I was surprised it didn't fall off my shoulders.

There he stood. Bentley Roycroft, wearing a pair of blue jeans, a V-neck navy blue T-shirt, and a smile that said, *Don't be too mad*. Beside him, a blonde woman walked with her hair in a bun, wearing a blue floor-length turtleneck dress.

"You've gotta be shitting me," I said under my breath.

In a hushed tone, Phoenix said, "Do you know him?"

"Sorry, Ophelia," the woman beside Bentley said. "We were just setting up his tent. He brought one of his own."

"How nice. I'm sure you'll be very comfortable tonight."

"I know I will, ma'am," Bentley said. "It's roomy too. If you're short on tents, my girlfriend could stay with me." He gestured my way. "Plenty of space for us both."

My jaw tightened, and my eyes narrowed.

"Is that right, Maddie?" Ophelia asked, but my eyes were still on him. "Is this the boyfriend you were telling me about?"

Bentley wiggled a brow. "I hope there wasn't another in the lineup."

The boyfriend I came here to get away from. "Yes, this is him."

"I see." Silence snuck in, only the wind rustling through the trees. "Would you like us to set you up a tent in that case?"

"Yeah, would you, Mads?" Bentley asked.

Tracing my tongue along my teeth, I weighed my options. A sheet suspended over a couple branches, or a plastic weather and bug proof tent. "I'll stay with him."

"Are you sure?" Phoenix asked. His tone was gentle, concerned. "If you want to bunk with me, I've got room."

I appreciated it. And so far, I liked Phoenix. He seemed more stable than Ophelia, and he had been here long enough to show me the ropes. Just before we came this way, he was about to tell me something vital, something that would steer me away from this place. Something that might have given me answers.

But Bentley and I needed to talk. Damn it.

"No, that's alright. Thank you." I turned my attention to Ophelia. "Is it okay if he and I head to his tent for a while? Just catch up on things before dinner?"

"Surely." Another smile, but a darted glance at Bentley. "Holler if you need anything."

Chapter 9

"What the hell is wrong with you?" I stood inches before Bentley, speaking barely above a whisper. Now that the sun had set, only a small lantern hanging from the tent pole illuminated the space. Didn't make it easy to read his expression. "Did you give them your real name?"

"No, did you?" His volume was as low as mine. "And nothing's wrong with me. You wouldn't talk to me, so—"

"So you followed me here like a stalker?"

"I didn't follow you," he said. "I copied you. Daisy told me you were taking the case, so I googled this place, and I filled out the contact form."

"Yeah, because that makes it better, Bentley." I crossed my arms against my chest. "I told you very specifically that I was not ready, so you forced me into a conversation with you? You think that's fair?"

"It's been more than a month, Maddie." His lips tugged downward, but his brows furrowed in annoyance. "You've had plenty of time. At some point, we're either gonna have to talk, or you're gonna have to cut the cord."

"I told you I wasn't ready to do either."

Silence. Silence so loud, it hurt. Him more than me, judging by the softening of his eyes and his slightly parted lips. "That's where we're at? You're thinking about ending this?"

A stab ached through my chest.

Shoulders slouching, I propped my hands on my hips and shook my head. "I'm working. You shouldn't have followed me."

"Nice deflection." He glowered and sharpened his tone but kept his voice low. "You can't be mad at me. This place is bat shit. All those cars out there? I don't know about you, but I only counted a few dozen people. The girl showing me around was talking about star seeds and how she's a breatharian."

"A what?"

"Something about prana? Hell if I know. She doesn't eat. She thinks that once you've reached divinity, whatever the hell that is, you can survive without food and water." His tone switched to a mocking, slow rendition of Ophelia's quiet falsetto. "'Just breathing in the light and air of the world around you.' Anorexia, that's what she has. I think they all do."

"Or they're being starved. Or do drugs or have some illness from living in these conditions." I rubbed a hand over my face. "It's weird. It's really damn weird. But I would've been fine. I didn't need your protection."

"'Course not. You never do." He trailed his tongue over his lips. "And who was that guy you were talking to? The one whose tent you were about to sleep in?"

I rolled my eyes but had to fight the smile that twitched the corners of my lips. "Seriously? You're jealous?"

"Jealous? No. Concerned about your decision-making skills? Yeah."

"His name is Phoenix, and he's gay. So yeah, if you hadn't shown, I would've taken his offer, because he's one of the few people here who seems to have his head on at least somewhat straight." A bug whizzed by, and I swatted it away. "Right before he led me to the fire, he was about to tell me something. Something about how I should go home because this place gets really dark. He's been here so long, he didn't even know what year it is. And he's definitely on something. I think they all are."

"I thought the same thing." Lowering himself to the air mattress, Bentley scratched Tempest's head. She laid at his feet, patiently waiting for us to finish our argument. "I thought dope at first, but Sunshine—the girl who showed me around—her pupils weren't constricted. Weren't dilated either."

"And they would be if they were taking hallucinogens." I sat beside him. "I haven't even seen the girl I came here to find."

Bentley's eyes met mine, slightly widened, brows pinched in the center.

We were thinking the same thing. I wasn't ready to go there.

But he was. "You think one of those abandoned cars out there was hers?"

"I'm sure one of them *is* hers." I rubbed at the chills that swept over my skin. "Until I have a reason to, I'm not gonna talk about her in the past tense, Bentley."

Swallowing, he gave a nod. "Alright."

Another long moment of silence, only the sound of Tempest panting filled the space.

Bentley broke it with, "Who is she? The girl you came here for."

"Jasmine Armstrong. A little older than Daisy. Pretty, seemed like a good kid, but always kinda troubled." Letting out a deep breath, I trailed my hands down my thighs. "She started going down conspiracy theory rabbit holes in high school after her dad died. A back injury gave her chronic pain a year or so ago. She started looking for a career outside of the corporate world where she would have a little more freedom, stumbled upon this place, and told her mom some really cryptic shit about *the end*. Her brother also thinks she's on something but doesn't know what."

"What do you mean, the end?" Bentley asked.

"No idea. Something about how they'd be together again in the end?" Chewing on my cheek, I shook my head. "Brings that whole 'don't drink the Kool-Aid' thing to a whole new level."

"Do you think that's what she was talking about?" Concern wrinkled his forehead, a frown tugging at the edges of his lips. "Like a Jim Jones mass suicide?"

Willow Grove and Jonestown—later known as the Jonestown Massacre—weren't all that different. There was a similar basis, in that both walked the line between commune and cult, requiring members to sell off all their assets before they joined. Both cults had a religious aspect. Jim Jones claimed to be a Christian, while Willow Grove had a hogwash of a thousand different ideologies. Brainwashing seemed as common here as it did in Jonestown.

"Maybe? But Jonestown was different." Scratching my head, it took a few moments to put words to it all. "Jim Jones was a psychopath. His commune was all about control and power. But Ophelia doesn't have the personality type to lead a cult. Not from what I've seen at least. She doesn't own this place either. Her name isn't on anything. Money's a big component though. The business netted almost a mil last year."

"You don't think?" Bentley lowered his voice, looking toward the exit of the tent. "She definitely has that charismatic magnetism to her."

"She seems highly empathetic. Everything I've seen of her so far is passive and docile. I don't see any of the authoritarian or narcissistic attributes that are so common in cult leaders." I shot him a look. "But we only met for all of five seconds before you showed up."

"That's not fair," he said. "You didn't have to run in here with me."

"Yeah, I kinda did." I glared. "Wouldn't have been great if I called you Bentley Roycroft in front of them, would it?"

Licking his lips, he raised a shoulder. "Bentley Radcliffe."

"What did you tell them you do?"

"Registered nurse. Seemed close enough to what I do but far enough that it'd be hard for them to figure out who I was." As I nodded my approval, he bumped his elbow into mine. "Just a dog trainer, huh?"

"Doubted they'd let me in if I said I used to be a cop."

"Probably not."

A deep breath eased from my nostrils, softening my tense shoulders. "At least we're on the same page now."

And as much as it pained me to admit, I was glad I wasn't alone here. Would I have survived on my own? Obviously. It'd take more than a bunch of drugged up hippies to take me down. But Bentley had medical training I didn't. Maybe he could help me pin down what drug these people were taking.

"Are we?" He cocked his head to the side. "On the same page? Because when you confirmed that we were a couple, Ophelia seemed kind of worried about you."

"She did, didn't she?" Further illustrating my point that she seemed more empathetic than most cult leaders.

"Can't help but wonder why." He propped his chin in his hand. "What did you tell her about me?"

Something between a laugh and a snort escaped me. "You're worried about the cult leader's opinion of you?"

"If she thinks I beat you or some shit, yeah, I'm kinda worried." He glanced behind him. "Especially after seeing that field. You gotta get pictures of that and investigate all those license plates."

"Maybe we'll try to sneak out tonight after everyone's in bed."

"Sure, it's not a far walk. But you're still evading my question here."

"I told her we were going through something right now." Nibbling my lower lip, my eyes flicked between his. "And we are, aren't we?"

For a few heartbeats, we just looked at one another. And I hated how warm my chest became.

Before Bentley was here, there were chills all over my arms, hair standing on the back of my neck, but now? My shoulders were lax. The warmth of his body radiated toward me, heating up all that unpleasant ice in the air. It was like we were on any other camping trip. Better yet, like we were just sitting in my living room.

No matter how much time apart, we always fell back to this. Familiarity. Friendship. An invisible tether that had connected the two of us for as long as I could remember. Every time we sat beside one another, it was like we had never been apart.

"We were," he said. "We don't have to keep going through it. We can just work it out, Maddie."

I couldn't stop my scoff. Turning away, I clenched my fists and shook my head.

"What? What did I say?"

"You want to move past it, Bentley?" I stood. "Maybe take some accountability. Stop acting like this was a small thing. You weren't just late for a date, you helped Sam—"

"Knock, knock." Phoenix's voice sounded behind me. The tent was zipped shut, but the outline of his frame—and Dude's at his side—cast a shadow inside. "Sorry to interrupt. We're all heading to dinner. Are you guys coming?"

Bentley said, "No," while I said, "Yes."

I shot Bentley a wide-eyed, teeth gritted glare. "Yeah, sorry. We'll be just a minute."

"No problem. Just meet us at the Willow," Phoenix said. "I'll show you the path from there."

"Great, thanks," I called. I spun back around to Bentley, pointing a finger at him, lowering my voice. "I'm at work. There are young, impressionable kids who have been manipulated into joining this thing. Whatever the hell it is, it's dangerous, and I want to help them. I don't have time for this right now. So either stay here by yourself or come with me and play the part. But do not screw this up, Bentley. I can't help these people if you screw this up."

For half a second, his jaw tightened. Then it released. The slightest bit, his eyes softened. "Okay. I'll play the part."

"Thank you."

"But we have to figure this shit out, Maddie."

Shutting my eyes, I massaged down the bridge of my nose.

"Figure out what you did wrong, then maybe we can figure this shit out."

* * *

WITH AN OIL LAMP FOR LUMINANCE, PHOENIX LED US PAST THE barn and fenced-in field. An occasional moo sounded inside, suggesting that was where the cows lived. On the other end of the field, we walked past a chicken coop. By the time Phoenix led us onto a trail at the edge of the field, we were just getting past the small talk.

Holding a branch up so it was easier for me to get past, Phoenix glanced at Bentley behind me. "So you're an RN, right?"

"Yeah, but I don't know how I feel about it all." It shocked me how natural Bentley's voice was. If we'd only just met, I'd have no reason to believe he was lying. "There's so much wrong with the medical industry."

"I think everyone can agree with that." Now that Bentley had passed, Phoenix cut ahead of me again. "Everyone here, obviously. But even the outside world. Doctors and nurses don't have any compassion usually, you know? No offense or anything."

"None taken," Bentley said. "That's actually what made coming here so appealing for me."

"That right?" Phoenix arched a brow at him over his shoulder.

"Yeah, my sister-in-law was in the hospital for a while. Long story. But she had a long recovery, and only a couple of the nurses really gave a shit about what she was going through." Maybe Bentley wasn't playing a part after all. "She had some psychiatric things to work through. But no denying she had physical injuries too. Some pretty bad nerve compression in her back. No loss of sensation, just pain that radiates down her leg. She's got a history of drug abuse, so they wouldn't give her anything strong. I'm a nurse too, so I get it, but when she complained of the pain, they said stuff like, 'We can give you ibuprofen, but just know, if you're taking it so often, you're running the risk of ruining your stomach lining and ending up with a bleeding ulcer.'"

Phoenix huffed. "Basically saying, 'that sucks.'"

"Pretty much." Bentley stumbled over a small rock and cursed under his breath. When he recovered, he continued. "But it was more than that too. Like they thought she was just drug-seeking. She wasn't. She never even liked downers. It's just—hell, I don't know. Walking into a hospital or doctor's office these days is a lot like walking into an airport. You're treated like a criminal, no matter the circumstance. And I guess that's where my head is. I got into health-care because I want to help people. But I'm not sure modern medicine does much of that."

"I hear you on all that." Phoenix slowed to a halt and lowered his voice. His eyes stayed on Bentley as a deep breath lifted and softened his narrow shoulders. "But you're not against all modern medicine, right? I mean, you just got here, so you still gotta have some faith in science."

Concern scrunched up Bentley's face. Cocking his head to the side, he glanced at me.

Sure, I had told him not to screw this up. That meant playing the part as best he could. But going undercover required improv.

Quickly, too fast for Phoenix to notice, I gave a short nod of approval.

"I don't think science is the problem." Bentley shrugged. "I think the medical complex is. It'd be stupid to throw out the baby with the bathwater."

Phoenix's shoulders dropped further with relief. "I was hoping you'd say that. Before we get any closer, and before we go back to camp, could you take a look at something for me?"

Bentley cocked his head to the side but nodded. "Sure. Like an infected scratch or something?"

Phoenix licked the inside of his teeth, wiggled a brow, and shifted his head from left to right. "Or something. Mind holding this, Maddie?"

I accepted the oil lamp from his palm.

He lifted the back of his shirt, tugged down the top of his pants, and spun around.

As soon as the yellow light of the oil lamp touched his upper glute, I gasped.

I didn't mean to, and I knew I should've bitten back my shock, but how could I?

WG, roughly the size of my open palm, stamped onto his ass in beautiful calligraphy. The rest of his skin was a pearly, pale white, but that WG was blacker than the night sky overhead.

"Holy shit," I said, bending for a better view. "These assholes branded you?"

"I'm not supposed to tell anybody, especially not newcomers, so keep it quiet, if you don't mind." He glanced over his shoulder, holding a tree for stability. "But kinda standing here with my ass out, and this shit hurts. Does it look infected?"

It's not like I was the medical professional here. But judging by the swelling that made one of his cheeks look almost twice as big as the other and the yellowish puss draining from the blister at the bottom edge of the W, I would guess yes.

"Shit, man." Bentley kneeled, gesturing for me to bring the light closer. Given the flickering nature of an oil lamp, I had to get close to give him a good view. When the metal lip touched the inflamed, fiery skin, Phoenix yelped. "Sorry, sorry."

Phoenix breathed deeply through the pain. "All good."

"I can't examine it really well in this light at this angle without PPE," Bentley said. "But this is bad, dude. Any burn that leaves charred skin is *really* bad."

"Yeah, kind of figured," Phoenix said. "Hurt pretty bad too."

"This is the sort of thing you should definitely see a doctor about. Which I'm not, unfortunately," Bentley said.

Phoenix's breath was so deep this time, it formed a cloud of steam before his face. He lifted his pants back to his waist, let his shirt fall, and spun to face us, wincing. "Doctor's not an option."

Of course not. Because this was a punishment.

If he were a newer member, I'd suspect an initiation of some kind. But he had been here all his adult life. If it were just any regular wound, I might have cracked it up to a ritual of some kind. But it was a brand. Their business's brand. One he wasn't allowed to tell anyone about.

Bentley's frown suggested he'd come to the same conclusion. "I've got some antibiotics. That might be enough to stop the infection from spreading? But if it gets worse, man, you gotta go. Infections aren't a joke. Antibiotics were one of the biggest medical developments in human history. It's why we live to a hundred now."

Phoenix didn't roll his eyes or wave a dismissive hand at Bentley. His face stayed neutral, suggesting he already knew everything that Bentley explained. "I'm allergic to penicillin. Any chance you've got something else?"

A long moment of silence as they stared at one another. Eventually, Bentley gave a nod. "Yeah. I've got options. You can take your pick when we get back."

"Thanks," Phoenix said. "I've got some damn good apple butter in my tent if you want it. Maybe not a fair trade, but it's amazing. Made it myself."

Bentley huffed a laugh. "Appreciate it, but dinner'll be enough for me."

"We better get to it then, huh?"

Chapter 10

A SOLARIUM BIGGER THAN MY HOME.

That's what Phoenix led us to.

The edge of the trail opened to a small field. Most of it was a black blur in the dim moonlight. All I could clearly make out was the large glass building. Vines climbed the windows and trellises, disguising the interior. Potted plants covered the space, brightened by blowing oil lamps that hung on metal posts.

Phoenix held the door open for me and Bentley. Three wooden tables stretched from end to end. Long benches perched before them. A fourth stood parallel to them. There were only three chairs in the whole room, and they were before that one. The table at the end, the one that gazed upon the people of Willow Grove. Ophelia sat in one wearing a dress like all the other women's, Bronwyn in the middle wearing a flowy blue shirt, and Jasmine in the last.

An audible breath of relief left me when I saw her.

Like I had discerned from her pictures on social media, she was a pretty girl. All her life, she had been petite, thin. Couldn't have topped five foot three.

No way she was more than a hundred pounds soaking wet now.

She, like the others, wore a high-neck, floor-length skirt. Her dark brown waves lacked all the luster and volume they'd had in her photos. While everyone else's hair was tied in a bun, hers fell in messy curls to the middle of her waist. Dark circles lined the undersides of her brown eyes. The creamy white of her skin from the photos was grayer now with deep purple undertones. A white sling hung over her shoulder, propping up her left arm.

Her mere presence had my heart pumping harder. That sling did nothing to soften my anxieties.

The three of them sat before the few dozen of us like royalty ahead of their servants. Jasmine wasn't just a member of Willow Grove. She was a leader.

"Here." Phoenix gestured over his shoulder for me to follow him. "They want us up front."

The chattering crowd quieted as the three of us and Tempest ascended the aisle. Jasmine glanced at me, then at Bentley, only to whisper something in Bronwyn's ear. Ophelia looked their way, smiling, and said something. Bronwyn gave her a glance before returning to Jasmine with a smile.

My feet clapped against the straw covered stone floor, knee aching with each step. I tried not to study the three of them too closely. If it looked like I was staring, they might catch on to why I was really here.

Instead, I took note of the spreads on the tables. A hell of a lot more food than I expected given everyone's lanky frames.

Each of the three tables had an entire turkey, chicken, and ham. Bowls of salad and dressing sat neatly between them. Buns and loaves of bread steamed from the baskets every few feet apart. Logs of butter laid beside each one. Not to mention the fruit bowls.

More than that, the tables were staged. It wasn't just food thrown onto a block of wood. Pretty silverware and cloth napkins laid beside each plate. Garnishes of flowers and ivy climbed every surface, reminding me of wedding Pinterest boards. They matched the lines and flowers that climbed up the glass walls perfectly.

Why were they so skinny if they had all this food?

As we moved closer to the edge of the room, my stomach spun. There were no open seats on my left and right at the benches. The only place to sit? The bench directly across from Bronwyn, Ophelia, and Jasmine.

"Sorry we're late." Phoenix hoisted a leg over the bench, sat, and gestured for us to do the same. "Had to stop for a bathroom break."

"Don't apologize, dear." Ophelia stretched across the table and gave his hand a big squeeze. "Thank you for showing them around."

"No worries." Phoenix stifled a yawn and reached for the tin pitcher of water.

As he poured his cup, Ophelia frowned at him sympathetically. "Oh, poor thing. You're exhausted, aren't you?"

"Eh, it's just those fire drill nights." Phoenix gave her a smile. "Don't worry, I'm fine."

"Fire drills?" Bentley asked, sitting beside him.

"Yes, with the forest fires up north lately, we felt it best to implement monthly drills," Bronwyn said. "Phoenix stays on crowd control. Always does an excellent job."

"Do my best." Phoenix took a sip of water, then lowered his voice to a snippy whisper, like a teenager quietly feuding with their parent. "I'd do a better job if they weren't always at three in the morning."

Bronwyn's smile at Phoenix was tightlipped, but almost genuine when he looked at me. "Tomorrow though, if you don't mind, could you tie him up outside?" He glanced at Tempy. "We don't like dogs in the dining hall. I'm sure you can understand."

It took everything in me to return his smile. Sitting on the edge, directly across from Jasmine, I gave Tempest's head a scratch. "Yeah, definitely. Sorry for the inconvenience. She's actually a service dog, so maybe tomorrow, I'll just sit outside with her to eat."

"Wow, is that right?" Mouth falling open, Ophelia propped her elbows on the table. "She's a guide dog?"

"More like an accessibility aid." Talking about her like she was nothing more than a tool for my convenience made my chest tighten. I stroked my fingers through her scruff to loosen it. "When my knees are bad, she helps me walk. If I fall down, she can alert people for help."

"Why didn't you say so?" Bronwyn's eyes softened. "Forget I said anything. If you need her for those sorts of things, she's welcome wherever you are. We want you to feel as safe and at home here as we all do."

"That so kind of you." Actually sounded like a load of bullshit, but I had to play the part. "Thanks so much for your understanding. And for this place. I could tell it was beautiful already, but then I stepped in here." Laughing, hoping it sounded legitimate, I lifted my arms at my sides to gesture. "This is like something out of a fairytale. Or a wedding magazine. All the decor, the food—it's like a work of art."

"Aw, that's so sweet." Ophelia pressed a hand over her heart. Tears bubbled in her eyes. "Thank you so much. I always wanted to do that sort of thing. Decorate for parties or people's homes. Now I get to do it here every day, and it's a dream come true."

"I like to think all our dreams come true here. That's what Willow Grove is all about. A simple, beautiful life for everyone who enters." Using the wooden tongs, Bronwyn scooped salad to all three of our plates. Onto mine, he spooned some of the white dressing. "You've gotta try this. Everything is made from scratch, but the ranch is sourced entirely here at the Grove."

I dipped a piece of lettuce into it and popped it into my mouth. The flavor was fine. No better than Hidden Valley, but nothing worth complaining about. Still, I said, "Wow, it's amazing."

"Jasmine's recipe." Ophelia gestured to her, voice as warm and inviting as it had been when we first spoke. "It's the darndest thing. I made ranch all the time, but with dried ingredients. Always organic, never any GMOs, of course. Then when Jasmine came, she looked at all the herbs I already had growing, and she said to me, 'Ophelia, you don't need to use that prepackaged garbage. You have all you need.' Isn't that right, sweetheart?"

"It's one thing we all have in common." Jasmine's cadence

reminded me of the flap of a hummingbird's wings. Quiet but quick. "An affinity for simpler. Simpler is so often better. We have the cows here already. Why buy milk when we can use theirs?"

"Wish I weren't lactose intolerant." Bentley pointed at two glass bottles. "Are those vinegar and oil?"

Bentley ate milk and cookies with me almost nightly. He wasn't lactose intolerant.

While I didn't slide the plate away, I rested the fork inside it. There was a reason he wasn't eating that ranch dressing. Probably best I did the same.

"Sure is." Bronwyn passed them to Bentley. "More of a vinaigrette guy?"

"Usually." He wasn't. Still, Bentley poured it over the leaves of lettuce, giving a smile. "Thank you guys again for inviting me in. I'm having a really good time. Best camping trip I've had in a while."

"Thank you for joining us," Ophelia said.

"You two are the guests of honor." Bronwyn stretched across the table for the knife that sat beside the chicken. I tensed as he pinched the tip of the blade between his thumb and forefinger, holding the handle toward Bentley. "Would you like to do the honors?"

Halfhearted laugh escaping, Bentley thanked him again. He stood so he could reach the bird better. "It smells amazing. Are these chickens from the farm too?"

"Everything we eat, we had a hand in growing." Jasmine trailed her fingertips over Bronwyn's upper back, down his arm, and onto the tabletop. "He finally let me butcher one today."

Chuckling, Bronwyn rested his hand on the back of Jasmine's. He patted it a few times before twining their fingers together. "Don't make it sound so sinister, honey. It's just a lesson of life, one she wasn't ready to learn yet."

Holding hands. The middle-aged man and the twenty something-year-old girl before me were holding hands while his wife sat on his other side. All while one of the young girl's arms was tightened against her chest in a sling.

God, what had I walked into?

"One I'm afraid I'll never learn." Ophelia frowned at the chicken. "This little guy was Sapling. Such a shame he's gone now."

"He did live a good life though." Jasmine's eyes were sympathetic when they met Ophelia's. "It is the cycle of life, isn't it? Things live, and things die. Along the way, they provide new."

I couldn't stop staring at their hands twined together on the table.

Was this a polygamist cult? Polygamists were typically Mormon, a denomination of Christianity. I had yet to see anyone wearing a cross or holding a Bible.

Clearing his throat, Bentley nodded at Jasmine and made his first slice through the chicken's breast.

"Oh, I know dear." Ophelia rested her head on Bronwyn's shoulder, still frowning at dead Sapling on the table. "I just have to stop naming them."

Bronwyn kissed Ophelia's forehead, his hand still intwined with Jasmine's. "I keep telling you to, sweetheart."

"Maybe I'll learn one day." She cozied up against her husband and smiled at me. "You're not a vegan or anything like that, are you?"

"Animal lover, yes." I rubbed Tempest's ear and held her face closer when she relaxed into my palm. "Vegan, no. I tried to cut out meat once, and it was just too expensive. And too difficult. I'm not much of a cook, so pre-packaged stuff is my usual."

"No, you can't put that poison in your body." Jasmine leaned toward me, tone urgent. "Especially with your pain. All those seed oils and preservatives are just going to increase the inflammation."

Shit. Shouldn't have let that slip.

"That's what I keep telling her." Bentley made a *tsk* noise at me. "Luckily, she lets me cook for her now. We get everything from a butcher down the street. As much as I can, I pick up the produce at farmer's markets."

Damn. He played the part better than I did.

"You know, I gotta admit, I really respect that, Bentley," Bronwyn said. "We all have our places, right? But out there, in the outside world, we don't get to really embrace where we belong." He gestured between Ophelia and himself. "I know we didn't back in the day."

"Gods, no." Ophelia clasped a hand over her chest, still cuddling up to Bronwyn. "It was all work, pick up a pizza for dinner, rush home, sleep, work, pick up a pizza, and so on. Every day, the same thing. And I was never really fulfilled. Doing all this?" She gestured around the solarium. "Surrounded by all these friends—family, really—cooking together and building together. That's where we belong. It's our place as women, you know, Maddie?"

I opened my mouth to speak, but no words came out.

"Yeah, we've been talking a lot about that lately." Bentley laid a piece of chicken breast on my plate. "That's part of what made this place so appealing. Maddie wanted to check it out on her own, get a feel for this kind of lifestyle, but I knew we really had to immerse ourselves together for a couple of days. See if this is the type of life we both want to live."

What—barefoot, pregnant, baking bread each day? That was the "lifestyle" we were debating? That wasn't a lifestyle. It was systemic oppression women had only begun to escape in the last hundred years.

If my options were death or living like this, death was the clear winner.

But I'd demanded Bentley play the part. Gracefully, he was doing just that. I couldn't argue with him about views that I knew we agreed on. A single woman raised him, and he respected her more than anything. He was raising his daughter to be a strong independent woman too. Women were equal to men in every way, a fact he never debated.

It just came out of his mouth so easily, so smoothly, that I was silent for a moment.

"And so far, I'm really enjoying it." A knot thickened in the back of my throat, and I fought the urge to swallow it. "It's something we've really been considering lately. But giving up on my clients, that would be hard. Each week, I get to see all my puppies improve on their behavior and skills training. I don't know if I could never see all those dogs again."

"Oh, how sweet." Ophelia tapped her hand against her chest, eyes sympathetic. "You already have the knack for it. Caregiving, I mean. A lot like myself. I was meant to be a mother, and—well, everyone here. They're like my children. All the animals here, they'd love the kind of guidance you could give, Maddie."

"And you wouldn't be stuck here, of course," Bronwyn said. "Once a month or so, we take a trip into town for things we can't grow or make ourselves. We could always take an extra long one, just for you to go see all the animals you love so much."

A chill quivered up my spine.

Restricted entry and exit. Supervised activity in the 'outside world.' Common enough in a commune or cult, but this was the closest confirmation of it since I'd arrived.

"How sweet." Doing my best to match Ophelia's warm ambience, I patted a hand over my heart. "That's so considerate. It will definitely play a part in our decision."

"Absolutely." Bentley held the chicken leg up, sandwiched between the blade and a fork. "Who prefers dark meat?"

"I'll take that." Bronwyn held up his plate. As Bentley dropped the chicken leg onto it, Bronwyn glanced at Ophelia and Jasmine. "The dark meat's denser."

"Do you like the skin?" Jasmine squinted at my plate. "It's just— well, I'm sure you know. The light meat, without the skin, is far more nutrient-dense, far fewer calories."

Did she just call me fat? I fought the instinct to tighten my jaw. Instead, I forced a smile. "Oh, no. I'm saving it for my dog."

"Thank Gods," Jasmine said, chuckling. "We don't need much to survive. No one does. Nothing, really. That skin alone would be enough to last for the whole day." Jasmine nodded to Tempest. "The world these days is so full of consumption. That's all anyone does. Consume, consume, consume. What kind of life is that? And what will we be leaving for everyone and everything else?"

Concern about overconsumption? Was that the conversation we were having?

A valid discussion, I'd admit. Consumerism damaged the planet. Constant online shopping affected the reward system in our brains, triggering a type of psychological addiction in some. Not to mention the people who were harmed by it all. Exploited employees paid two cents an hour in horrible conditions just so corporations could make more money; the poor who couldn't afford to eat, couldn't find a steady address long enough to land a minimum-wage job while the heads of the companies hoarded wealth.

But that wasn't the conversation Jasmine was trying to have. She seemed to genuinely believe that my hundred-pound German Shepherd could survive on a single piece of chicken skin for the entire day. Survive, maybe. For a week, or two, possibly a couple more. At some point, she would starve to death. She would die.

This wasn't a simple difference in opinion. It was fact and fiction.

How the hell could I say that without blowing my cover?

"Yeah, Sunshine mentioned something about breatharians earlier," Bentley said, laying a piece of chicken breast on Jasmine's plate. "I gotta admit, I'm kinda confused by how that works."

"We were too, in the beginning." Bronwyn sliced into his chicken leg. "And it's not that simple. Breatharian makes it sound as though that's all we eat. Just air and sunlight. As you can see from this spread, that's not the case."

"It's about vibrations, you know?" Jasmine asked. "After you've had a big meal, you almost feel like you're hung over. Eating, like all things, has to be done in moderation. It's a necessary but regrettable act, really."

She couldn't be serious. There was no way these people were serious.

"Enlightenment is about letting go of earthly needs." Ophelia sat forward and held up her plate for Bentley. When he dropped some chicken onto it, she laid it back on the table. "The less attached we are to these forms, the closer we are to reaching our higher selves."

"So the less of you there is, the closer you are to your Gods?" I asked.

It just slipped out. Maybe a bit backhanded, maybe like an insult, but I needed to understand why they were so thin. Were they sick? No one withheld food from them. Did that mean they were actively choosing to be thinner because it was closer to an ethereal form?

"There are plenty of other benefits." Bronwyn carefully sliced the meat from the bone. As he did, it was hard to ignore the fullness of his own cheeks while the women beside him looked one sharp movement from breaking skin and exposing bones. "We feel better eating less. It's spiritual for us, of course. Like you said, the less of us there is, the more our spirit can move through us. But going to the bathroom is so much smoother." *Gross.* "We don't feel as dragged down throughout the day. There's a whole process we go through as we transition to breatharian living, and I'd love to walk you through it, Maddie. It's a few weeks long, but I know by the end of it, your pain will be so much lighter."

Sure. My chronic pain may improve if I stopped eating. Because the brain can only focus on one type of pain at a time. If my stomach ached from hunger, how could it center on the throbbing in my knee?

"Uh, yeah." Forcing a smile, I nodded slowly. "Yeah, maybe I'll try that."

"It's tough in the beginning," Phoenix said under his breath. The first time he had spoken since we'd sat down. When all eyes turned on him, he poured a bit more ranch into his bowl of salad. "But worth it in the end. I practically live on leaves these days, and I've never felt so light and closer to the spirit."

"So true, Phoenix," Ophelia said.

"Be careful with that dressing though," Jasmine said, sipping from her glass. "I added a little something to it tonight."

My stomach twisted. "Oh? Like what?"

She laughed softly, eyes flicking over me for a few long moments. "You'll see soon. It'll be a fun trip."

Ah, shit.

Chapter 11

I DIDN'T EAT ANYTHING ELSE AT DINNER.

I didn't talk much more either.

Before the effects had even set in, my heart hammered against my ribcage and sweat dampened my hands. Ophelia, Bronwyn, and Jasmine kept talking about enlightenment and ethereal realities. If I leaned into this, I would feel it too. If I focused on them, I could transcend consciousness.

That freaked me the hell out.

I wasn't lying when I said, "I'm feeling a bit queasy," and bolted out the entrance we had come in. Tempest rushed to my side, Bentley was close at my tail, and Phoenix stayed on his. Couldn't say if it was the drugs or the anxiety, but as soon as I burst through that door into the cool evening breeze, my stomach lurched. Grabbing hold of a tree for support, I emptied the contents of my stomach onto the forest floor.

Bentley's hand trailed over my back. "It's alright. You're gonna be alright."

"No the hell I won't," I snapped, digging my nails into the bark. "Hallucinogens and me don't mix. They never have."

"It'll last a few hours and then you'll be alright." He pulled my hair back, but it was too late. Vomit already contaminated a few strands. "Just gotta stick it out for a few hours."

"Not in there." Panting hard, I held onto the tree and shut my eyes. "I can't do all the hippie-dippy shit right now. It's gonna freak me the hell out."

"Shit, man, I'm so sorry." Phoenix's voice came from somewhere in the vicinity, but I kept my eyes shut. "It's probably acid. Might be DMT? Could be shrooms. By morning though, you'll be back to normal."

"I know how drugs work, thanks." Biting his head off wasn't my intention. He didn't do this, and I knew that. But damn it. "What's today's date?"

"It doesn't count, Maddie." Bentley's fingers still swept over my back. "You didn't do this intentionally—"

"Twice in one year," I said under my breath, eyes still sealed shut. "How the hell do I get drugged twice in one year?"

"It's really screwed up," Phoenix said. "Jasmine, she's not right these days. But Bronwyn had a hand in that. I know damn well he did." Annoyance tinged his voice, maybe anger. "They should've told you. You should never slip someone hallucinogens. Of all the drugs, you shouldn't slip someone those."

"Especially someone in recovery," Bentley said.

I flung my eyes open and shot him a look.

"It kind of matters at the moment." His frown was hardly visible in the dim moonlight and glow of oil lamps from inside the solarium. "I'm sorry to betray your confidence, but it does matter."

"Shit, really?" Phoenix spoke on a heavy breath. "I'm so sorry. That really sucks. But I agree. If your clean date's really important to you, this doesn't count. You didn't choose it."

Maybe not, but didn't I, in some respect? While I didn't consent to using the drugs, I came here to find out what they were. Here was my answer.

My stomach lurched again, and I bent over to spill it all out.

With every spasm, my heart hammered harder. Sweat pearled my brow at first, then erupted all over and poured down me like rain. Each breath got harder to take, like my lungs couldn't fully accept air.

"This isn't acid or mushrooms," I said between dry heaves. "It's— it's something else. This is different. This is—Ah, shit." I bent over hurling again.

"I mean, I don't think anybody has real acid these days," Phoenix said. "Maybe some type of upper mixed in? I don't know, but it's not gonna kill you."

"Feels like it is." The sweat drenched every inch of me now. That cool breeze feathered through my clothing, chilling me to the bone, yet it was like fire sat on top of my skin. Angrily ripping at my hoodie, I struggled to get it off my arms. "Get this off. Get it off!"

"Okay, okay." Like he had so many times, Bentley lifted the hoodie off my frame. He passed it to Phoenix and pressed a hand to my neck. As he stared at me, concern riddling his brown eyes, a pale yellow glow illuminated the edges of his face. Gradually, it encompassed his whole head until a mystical halo became clear. "Your heart rate's a little fast, but not heart attack level. It's probably a panic attack."

So stable, so steady. Everything else swayed and throbbed, but not Bentley. I grabbed hold of his forearm for support. "How did you know?"

"How did I know what?" His voice was like that of the breeze. Calm, soothing. When he trailed his fingers from my neck down my arm, they felt just the same as his voice sounded.

Which told me it was kicking in.

"That there was something wrong with the dressing," I said. "You're not lactose intolerant. How did you know?"

"I didn't think it was drugs." Shaking his head, he raised a shoulder. "They said it was all made here on the farm. Figured it was fresh milk from the cow. Unpasteurized." He looked at Phoenix over his shoulder and wagged a finger. "Another thing to remember. Antibiotics did the most to expand our lifespans, and pasteurized milk is right behind it. It kills so many diseases, and you can probably do it yourself. Just boil it until it reaches a hundred and sixty-one degrees and keep it there for a while. If you want to not get sick in this place, try to remember to pasteurize your milk."

"Noted," Phoenix said. "You should probably eat, Maddie. Or at least drink something—"

"I'm not eating or drinking anything else that those people touched," I said.

Pressing his lips together, he nodded slowly. "I can't blame you there."

"I've got some bottled water in my cooler. And some other stuff that might help you calm down." Bentley wiped some sweat from my forehead. "How about we go back to camp and ride this out in my tent?"

* * *

IT ONLY WORSENED ON THE WALK BACK. TIME MOVED SO slowly. Every lift of my foot to take a step felt like a minute passed.

From the shrubbery that lined the trail, a ruckus sounded. Whispering, singing, laughing. When I asked if anyone else heard it, Phoenix told me that yes, it sounded like there were already some people back at the tents, and they were speaking.

But it didn't sound like normal voices. It was the hushed whispers and giggles of horror movies.

Worse than that were the visual hallucinations. This wasn't my first time taking a hallucinogenic. The effects had usually made the walls breathe and the lights shine brighter.. Everything just looked a little different, a little more fluid.

All those times before, as a teenager tripping face, I'd been in mine or my friend's house. A familiar place, with familiar people, and a general sense of safety.

Now, every time I looked to my left or right, the bushes and trees wiggled and spun. Leaves became faces. Their lips released those giggles and whispers. For a moment, they would resemble something from a fairytale, and the next, their eyes would stretch into their fore-head, their mouths would hang open, and their giggles would grow louder.

Not to mention the circles. Every hallucinogenic trip came with circles. It was like my mind was on a racetrack, spinning donuts around it over and over again.

We're walking through the woods. That tree has a face. The face's stretching, morphing into something else. It's laughing at me. We're walking through the woods. That tree has a face. Its face's stretching, morphing into something else. It's laughing at me again.

As if I was stuck in a time loop. We were in these woods, and we were never going to get out, because we were just going to keep walking past trees with faces that stretched and morphed and laughed.

Of course, that was the drugs. Because eventually, we did break from the foliage into the open field that framed the barn and farm-house. In the different surroundings, time sped up. Step by step, eyes on the camp ahead, I could see the progress we were making and had already made.

The loop now said, *Get to Bentley's tent. Lay on the air mattress. Close your eyes. Get to Bentley's tent. Lay on the air mattress. Close your eyes.*

My thoughts were music, singing to themselves in a rhythm.

Eventually, we got to Bentley's tent. I lay on his air mattress. I closed my eyes.

But all I could see again were those trees with faces. Bentley spoke, but all I heard were their giggles. Their giggles and their whis-pers. Rain droplets pattered the tent's peak, and music still sounded somewhere in the distance, but their giggles and whispers were loud enough now that I could understand them.

"Sober? You can't call yourself sober." Against the back of my eyelids, those trees got bigger, faces growing and shrinking. "You're a junkie, and you'll always be a junkie. Just like your mom, just like your dad. You're a killer just like him too. You're a junkie, and you'll always be a junkie. Just like your mom, just like your dad. You're a killer just like him too."

"Maddie." Bentley grasped hold of both my hands. "Maddie, open your eyes. Look at me."

I did.

There he was, with that white glowing halo around his head. The glow remained, but his features morphed too. My throat thickened, worried that he would morph into one of those trees and say all the things that they had. But he didn't. He morphed into the Bentley he'd been a decade ago, and then two decades. Then he was back to the modern Bentley, and morphing again, back and forth, aging and growing younger, until gray streaks lined his beard and wrinkles crinkled the corners of his eyes, and all those brown curls that framed his face turned gray. They dissolved back to brown, sharpening his jaw, then softening again when his face grew youthful and childlike.

Those whispers quieted. They were still there, bouncing between my ears, repeating those same three sentences on a loop, but softer now.

If I looked at him, they quieted.

"I'm losing my mind," I said, shaking my head, my own voice sounding like I was under water. "I—I don't understand. This is the worst thing I've ever felt. This doesn't feel like my head." An icy hand clapped against my forehead. It took too long for me to realize that it was my own. "This isn't—I've never taken a drug like this, Bentley. This is the most intense thing I've ever felt."

"That's how everyone describes their bad trips." As he spoke, his face I knew so well returned. Boyish cheeks, framed in a deep brown beard. Round brown eyes, soft with concern. "It'll stop in a few hours. Just relax and talk to me, okay? Whatever you're hearing, don't talk to them. Talk to me."

"I was talking?"

He rubbed a cold cloth down my cheek, giving a sad smile. "We used to have a lot of fun doing this back in the day."

"We were idiots." I grabbed the cloth from his hand and trailed it all the way down to my chest. Lying it there gave me more relief from the hot sweat than the cool wind outside. "Why would anyone do this for fun?"

Bentley chuckled. "Like you said. We were idiots."

"Kids. All kids are idiots." As I breathed in, those voices in my mind quieted further. They were hardly louder than a single headphone in my ear at one point volume. "It goes so fast. Everything goes so fast."

"Your current state is going to affect your perception of time." Still sitting on the edge of the bed, head blocking out my view of the top of the tent, he touched the side of my neck. "How are you feeling?"

Even in my state, I wouldn't admit aloud that I was terrified. Maddie Castle dared never admit to weakness. All I could do was shake my head.

"Yeah, figured," Bentley said, apparently reading my mind. "Your heart rate is still pretty high. I'm guessing your blood pressure is too. It's cold in here, but you're sweating, and your teeth are chattering." Were they? I hadn't noticed. "I think you need to sleep this off."

"Ever tried to sleep off acid?" I snorted. "I haven't even peaked yet. It's going to get worse before it gets better, and—"

"You'll sleep through it if I sedate you." With narrowed eyes, I opened my mouth to argue, but he continued before I could. "I know you're worried about your sobriety. But if we were at a hospital right now, a doctor would recommend doing the same thing. You're putting your body through more stress than it needs to be in. This panic attack won't give through your trip, and I don't want to torture you with it for another eight hours 'til it wears off. I've got everything I need, and I'll make sure no one comes in here to mess with you. Tempest is sleeping on the floor beside you. Just let me do this, okay?"

My sobriety was ruined anyway.

With all the feelings rushing through my body, the voices whispering when Bentley stopped talking, I would do damn near anything for relief. For my thoughts to slow, for the loops to cut, for my brain to feel like my own again.

Shutting my eyes, I stretched my arm out, veins up. "Do what you got to."

I didn't feel the needle go in. Just Bentley's warm fingertips. Then the chill that turned warm as it traveled up my arm and through my body.

The voices silenced. The racetrack vanished.

Darkness washed over me, and I had never been so grateful for it.

Chapter 12

TICK. TOCK.

A warm, wet tongue slapped against my cheeks. Eyes shut still, I waved her off. "Go lay down, Tempy."

More lapping licks.

Something between a grunt and a laugh escaped me. I reached up to stroke her fur, but thick nylon met my fingertips. Tempest wore a slip lead most of the time. Not a vest. But she was wearing a vest, and...

Eyes opening, I blinked hard. The darkness still enveloped me, enveloped us both, but light shone from below. As if the ground itself was glowing, illuminating the dog's face.

It did look like Tempest. The same dark brown eyes, the same black fur, but the smile was bigger. The ears pointed higher. The face, though almost identical, was broader. And that nylon, it was a harness that wrapped around the chest, the neck, with K-9 printed on its side.

"Bear?" I whispered.

His tail wagged, and he came in for more kisses.

My chest warmed while my heart hollowed. Bear was dead. He

had been dead for two years now. But he was here, and he was licking me, and—

Tick. Tock.

Tick. Tock.

Rubbing his ears, I sat forward.

A white, glowing floor. It stretched a dozen yards in each direction, with big black pillars every few feet apart. Beyond them was nothing. Pure, utter blackness.

What the hell was this?

Tick. Tock.

Using Bear for support, I brought myself upright.

Tick. Tock.

I spun around.

A long black rail, suspended from a bearing in the center, inched closer. The edge twinkled silver in the light of the disk. Like a blade.

Tick.

It inched closer.

Bear whined.

Tock.

Bear sprung onto all fours. The sudden jerk, having ahold of his harness, yanked me forward.

Tick.

"Bear, come!"

He ran, and he kept running. Straight to that black pillar at the edge of the disk.

Tick.

I bolted after him.

Each step altered my view of the pillar. From where I was sitting, it was only a tall black pole. But now, it warped and swayed and morphed in to more. A letter, maybe? B, or a—

3

It was the number three.

Bear ran straight through it.

Without thought, I followed him.

No more glowing white disk. No more tick tock.

My eyes pinched shut. Indiscernible yells and screams sounded. A few rooms over, maybe?

"You can't keep her from me, Natalie!" Sam.

That was Sam's voice.

Curled up in the crease of my legs, Bear whimpered.

Sitting up to comfort him, I jumped at the slam of the door. My Barbie nightlight shone in the corner. It gave me just enough light to see, just enough to run my fingers through Bear's fur as I stretched across the bed to reach the window. The touch was softer than the flap of a butterfly's wing, careful not to rattle the rings of the curtain.

Then Mom would know I was awake. She was already fighting with Dad, and she would be mad if I was up so late.

I knew better than to make her mad.

Out the window, Sam slammed the trunk down. He cussed under his breath.

Take me with you. Don't leave me here. Take me with you.

He stepped around the car, swung open the driver's side door, and sat inside. The engine roared to a start. Tires spun, and a plume of dust floated closer to my window.

Don't leave me here. Take me with you.

I touched the cool glass.

As if someone pushed me from behind, I fell straight through it.

I landed on the disk again.

Bear sat before me. Butt up in the air, tongue hanging out of his mouth, he wagged his tail.

Tick.

"What is this?" I whispered. "What's going on?"

Bear bolted to the next pillar.

I couldn't let him go in there alone. I couldn't *do* this alone. Whatever the hell this was, I needed him for it.

I rushed to my feet, and I ran, and just as I touched the black pillar, the next number, I fell again.

I sat on my cigarette-burned floral print sofa. Bear panted beside me. But he was so big now. He had to have been as big as I was. My feet didn't even reach the edge of the cushions.

Mom stood at the front door. She was big too. Twice the size of me.

"Can Maddie come out today?" A little boy's voice. He stood on the other side of the door, blocked by Mom's frame. His voice melted into the warm sunlight that trickled in from behind her silhouette.

"She's got to do chores first, kid," Mom said. "Come back in an hour, and—"

"What if I help her with her chores?" The little boy poked his head around Mom, and my heart warmed. Tears burned across my eyes when he smiled at me. "Then can we play?"

Mom made a sound I couldn't distinguish. "Whatever, Bentley. You two can do chores together when you get back. But don't think you're going straight to bed, Madison."

"We will, Miss Castle," Bentley said, smiling up at her. "I promise, we will."

I hopped down off the couch, and I ran to the door, and Bear was right behind me, and I walked through it—

And I fell onto that glowing white disk once more.

Tick.

Bear stood before me. Tail wagging, he barked.

Tock.

I was on my feet again, and Bear was running. At full speed, he burst through another one of those black pillars. That one, number six.

Tick.

I looked over my shoulder, and there it was again. That black bar and its sparkling blade. Only inches, maybe centimeters, from the number three.

Tick.

The black bar slashed through the pillar.

It popped, as though it were a balloon. Ashes erupted and rained all over.

I ran after Bear, straight into number six.

And it was dark.

Stars twinkled above me. The hot summer breeze plastered every hair on my body to the skin. Laughs billowed from my lips, and more from the boy who lay beside me on my right. Nuzzled up against my leg, Bear panted.

"Two more weeks," the boy said. "Two more weeks, and we never have to come back to this place."

"Counting down the days." Stroking my fingers through Bear's fur, I rolled my head to face him. "There's one thing that sucks though."

Bentley propped himself on his elbow, hand cradling his mess of brown waves. "What's that?"

"After we graduate, and you go to college, and I go to the city, we'll never be neighbors again." I blinked at the tears that bubbled in my eyes. "I'm gonna miss being your neighbor, Bentley Roycroft."

Tick. Tock.

That cerulean sky speckled with stars crashed down around me, and my back slammed again onto that white disk.

And the process repeated.

Bear and I ran to number six, then I was at the breeder's house the day I got him. I was holding that little puppy in my lap, stroking the full-grown version of him on my side, and when I stood, the puppy vanished, and I looked down at Bear, and I was in a field.

A restrictive uniform pinched my skin all over. The radio on my chest crackled something about the Country Killer, and when I looked up, another version of me was running out of that farmhouse. Bear and I stood on the outskirts, watching as that monster fired the gun that blew my knee apart.

Bear ran.

He ran after that sick son of a bitch.

I chased him, screaming for him, but he kept chasing Eric Oakley, who fired his gun again, and in the flash of it, I fell again onto that white disk.

This time, Tempest was waiting for me.

Tick, tock.

She darted for number seven, and I was right there with her.

We stood on the grass, watching Sam knock on my door. All the words he spoke were a blur, so were mine, but when he turned around and walked to his truck, tears glistened down his cheeks and more glistened my own. I took a step toward him, and I fell, so hard and so fast that I landed once more on that white disk.

Tempest was there already, laying on her belly, panting with a smile just like her brother's.

Tick, tock.

As if it were a command, she rushed to her feet and ran at full speed to number eight. Suddenly, I was behind her, and we were in my kitchen. I sat on that floral print, cigarette burn-covered sofa. Tempest lay at my feet.

Grace stood in the kitchen, mixing a bowl of cookie dough. Bentley sat at the table, bouncing Bella on his knee, while Daisy sat beside me, talking about something that didn't register. Dylan was in an armchair, facing Daisy and me, quiet as he flipped the page of a book.

Sam stood on a ladder just before the TV. Fiddling with something on the wall, he cursed under his breath. He took two steps down, eyes glued to whatever it was in his hands.

A circle. A disk.

"What is that?" I asked.

"Damn thing stopped ticking." Sam spun it around, revealing a clock. "Sure would be nice though, wouldn't it? If we could stop the clock for a while? Or rewind it. That's what I wish. That we could rewind it."

"It's not like its run out yet," Bentley said. "We can't get back what's gone, but we've got time to make things right."

Tick.

Tock.

"Would you look at that," Sam said, chuckling. "Maybe it's not broken after all."

Chapter 13

Birds sang in the distance, a chorus of frogs' chirps joining them. Morning light pulsed against my eyelids. Slowly lifting them, the familiar blue canvas tent stared down at me. The weight of the deflating air mattress below me shifted, rolling me with it.

I rubbed at the crust in my eyes and struggled to wiggle onto my side.

Bentley shuttered his phone and gave me a smile. "Morning."

"Morning." I stifled a yawn. "What time is it?"

"Just after seven." He twisted onto his side. Shades of deep blue weighed the undersides of his brown eyes. "How are you feeling?"

"Normal mostly." My vision was still a bit fuzzy, but no more than usual morning sleepiness. "Do you have service?"

"Nah, I was reading a book. But my phone's about to die anyway, so." A shrug. "Why?"

"I just figured maybe I could send some license plates from that field to Dylan. Sucks we didn't get to go and check it all out last night." Squinting at those dark circles that lined his eyes again, I cocked my head to the side. "Did you sleep?"

"I'm good. Do you want to go do that now?" He tossed the

sleeping bag off his body. "I gotta piss anyway. Tempest probably does too."

"You didn't sleep at all." I almost said it as a question. "Not even a little bit."

Yawning, he gestured over me. "You were drugged. We didn't know what with, and then I gave you benzos. I had to watch your vitals."

No matter how heartwarming that was, I frowned. "You need to get some rest."

He laughed as he stood, keeping his voice quiet enough that it wouldn't disturb anyone else. "It's not my first all-nighter. I'll live. Come on. Let's go before anybody else wakes up."

Bentley grabbed his hoodie from a pile on the floor, then sat on the edge of the bed to pull on his socks.

I stayed still, just watching him. My chest was both hollow and warm at once.

Before last night, I couldn't put it into words. But it all made sense now. Everything I had pushed away since Sam had killed Deangelo.

Maybe I was ready to talk.

A crooked smile played at the edge of Bentley's lips. Tying his shoes, he narrowed his eyes. "What are you looking at?"

I flipped him the bird.

Apparently, not *quite* ready.

* * *

THE MORNING DEW DRENCHED MY SHOES. THE ANKLES OF MY sweatpants were no better. But that sunrise draped in pink and orange light made up for my cold feet. Crisp dying leaves crackled beneath us as we walked to the tree-canopied road in near silence. The cool autumn breeze burst past my sweatshirt, bringing a layer of goose bumps to my skin.

Tempest didn't seem to mind. She chased after crickets on her long lead, never even glancing at Bentley and me.

With each step down the quiet, gravel road with Tempest in my line of sight and Bentley at my side, this place began to make sense. Even considering last night's drug-induced panic attack, I understood.

Willow Grove was the antithesis of the modern world. No cell service. Birds singing in the distance. Quiet sunrises and sunsets. Nature was a canvas, and here, you could make out every inch of it. Back home, it was a blur of colors as you pressed the gas on the highway. Here, the air was like a blanket against your skin, the smell of dead leaves like a candle.

And as grateful as I was for my sobriety, despite that last night had been the worst trip of my life, I understood why people enjoyed it. I understood why they considered it spiritual.

It hadn't been for me. There was nothing spiritual about the dream I had last night.

The terror had simply opened my suppressed subconscious. It allowed me to come to terms with something I'd been avoiding for over a month.

Hell, maybe longer.

My therapist said most of us had an avoidant attachment style. Even people who thought they were more anxious and obsessive were most often fearful avoidant.

When she'd told me I was fearful avoidant, I'd scoffed. Me? Afraid? I feared nothing.

That's where the avoidant came in. I avoided my fear because it was easier than facing it.

I'd wager that ninety percent of the people here had taken a similar drug induced journey and came to a similar revelation to the one I'd had last night. Taking some drugs probably would've helped me open up about it too, because I had been walking with my mouth open for at least a minute now, debating how to bring it up.

I started with, "Thank you. For last night. I'm sorry I was such a mess."

"Nothing to thank me for." Bentley's hands were stowed into his jacket pockets, eyes watching each step we took on the gravel road. "And don't apologize either. Pretty sure I would've been in the same state you were in if the roles were reversed."

"Yeah. I guess." Something stiffened in the back of my throat. I had to swallow to keep my voice from cracking. "But I don't think I thank you enough. In general. For everything. You're one of the few people in my life who's stuck around, and that means more to me than I have words for."

His eyes finding mine, they brightened. "I could say the same about you."

"You already do though. You're good at that stuff. Talking about what you think and how you feel, and—" I snorted a laugh. "And I'm not. When something surfaces that isn't happy, I push it away. Just like I've been pushing you away."

Those big puppy dog eyes remained soft, but his shoulders sunk. "You had a pretty good reason this time."

"Not gonna argue with you about that." I pressed my lips together, pivoting to the left when we made it to the road Phoenix had me leave my car at yesterday. "But I don't think I ever really got your side of the story, anyway."

"I didn't know Sam was going to kill him." Bentley spoke those words on a deep breath, quiet enough that even if someone was in the bushes, they wouldn't have overheard. "You just couldn't be in two places at once. If we would have had more time, if we weren't watching the clock, I would've gone to that college town myself to question the first guy. The motel owner guy?"

My forehead scrunched up. "Sam questioned him too?"

Bentley chewed his lower lip. "I think he beat him up."

Licking my teeth, I shook my head. "New information to me."

"But I didn't know he was going to do that. I just thought he was gonna go talk to him, get some information. And he did. Maybe not with the best methods, but he didn't kill the guy. He didn't tell me any of this until afterwards anyway. All I knew was that he got information, and it helped you."

He wasn't wrong. I sure as shit didn't like it, but he wasn't wrong. "Go on."

"Then you had a solid lead, and you were chasing it, and before long, we had her. Daisy was back, but the baby wasn't, and—" A sharp inhale. He pinched his eyes shut and stayed quiet for a heartbeat or two. "And I didn't care anymore. I didn't care what had to be done. It didn't matter if Sam killed that guy for the fun of it to me. I know that's messed up, and I probably shouldn't admit it out loud, but I would've done anything to get her home."

"I would have too, Bentley," I said, tone sharp.

He frowned at me. "I just told him what I knew. I guess Sam found him at that hotel. The one he had taken Daisy to that day. I don't know how it went down. I didn't tell him what to do, and he didn't tell me exactly what he did. He just called me a little while later and said you were on your way. You were getting Bella. And that was it. Then you answered my phone in the hospital, and you know the story from there."

It didn't change my perspective. Since the get-go, I'd been aware of who my father was, and who Bentley was. Sam had done it. He'd done it for Bentley, and for me. And for Daisy, and for that little girl, because he had a strong sense of justice. Not because he was malicious. Not because he wanted to cause harm. Just because Deangelo didn't deserve to live, but those girls did.

Not the brightest bulb, though. We still had no idea where Deangelo's partner was, and we probably never would. That was thanks to Sam, too.

"I'm not happy about it," I said. *But not for the reasons you think.*

"I know how messed up it sounds, but why, Maddie?" No accusation touched his tone. Just genuine confusion. "We both know and work with Simeon. We know what he does. We know he's a murderer, and that's not a moral issue for you. But killing Deangelo was?"

"Simeon's a different beast. He's barely a friend, let alone family."

"So you only have an issue with murder when your friends and family do it?"

In blanket terms, I had an issue with murder altogether. But there were a thousand layers of gray here. "That's obviously not what I meant."

"Then what do you mean?" No anger in his voice or expression. He was just confused. "Why are you so upset with me? You weren't upset about The Country Killer. Knowing you, there're probably dozens of other murders I don't know about, and you're not angry about those either."

"Deangelo deserved to die a thousand deaths, a thousand brutal ways. It's not about the morality of it, Bentley. It's me being selfish."

He stopped and stood still. "What the hell does that mean?"

"Maybe selfish isn't the right word." Halting, I rubbed a hand down my face. "It's about time. I've already lost so much time with my dad. Because he was stupid. Because he has a twisted sense of right and wrong, and so do I, and I probably get it from him. But I'm smarter. I don't say that to be vain, I say it as a fact. Sam went to prison for killing a guy he claims deserved it, and I believe him.

"But when I killed Eric Oakley, we did it right. Not only was it the right thing to do, but we were also smart enough to cover our asses. I'm not convinced that Sam is. I love him, and I can honestly say that I respect what he did. But it's because I love him that I'm angry. Not just at him, but you, because—" My voice quivered, and my eyes stung. I squeezed them shut and cleared my throat. "Because someone could have found out. He could've wound up in prison again, and I could've lost him for longer. Because Deangelo could've killed him first, and I could've never seen him again. Because someone could still find out, and the same thing could happen to you. You could go to prison for this. You could ruin the life you've worked so hard to build. And I could've lost you. I could've lost both of you. And I can't lose you guys again." My voice wavered, throat continuing to clog with emotion. "Alright? Do you get it now?"

Bentley's expression turned downward and he tucked some hair behind my ear. "I'm not going anywhere, Maddie. Neither is Sam."

"You won't have a choice if you go to prison." I pushed his hand away. "Sam could get the death penalty. He's already killed someone, and I can't see a DA going easy on him. No matter the reason. You may not have told him to do it, but you took part in it, Bentley. Behind my back, you encouraged him to do something that could take his life."

His frown stayed in place. He studied me for a few heartbeats. Eventually, his Adam's apple bobbed with a swallow. "Yeah. I guess so."

"I get why you did it." Now it was my turn to reach across the aisle. I took his face in my hand. "How much you love those girls, how much you're willing to do for them—I respect that too. But I was trying to put your family back together, and you were risking tearing mine apart."

He nodded. "You're right. I'm sorry. If I could do it over, I would've told you everything. I can't apologize enough for the fact that I didn't." His hand came to my cheek. "But if you are so afraid of losing us, why did you push us away?"

I harrumphed. "Dig up Freud and ask him."

A half laugh escaped Bentley. "He was discredited, you know."

"I do, but that's not the point." Releasing his face, I lowered my hand to my side and wiggled my fingers. He took them. "It's my instinct. When things are going bad, my instinct is to run."

"Any chance I can get you to run toward me next time?"

"Don't lie and go behind my back, and we won't have any more problems." As we resumed our pace, the field of cars came into view. "Deal?"

He squeezed my hand tighter. "Deal."

Beneath the Grove

* * *

THE BATTERY EMBLEM AT THE TOP RIGHT CORNER OF MY PHONE said eighteen percent. By the time we walked through the first line of cars, taking pictures of each license plate, it was at thirteen.

So far, Bentley and I had counted twenty-six vehicles. We still had three rows to go.

The clock said 7:45 when we made it to the second row. That's when music sounded back at camp. Nothing crazy, certainly no party, but enough to inform me that the others were awake. Just a matter of time before they started looking for us.

With limited battery, and limited time before the others realized we were gone, we had to work fast. I switched to video instead and recorded every license plate we came across. It took about twenty minutes to walk all three aisles. I was sure the video would be blurry at times, but hopefully this would amount to something. Either searching for the owners of all these vehicles would ease my anxiety and prove they were alive, or prove they were dead. That would be enough for a warrant. If even one owner of these cars was missing, a judge would sign off on a search of this place.

My phone was at eight percent when we headed back to camp. I shut it off to preserve what was left.

Not like I needed it anyway. Last night, I'd gotten a decent idea of the cult's belief system and the practices they followed. Today, I hoped to learn what it was like living here.

It was quieter in the morning. Someone somewhere played a guitar, a dull background noise that blended beautifully into the songs of the birds. People sat on blankets outside their tents doing simple, monotonous tasks.

One woman had a baby in her lap who kept fiddling with her knitting needles. The yarn attached to it draped over both of their legs, forming a fuzzy pink blanket that would've easily fit a queen bed. Must've been aiming for a king.

A man near my age, situated on an old, tattered sheet, placed little glass beads onto a string of hemp. Each touch was careful, slow. As Bentley and I walked past, he didn't so much as glance at us. The task before him outranked everything else.

I recognized that intense focus. I'd seen it in the trailer park, even on college campuses. Usually, stimulants were to blame.

"Oh, Maddie!" Ophelia walked off the porch, wearing her ever-present smile and floor-length skirt. This time, she paired it with a handmade beige cardigan. When I stopped at the foot of the steps, she stretched her hands out for mine and squeezed them tight. "How was your evening?"

"Eye-opening," was all I could come up with.

"I bet." Giggling, she shook her head. "I am sorry about it though. Jasmine should've warned you. If she had told me, I would've let you know first."

Phoenix had said something similar last night. It hadn't registered until now.

Maybe the sweet old woman persona wasn't a persona at all. Maybe she was kind and gentle-hearted at her core. Even when Bentley had arrived, she had seemed concerned for my well-being.

Jasmine was the one who dosed the food. She'd admitted to it.

Had the brainwashing gotten to her that quickly? She hadn't been here long enough that I could believe she was this cult's leader.

She sure did get in bed with him though.

"Yeah, it probably would've been a better experience if I'd have known what I was walking into." Softening my voice, I gestured to mine and Bentley's hands. "It was for the best though. We really leveled on some things last night."

"Aw!" Ophelia released my hands and clapped quickly. "How wonderful. I always love a happy ending."

"So do we," Bentley said.

"Where is Jasmine anyway?" I glanced around. "I was hoping to thank her."

May not have been a truthful show of gratitude but would hopefully give me a few moments alone with her.

"Well, she and Bronwyn were up late." Something dismal flashed through her eyes, her tone remaining steady. "But they'll be up by noon. You two can talk then, if you'd like."

"I'd love that, thank you."

"Would you like to join me for breakfast in a few minutes? Many people continue fasting through lunch, but I need my sustenance early." She shrugged. "Or I could show you around some more before—"

"Help!" a woman called, far off in the distance. "Somebody help!"

Ophelia's mouth fell ajar. Bentley's head twisted around.

Tempy and I were already running toward the source of the sound.

Chapter 14

HER SCREAMS CAME FROM AROUND THE OTHER SIDE OF THE house, past the Weeping Willow. I was halfway there when she came into view. She looked like all the others. Dusty blonde hair braided at the nape of her neck. Rail thin, wearing a floor-length dress that reached her collarbone. A toddler sat on her hip, bouncing with every strained, hurried step.

"Starlight," she said between panting breaths. "She collapsed. Just—just collapsed out of nowhere."

"What do you mean she just collapsed?" Ophelia asked, winded at my side. "What was she—"

"Where is she?" Bentley asked.

"At the ovens." Tears came down her pale cheeks in floods. "The —the red shed by the woods."

"I'm grabbing my bag." Bentley trailed a hand over my back. He whispered, "Start CPR if she's not breathing."

I nodded and said to the woman, "Show me where."

She spun around, and I followed.

No matter how slippery the grass was underfoot, I maintained a steady jog. Adrenaline pumped enough natural painkillers to my knee, allowing me to keep up with Tempest's pace. She beat all three of us to the shed.

Smoke spit from the chimney at the little red shed's peak. The heat blasted me before I made it inside.

Starlight lay on the plywood floor. On her left and right, wood-burning stoves blazed away. Half a dozen wicker and cloth baskets sat on a wooden table, covered in white terrycloth towels. Sweat dampened every inch of Starlight's blue gown. It matched her thin lips. Even her cheeks had a bluish tinge.

I dropped beside her, motioning for Tempest to get back. The heat of her skin had me furrowing my brow. My two fingers on her neck eventually found a pulse, fast and thready. Her chest hardly rose or fell with breaths. I lifted her closed eyelids. Vacant blues with pinprick pupils stared back at me.

"Starlight," I said, shaking her shoulder. "Starlight, wake up for me."

Nothing. Which was what I expected.

"This looks like a heroin overdose," I said, looking up at Ophelia and the other woman behind me. "Is she an addict?"

"Gods no." Ophelia clapped a hand over her chest, as if to clutch her pearls. "That garbage isn't welcome here."

"Yet drugging guests at dinner is perfectly okay," I said under my breath, moving around Starlight to better reach her shoulders. "Her temperature is way too high. We need to bring it down." I looked to the other woman with the baby. "Ma'am, what's your name?"

"Raven." She passed the baby on her hip to Ophelia. "What can I do?"

"Grab her feet, Raven." I stuck my hands under Starlight's armpits. "We just need to get her out of here, onto the grass where it's cooler."

Raven sprang into action. My back ached as we lifted Starlight into the air, but I worried more for her dangling head. Luckily, it was only a few seconds before we had her in the grass outside.

Starlight's breaths were still quiet, ragged. A rasp accompanied each exhale. But this was Bentley's area of expertise. She was still breathing, so I wouldn't start CPR. Not yet. Not until he administered naloxone.

Those lips stayed blue, but more sweat poured from her forehead, underarms, and everything else visible.

Thready heart rate, low respiration rate, tiny pupils—trademarks of an opioid overdose. But why was she so hot? And why was her heart beating fast? Out here, the temperature couldn't have been higher than seventy. In that shed, it was at least a hundred. It still didn't make sense.

"Who is she to you, Raven?" I asked, keeping my fingers on the thready pulse at Starlight's neck.

"My big sister." Lips quivering, she grasped hold of Starlight's hand. "I—I don't understand. She was fine. She was completely fine, and then she just dropped."

"What did she take?" I made sure my voice was neutral. This was not a passing of judgment. "I can't help her if I don't know what she took."

Raven looked at me, then behind me at Ophelia. Ophelia nodded.

"Glow," Raven said. "But I took some too. We take it all the time, and it's fine. It's not dangerous."

Clearly, it was. "Glow," I repeated, looking between them. "What the hell is glow?"

"It's not dangerous," Ophelia repeated. "That's not what caused this."

"If it's a drug, it's dangerous." I shot Ophelia a look. "Of all people, you would know that. I thought this place was against pharmaceuticals."

"It's not a pharmaceutical," she said, face screwed up in some combination of confusion and betrayal. As if I were a villain for questioning her. "We all take it, and we are all fine. It's enlightening. It opens the door in your mind to—"

"Is it an opioid?" I didn't have time for her hippie-dippy bullshit right now. "Is it something else?"

"It has uplifting effects." Shaking her head, she raised her shoulders. Maybe her way of saying that she didn't know what the hell it was. "It's perfectly safe. I took mine earlier, and I'm fine."

"She doesn't even know what it is, but she's high on something, and you're letting her hold your baby?" Raven's open mouth caught a fly or two, tears streaming faster down her cheeks. The moment I saw them, guilt pinched my chest, and I knew I should've kept my mouth shut. But god damn, somebody needed to be the voice of reason here. Shaking it all off, I said to Raven, "Do you have a pair of scissors nearby?"

"Scissors?" Raven asked, blinking hard. "Are you going to cut her—"

"No, we need to cool her down. I don't want to move her and risk hurting her spine if there's something more serious going on. If we can cut at least the sleeves and legs of the dress off, we can lower her body temperature."

"Right." Raven rushed to her feet and ran into the shed.

"I'm not sure that's appropriate," Ophelia began. "Our earthly bodies are—"

"Are you about to tell me that her modesty is more important than her life, Ophelia?" I whipped my head around to face her. Just the look I gave her left her backpedaling. "I'll make sure the sensitive parts of her stay covered. But she is overheating, and I'm not going to let her die for your modesty rules."

A hard swallow. Then silence.

Silence that allowed me to hear footsteps and rustling leaves.

A few dozen yards behind Ophelia, Bentley jogged toward us at full speed with a blue duffel bag over his shoulder.

"Here." Raven dropped to her knees on the other side of Starlight. She held out a small blade. "We use it to score the bread. Will this work?"

It was better than nothing. I grasped hold of the heavy linen around her arm, stuck the blade through, and tore. By the time I was on to her legs, Bentley skated to his knees beside Raven.

Yanking supplies from his bag with one hand, he searched for a pulse on her neck with the other. "Bring me up to speed."

"Pinprick pupils, blue lips, thready, fast pulse, and she took something earlier. They call it glow. No one seems to know what it is."

"Barely there pulse, barely breathing," he murmured, tossing me a paper box. "Definitely some opiate."

The label said Naloxone. I ripped it open, peeled the plastic at the tip, and spun off the lid. When I passed it to Bentley, I turned to the others. "What are the effects? What do you feel when you take it?"

"Happy," Raven said. "Relaxed, but happy, and energized at the same time? It's hard to explain."

"Speed balling, maybe?" I asked Bentley.

He pressed the tip of the bottle into Starlight's nostril and squeezed. "Possible. But meth and coke don't usually make you hot. Not this hot, anyway."

"MDMA does." Still ripping at the fabric around Starlight's legs, my eyes found Raven's. "Have you ever done Molly? Is that what this feels like?"

"Kind of, yeah," Raven said. "It's like—"

"We don't do drugs like that here." Ophelia bounced the baby on her hip. "I don't even know what MDMA is."

"Then how do you know you've never taken it?" Again, I tried to keep the judgment from edging my tone. It wasn't that I had a problem with people using drugs. As an addict, I'd be a hypocrite if I did. But this was different than an addict on the street.

"Because Bronwyn wouldn't allow it," Ophelia said. "Last night, what Jasamine put in the dressing, we grew it ourselves. I watched those mushrooms blossom. I—"

"Really not the priority right now." Bentley motioned us all to silence, nodding slowly as he felt the pulse at Starlight's neck. "Still fast, but stronger." He peeled open her eyelid. "Pupils are getting bigger. Definitely an opiate." With a touchless thermometer, he got her temperature. "Hundred and four point two. We've got to get that down." He dug around in his bag and came out with a few ice packs. "Snap them in half, and they'll start cooling. Put them all over her body." As Raven and I took two apiece, Bentley went back into his bag and came out with a smaller clear bag. "I don't have a stand, so someone's gonna have to hold this above her body—"

"Absolutely not." Ophelia shook her head quickly. "You already put that stuff up her nose. You can't give her anything else. Especially not in her vein."

I never understood that. As a cop, I'd handled more overdoses than I had fingers and toes to count with. Someone, whether a friend standing nearby or the person we'd revived, made certain to inform me they hadn't shot it. They'd confessed to snorting a drug, or eating it, or even shoving it up their ass. But because they didn't put it in their vein, they had some moral superiority complex. As if the route made any difference in the effects on the body.

As if they were better than those other depraved junkies who shot it in their veins and got those filthy diseases from dirty needles.

Just as Ophelia behaved now. Like her drugs were better because... Bronwyn said they were?

It amazed me in the worst way. These people's belief system made no sense. There was nothing natural about any of this, aside from the bread baking inside the shed.

But now I had a broader understanding.

None of this made sense for the same reason those addicts who boasted about boofing their drugs instead of shooting them made no sense. Because addiction was, by nature, senseless.

"If I'm right, and this is some cross of opiates and ecstasy, I've only helped half the problem." Bentley's voice was far kinder than mine would have been. "The opiates are out of her system. That's what naloxone was for. It instantly reversed the effects. That's why her breathing is picking back up. But if I don't bring down her body temperature and rehydrate her, her brain is going to fry. Her eyes will start to bleed. Her organs will shut down. She will have brain damage that she will never recover from."

I'd never seen an MDMA overdose result in bleeding eyes. But maybe Bentley dramatized the effects to show Ophelia why this was necessary. To show why medicine was the real magic.

Ophelia's eyes filled with tears, lower lip swelling. She clutched that baby on her hip tighter. "Maybe the spirit is calling for her."

I opened my mouth to say something, to cuss something, to scream something, but Bentley chimed in first. "Wouldn't the spirit want us to help her? Because this isn't nature running its course, Ophelia. This is the basic laws of physics. Cause and effect. If we do nothing, she dies. It if I help her, she lives."

"Even if you're right," Ophelia said, "and chemicals did cause this, adding more will just make it worse."

"The chemicals I just administered are helping," Bentley reminded her, gesturing to Starlight's lips. "See that? See her color coming back?"

"But she's still unconscious," Ophelia said. "She hasn't woken up, and, and—"

"Because she's severely dehydrated." Bentley held the clear bag of liquid for Ophelia to see. "It's just saltwater. That's all I'm going to inject. For now, anyway. I'm gonna monitor her blood pressure and heart rate, and if they don't improve, I might administer a beta blocker. Which, hopefully, will regulate her body. If it doesn't, we need to get her to the hospital as soon as possible, or she's not going to make it. You don't want that, do you? You care for these people. All these people here, you look at them like they're your children. You told us that yesterday, and I can see it in your eyes. It's the same way I look at my daughters. You don't want her to die."

Ophelia's forehead pinched with sorrow, nostrils flaring at the tears she fought back. "I don't have a phone. Bronwyn won't let us call an ambulance."

"Then I have to do this," Bentley said slowly, nodding. "I have to save your girl. Right?"

"Do it," Raven said quickly. "Save her. Do whatever you have to. Just save her."

Bentley tied the tourniquet above Starlight's elbow and tapped for a vein.

"Right," Ophelia whispered. "Okay, right. But we need to move her. Into your tent or somewhere else that she won't be seen. Bronwyn won't like this."

Doubted Bronwyn would like the gun that burned up my hip either, but if he came out here and stopped this, he could call the cops himself with my barrel to his head.

"Alright," Bentley said. "As soon as I get this line started, we'll move her to my tent, and we'll take care of her in there."

* * *

A FEW MINUTES PASSED, AND STARLIGHT'S TEMPERATURE reached one hundred-three point seven. Half an hour later, her fingers twitched, and she began murmuring to herself. Her temperature was down to one hundred-two point six. By the time it reached one hundred, she was in and out of consciousness, speaking to her sister.

It took almost two hours before it dropped to ninety-nine. By then, she was fully awake, but confused, nauseous, and hungry. Bentley worried about neurological damage. He pressed for her to go to the hospital. She refused.

She did, however, accept the protein bars he offered as well as another bag of saline. Since she wouldn't go to the hospital, he asked that she stay in the tent so we could monitor her. Apparently, serotonin syndrome was another concern he had. Starlight didn't argue.

With the exception of pissing in the woods, we spent the entire day in that tent. I tried to question them, to get a better understanding of why they stayed here, why this place meant so much to them. But I'd let my mask fall with Ophelia this morning; I had to tread lightly. Rather than interrogate, I made conversation.

Raven explained that she and her sister had grown up in the system. Sometimes they'd be in a family together. Most of the time, CPS had separated them. Starlight was older, and she'd tried to get custody of Raven when she turned eighteen. They wouldn't allow it.

So, at fourteen, Raven had run. Starlight had already found this place. Willow Grove had opened its arms, and two young, desperate girls fell into them.

When Ophelia sat beside Starlight, running a brush through her dampened hair, my heart warmed and ached at the same time.

That light that shined in Ophelia's eyes, the comfort Starlight felt at her touch... Of course I understood.

Ophelia desperately wanted children. She couldn't have them. Not without this place.

These girls desperately wanted a family. The outside world wouldn't give them one. Willow Grove did.

They were addicts. Barring the baby on Raven's hip, everyone I'd met here had a drug problem. Beneath it, they all had a pain problem. A loneliness problem. The world hadn't been so kind to them. Through drug use and esoteric spirituality, they escaped reality for a life of divinity and love.

When Starlight was steady enough to stand, just after sunset, Bentley helped her to her feet. Hand-in-hand with her sister, they wandered from our tent to a cloth one near the Willow.

"She needs help." Bentley spoke hardly above a whisper. "Maybe you could talk to her. Tell her how much better your life has been since you got clean."

A dozen or so tents perched all around the farmhouse. Outside them, people knitted blankets, strung beads on hemp, and embroidered inspirational phrases onto white cloths. Just as they had done since I woke up this morning. Even as the sun set, they all still sat there, doing their tasks, like robots or zombies.

That's what these people didn't understand. They may not have been working a soul sucking, corporate office job. But their souls didn't look so alive here either. Only numbed.

Was it really a simpler life? Or was it the same life in a different font?

Pressing my lips together, I rubbed at the goose bumps that rose over my arms. "They all need help, Bentley."

"Maybe we can get them some," he said, still whispering. "Maybe if we can get a warrant, the cops can raid this place, and then they'll have resources. They won't arrest them all, just the leaders. And—"

"Hey," a familiar voice said behind me. "How is she?"

Phoenix carried a woven laundry basket. All the linens reached the brim. One article, I recognized. The blue shirt Bronwyn had worn last night.

He was doing their laundry? Jasmine's and Ophelia's too, or just Bronwyn's?

Was it a punishment? Did it go hand-in-hand with that brand?

"Alive," Bentley said. "Wasn't so sure she'd stay that way earlier, so good news."

Pulling in a deep breath, Phoenix forced a smile. "Yeah. Good news for sure."

"We thought we were being inconspicuous." I cocked my head to the side. "How did you hear about it?"

"Raven told me when she came out earlier to get some clothes. Something about you needing to get Starlight's temperature down?" An awkward shrug. "Don't worry. I wouldn't tell Bronwyn."

"What would happen if you did?" I asked.

The storm door on the porch slammed shut.

Speak of the devil.

Holding Jasmine's hand, Bronwyn walked down the front steps. A duffel bag hung on each of his shoulders. I half expected him to continue around the house down the path we had taken last night to the solarium. Instead, the two of them continued straight, past the Willow, toward a narrow path that must've led into the woods.

Phoenix's heavy breath caught my attention. He watched Bronwyn and Jasmine continue on that path, speaking quietly to each other. They didn't so much as glance at us. Probably didn't notice we were there at all.

"He did it, didn't he?" I kept my voice low. "He's the one who branded you."

Phoenix glanced at me, then the two of them again. "Does it matter?"

"No. I guess it doesn't." I crossed my arms against my chest. "I'm just trying to understand what's going on here, because it doesn't seem to make much sense."

"It does when you're high." Eyes still on the two of them, his jaw clenched. Sympathy softened his forehead. "It does when you have nothing, and suddenly you have something."

"What do you mean?" Bentley's face scrunched up. "Jasmine? Is that who you're talking about?"

"All of us." Phoenix nibbled his lower lip. "I know how this place looks. I know how it is. And I know you don't understand, because you guys have each other. You got a life outside of this place that's good. It might not be perfect, but it's good. We didn't, and we don't. All we've got is each other."

"That's by design," I said. Maybe I shouldn't have, but the words came out, and they kept coming. "This place isolates you. It gives you a world of your own, and it takes the one you came from. You don't even have the choice to go back to it."

"You think I don't know that?" His tone wasn't accusative. Just flat, honest. "That's why I told you to forgive your dad. Don't stay here. That's what I tried to tell Jasmine, but she won't listen. She doesn't get it. She's brainwashed, and I can't get her to understand."

"Understand what exactly?"

"That it won't always be like this." He gestured to the house. "For now, she gets special treatment. She's his girl of the year. But there will be another whenever she's not good enough anymore, and then another after that, and another after that."

"What happened to the ones before her?"

Tracing his tongue along his teeth, Phoenix watched Jasmine and Bronwyn disappear into the forest. All he gave me was a shrug.

When I'd arrived, I'd thought that Ophelia led this group. In a way, she did. She was the mothering embrace all these people so desperately needed.

But that mark on Phoenix's flesh came from Bronwyn's hand. I knew it did. And I knew there was more to this place than the community Ophelia fostered.

That million-dollar profit didn't come from beaded bracelets and sauerkraut.

Maybe those duffel bags had something to do with it.

"These are Bronwyn's, right?" I gestured to the basket.

"Yeah, I'm on laundry duty," Phoenix said. "Why?"

I snatched the blue shirt from the top. "Because I want to figure out what they're doing."

"What Bronwyn's doing?" Phoenix asked. "Probably going to have sex under the moonlight or some shit."

"In that case, at least there will be some entertainment." I lowered the shirt in my hand for Tempest to sniff. "Track, Tempy."

"Whoa." Eyes wide, Phoenix shook his head slowly. "I wouldn't do that."

"Are you gonna tattle on us?" Bentley asked. "We'll take your silence in exchange for the antibiotics."

Phoenix huffed. "No, I'm not gonna tattle. But Bronwyn is a screwed up dude. If he thinks you're going to do something he doesn't agree with—"

"We can protect ourselves." Tempest pulled at the lead, and I followed behind her. "Thanks for your help."

"Maddie—" Phoenix began.

"Antibiotics are in my bag beside the bed." Bentley gave Phoenix a pat on the back. "Take your pick, man."

Chapter 15

TEMPEST'S WAGGING TAIL HAD MY HEART FLUTTERING AND A smile curving the corners of my lips.

Lately, I hadn't given her many jobs. Jobs like this, anyway. I did have her help me with menial tasks. Assisting me as I sat or stood, supporting my weight as I stepped from a vehicle. As a working dog, she needed a couple duties to keep herself occupied. She enjoyed those as much as jobs like this.

But the reality was, I wasn't a cop. She wasn't a narc dog anymore.

Not every case I had these days required her to sniff out drugs or track someone. There would never come a time when I would use her as an attack dog either. She had become a service dog, and she never failed to impress me.

Still, when I had a job for her similar enough to her old career, she enjoyed stepping out of retirement. And she was good at it—too good.

It only took us ten minutes to flank Bronwyn and Jasmine. Heading downhill, I could make out both of their figures. Tree branches and foliage disguised their details. Jasmine held a lantern in her free hand, the one that wasn't holding Bronwyn's, which gave me just enough light to be certain it was them. They spoke quietly, too quiet for me to make out what they said.

Tempest yanked the lead, as if to say, *Found them, Mom.* She stepped forward, and her paw crackled over a twig.

Bronwyn and Jasmine looked over their shoulders.

I grabbed Bentley's elbow and hauled him to the cold, damp ground. At the sight of us on the soil, Tempest crouched as well. The squat made my knee ache, but they couldn't know we were behind them. My calf trembled from the pain, but it could handle a few minutes of discomfort. It'd have to.

Bronwyn said something to Jasmine, placed a hand on the small of her back, and continued along the dark, overgrown path. He took our only light source with him. Now, we only had the bluish luminance of the moon to guide our way forward.

Once their voices muted, I dropped onto my ass, stretched my knee out, and breathed slowly through the relief.

"I get why you like this job." Bentley sat beside me, voice barely above a whisper. "You really do get a rush from this shit."

A half laugh escaped me. "You should come on cases with me more often."

"If I didn't have to go back to work next week, I would take you up on that." He was all but invisible in the lack of light, merely a shadow beneath the foliage canopy overhead. His hand found mine and laced our fingers together. "Probably would be better with a flashlight though."

"Good thing I prepared for that." I dug past the granola bar wrappers in my pocket for the small, battery powered flashlight I'd shoved in there earlier. "After last night, I wanted to be prepared."

"Of course you did." Something between a laugh and a huff left him. "Why have we been tripping our way down this trail then?"

"Because I knew we weren't far behind them. Didn't want them to see us." I patted around on the ground. "Do you still have that water bottle? Tempy probably needs a drink."

The plastic crinkled before the cold texture met my outstretched fingertips. "We should probably go easy on it. Looks like we have a long hike back."

Couldn't disagree with him there. My sip was mindful. So was the pour I made into Tempest's collapsible bowl.

She lapped it up, spun back around, and tugged.

But not ahead. To the left.

I clicked on the flashlight, but only bushes and vines stared back at me.

"They went straight." I patted her flank. "What's over there, Tempy?"

"A-woo-woo," she whined.

Using Bentley's shoulder as leverage, I stood and eyed the break in the foliage she stood before. It was a quarter the size of this trail, likely a little path deer had carved out. "What is it, girl?"

Another, "a-woo-woo," paired with a wagging tail that slapped me in the thighs.

"Shouldn't we stay behind them?" Bentley asked. "I mean, wasn't that the whole point of coming out here?"

"It was. But Tempest is well trained." I shrugged. "If she thinks there's something we need to check out back here, let's do it. She'll sniff Bronwyn's shirt and pick the trail back up when we're done."

"You're the expert." His hand came to mine. "But move carefully. One dip in the ground, and we're both breaking our necks."

"I'm always careful."

In my own way, at least.

* * *

Snout pressed to the ground, Tempy tugged me forward. Thorns and jaggers caught the bottom of my sweatpants. Mud dampened the ankles. A machete would've been nice right about now, because even with my flashlight, I could only see a few inches in front of me before another tree branch or vine obscured my view.

Tempest nearly hauled me to the ground, tail flapping back and forth. The black hair on her back stood at its ends. We couldn't have been on this trail for longer than five minutes before the smell smacked me.

"Shit," Bentley said with a chuckle. "Guess we know what she's leading us toward."

"Or there's a skunk nearby." I had to grasp hold of a tree branch to make it over a puddle of mud. Good thing I had, or Tempy would've hauled me to the ground. "Geez, girl. Take it easy."

The tension on the hands-free leash lightened when she glanced at me over her shoulder. A moment ago, her tongue had flapped in the wind, brown eyes widened with excitement. But now, her ears were back against her head. There was something in her eyes I couldn't quite describe.

A knowing. A certain sixth sense any handler found with their dog.

She saw or smelled something that my own eyes and nose couldn't detect.

Cannabis was growing somewhere nearby. That much, I knew for certain. But Tempest smelled that all the time when we walked around the trailer park. It wouldn't put her on edge.

On the other side of the mud, I rested a hand over my gun. Just in case.

"What is it, girl?" I asked. "Show me."

She turned around and continued forward, but her pace was slower. Cautious.

The smell grew stronger. Really wished I had vapor rub to put on my nostrils right about now. I hadn't smelled this much weed since that one time my mom had dated a pot dealer when I'd been in high school.

When I pushed one last big green bush aside, a clearing came into view. A quick wave of my flashlight confirmed what I had suspected. Cannabis plants, taller than me, a couple taller than Bentley, that stretched on at least fifty feet ahead and twenty-five to my left and right.

"How much charge do you have left on your phone?" I asked Bentley.

"Five percent I think." Standing beside me, he surveyed the plants as well. "Turning it on will probably use a percentage or two."

"Save yours then."

I dug in the pocket of my fanny pack—the same one Tempest's leash was attached to—and pulled out my phone. Once it powered up, I snapped a few photos. Luckily, my satellite access was on. I didn't need to go into my settings. Still, my phone was at seven percent when I opened the maps app.

I created a new folder labeled "WG Investigation - Oct 2023" and moved all the photos and videos there. Later, I'd need to transfer these to a flash drive and create a hash value to prove they hadn't been tampered with—basic digital evidence protocol I'd learned as a cop. For now, I just needed to preserve what I had.

I zoomed in on the little dot that signified where I was, flicked open the coordinates, took a screenshot. I flashed a quick photo of the field and immediately texted it to myself and Dylan with the note: "Evidence backup - marijuana field location, Willow Grove property."

"This will be enough to get a warrant?" Bentley asked.

"Definitely enough for a warrant," I said. "But until I know more, I'm not sure what the point of having cops come even is. If they question Bronwyn and Ophelia, everyone's going to tell them that they're here willingly. The drugs they do, they take willingly. And cops don't really care about pot anymore. I know there's more to this place than just some weed, but—"

Tempest whined.

She lay atop the soil, ears back, with that same look in her eyes. The one that told me there wasn't just pot plants here.

Only then did I really look at the ground.

My stomach twisted.

In front of the plants was a roughly six by four patch of tilled soil.

Most of our walk had been on soil or gravel, so it wasn't the dirt itself that stuck out. It was the shape. The size.

"Shit," I said under my breath.

"What?" Bentley placed a hand on the small of my back. "What's wrong?"

I gestured to the plot of soil. "Does this look normal to you?"

"Does what look normal?"

I unclipped Tempest's leash and passed it to him. Slowly walking the rectangle, I gestured to it. "The plants have been here a while. There's no reason to dig this up."

Bentley cocked his head to the side. "Okay..."

Pulling in a deep breath, I lowered myself to the ground. I lay beside Tempest and folded my hands over my chest. "See it yet?"

The warmth trickled from his face. A greenish tinge filled his cheeks. "You think this is a body?"

"Can't say without a shovel." I gingerly stroked my fingers over Tempest's fur. "If it were an animal, A. I don't know why they would've brought it all the way out here to bury it. B. Why would they need such a big plot for a pet? And C. Tempest wouldn't look so sad if it were a dead animal. This is the same face she made when we found Deangelo's cemetery."

Even from here, in the dim moonlight, I saw the goosebumps that rose over Bentley's arms. "But you marked where we are on the map?"

I struggled back to my feet. "I did."

"Then we can come back with shovels."

"And we will. For now, let's see where Bronwyn and Jasmine were going." I snapped my fingers for Tempest's attention and untucked Bronwyn's shirt from my belt loop. "Track, Tempy."

* * *

We went back to the trail we had come from. Once

Tempy had the scent again, she pressed her nose to the ground, and she all but ran after it.

Only cricket chirps and distant coyote howls sounded. No words formed on my tongue. What was there to say?

More than likely, Tempest had just found a body. If I had to hypothesize who they were or why they were there, all I had to do was remember this afternoon. Everyone here used drugs. They treated overdose like I treated the common cold. Unfortunate, uncomfortable, but a fact of life.

None of the research I had done about Willow Grove mentioned drugs, deaths, disappearances, or overdoses. I found it unlikely that Starlight had been the first. That's probably what we were dealing with here. Someone had OD'd, and instead of getting them help, or giving the body back to the family, they brought them out here, buried them next to their favorite flower, and went back to everyday life in the commune.

I hoped, anyway.

I hoped that whoever lay in that grave had died doing what they enjoyed. I hoped that their death had nothing to do with the brand on Phoenix's skin. I hoped their last moments were not painful or violent.

I hoped it had nothing to do with the end Jasmine had told her mother about.

Bentley must've been thinking the same thing, because he held my hand tighter than ever.

Our ascent for the last five minutes had made the hike easier on my knee. But now that we crested a hilltop, lights shined in the distance. I shut my eyes, focusing on the distant ambiance. A bass pumped. Not like the guitar they played at the campfire last night, but like a speaker. Maybe from a car?

I told Tempest, "Heel."

She stopped, spun around, and waited for her next command.

"Stay quiet," I said to Bentley.

A quick nod in response.

I clicked off my flashlight and stowed it in my pocket. As my eyes adjusted, I took in my surroundings. Nothing special. Trees and bushes to my left, trees and bushes to my right.

That light in the distance, though, reminded me of a streetlight. Nothing like the campfires and lanterns they used around the Willow. We hadn't walked long enough to reach society. So why was this area so well lit?

On my left, a sturdy tree with low-hanging branches stood tall. At least thirty feet tall, as high or higher than the canopy leaves and branches formed. Pine, which I didn't love because of the spikes. But the branches were close together. As easy to maneuver around as a set of stairs. Strong, too, judging by the thickness of the branches.

I unclipped Tempest's leash and passed it to Bentley. "Here, hold her for a minute."

"You don't think you're going ahead without me, do you?" His frown was audible. "Because I didn't come this far with you for—"

"I'm not going ahead of you." I tightened the knot of messy hair at the back of my head and nodded upward. "I'm going above you."

"Normally, I wouldn't argue about that."

Rolling my eyes, I grasped hold of the lowest hanging branch. "Just hold Tempest."

"What the—are you climbing that tree?"

"Yep." My feet were already at the height of his head. Digging my fingers into the next branch, I ducked to avoid hitting my head on another.

"My God, Maddie," he grunted under his breath. "You have a bad knee."

"And you're always the one telling me that my disability doesn't define me." Swinging my good leg onto the next branch, I approached ten feet in the air. "If I fall, at least I've got a paramedic waiting for me."

I squinted into the distance, to the source of that streetlight. But there were still too many branches in my way. I grabbed hold of the next branch, a foot or two above me, and relied on my upper body strength. Those pull-ups paid off, because my knee did none of the work to get me to the next branch.

"Your disability *doesn't* define you," Bentley said. "But even if you were perfectly able-bodied, I wouldn't like you climbing a tree in the middle of the night without so much as a flashlight."

"Well, I wasn't going to ask you to do it. You could get hurt."

He scoffed. "Damn you, Castle."

I chuckled.

Now, at least fifteen feet off the ground, I planted my ass on one branch and wrapped my arm around the trunk. Wasn't exactly a harness, but it gave me a bit more stability. Enough that I could grasp hold of the branch overhead and peer through it.

At the bottom of the hill, there was a clearing, a dirt road, and a building. Other things too, but I couldn't make it all out in the light. A gust of wind left me floating up and down, making it that much more difficult to level my vision.

All I had left was five percent, and it would have to do.

I powered on my phone, clicked onto the camera, pressed record, and zoomed in as far as the phone would let me. It was damn near impossible to tell what I was looking at with the camera so magnified, so I zoomed out a bit. Still holding the branch overhead, I did my best to remain steady enough to get a good angle.

There was a barn. Or garage, maybe. Not just any garage, but one of those big aluminum ones everyone in the countryside has these days. Two or three of my trailers could fit inside of it. Maybe four or six if you stacked them vertically as well as horizontally.

Smoke chugged from three chimneys inside the barn. Outside, a few men stood smoking cigarettes. One of them leaned against an old clunker, spitting smoke from its exhaust.

So much smoke for a place that claimed to hell and back to care about wellness and the environment.

My eyes caught on the clunker. I couldn't make out the exact make and model, but early two thousands? Late nineties? White with a purple racing stripe that started on the hood and ended at the rear fender. Had I seen that before? Did I know it from somewhere?

Two percent.

"Shit." I stopped the recording and shuttered the phone. "If I toss my phone down, do you think you can catch it?"

"Maybe if you shine the flashlight," Bentley called. "Why? Are you gonna drop it?"

"No, I want you to watch the video I just took before it dies. I don't think I'll make it down there before it does." Clicking on the flashlight, I waved it in a circle on the ground at his feet. "I'll drop it right there."

He dropped Tempest's leash and stepped on it. Holding out his hands, he said, "Ready when you are."

I let it drop into the illuminated circle. My heart hammered, but only for a moment. He caught it.

"What do you think I'm gonna see on here that you didn't?" Bentley asked.

"The car down there." Clenching a thick tree branch overhead with one hand and stabilizing myself below with the other, I clamped the flashlight between my teeth and talked around it. "Look familiar to you?"

"Shit," Bentley said. "Yeah. Yeah, it's Ken, one of Simeon's guys. I had a beer with him right before we went to Lancaster."

Still descending the tree, my words came out as an almost incoherent mumble. "Ken? He's a dealer?"

"Not a grunt worker, that's for damn sure. He's high up," Bentley said. "Simeon's careful about who he lets in his inner circle, but Ken's up there. If I'm not mistaken, he does a lot of the pickups."

Suddenly, those chugging chimneys made sense.

Nearly at the bottom of the tree now, I held the flashlight. "I get it now."

"You get what now?" Bentley asked.

"Yeah?" A woman's voice made me jump. A flashlight clicked on, illuminating her face half a dozen yards down the trail we had just come from. She looked far too much like a child holding a light beneath their chin at a campfire. Jasmine. "You get what now, Miss Kramer?"

Chapter 16

For obvious reasons, I wasn't going to answer that question.

When my feet thumped the ground, I expected pain to pulse through my knee. Supposed I had to thank the adrenaline for the fact that it didn't. I steadied myself against the tree with the hand that held the flashlight. The other fell to the gun on my hip.

As soon as Tempest saw them, the hair on her back stood at its ends. A low growl vibrated between her bared teeth. I motioned for Bentley to take her back a step, and he did.

A few feet behind, Jasmine and Bronwyn stood, the lantern illuminating the bottom of their faces. His crooked smile intended to instill fear.

But I knew exactly the kind of asshole I was dealing with now. He didn't scare me. I just had to fight the urge to swallow down a bit of vomit.

Something touched my ear. The distant rumble of engines carried on the night wind. Multiple vehicles, from the sound of it. How long had that been going on?

"What are you doing there?" I gestured over the hill. "What's that place for?"

"I'm not sure why you think that's your business, little girl," Bronwyn said. "A better question is why did you—"

"If I'm a little girl, what does that make her?" Returning the crooked grin, I waved over Jasmine. "She's at least five years younger than me. And you're, what? Thirty years older than the both of us? But you guys slept together last night, so what does that make you, Calvin?"

His smile dropped.

"Don't talk to him like that," Jasmine snapped. Her brows crunched down, and her eyes narrowed, and her lips pursed, but nothing about her scared me either. "Out of the kindness of his heart, he gave you a place to stay. He fed you. He was nothing but kind and respectful."

"He doesn't respect me." I shook my head at her. "He doesn't respect you either. He can't. To him, we are the weaker sex. We're no different than the chickens he slaughters for dinner. Our place is in the kitchen or on our knees in front of him. I don't owe him a damn thing, and neither do you."

"Watch your mouth," Bronwyn said, stepping forward.

"Piss up a rope." Bold, I knew. But it was over now. It had to be. There was no talking our way out of this. They knew we were watching them, they knew we saw what this place really was, and they knew we would never bow down in blind submission. "I'm not one of these weak little girls who's gonna fall for your bullshit niceties. But you already knew that. That's why you spent an hour over dinner telling my boyfriend to put a good leash and muzzle on me. That's why you let her drug me." I gestured to Jasmine. "Women like me, we make you so uncomfortable, don't we? That's why the guys smoke a little pot, but all the girls are sitting around with pinprick pupils baking you bread and threading beads on dream catchers that you are going to sell for a hundred bucks just to add some legitimacy to your money laundering operation."

He stomped closer, shouldering Jasmine out of the way. Teeth tightened into a line, his hands balled into fists at his sides. "You have no idea what you're talking about."

"I know exactly what I'm talking about." I brushed past Bentley. Bronwyn and I were only a foot or two apart. My eyes narrowed to slits. "I know men like you. You all think you're special. You all think you're different. You all think you're operating something no one has ever seen before. You all exploit the labor of women and minorities. You're all a little charming. You all have the same shit-eating grin, probably because you're all the exact same abusive pieces of shit."

He raised his hand.

Tempest growled and snarled and barked.

I grabbed his wrist just before it made contact with my face. Twisting it, I spun around him and pinned it to his low back. He groaned in agony, and I snorted out a laugh. "Hit a nerve there, huh?"

Jasmine gasped but stayed still with her hand clasped over her heart.

"Let go!" he squealed.

"Are you gonna be a good boy and keep your hands to yourself?" I yanked his wrist up higher, now wedged between his shoulder blades. He grunted in pain. "Because I can do a lot worse than this, Calvin."

"Let me go." His voice came out an angry hiss. "Now."

I chuckled. He still thought he was the one in power, that he intimidated me.

To prove he wasn't, and that he didn't, I shoved him just as I released his wrist.

He crashed to the ground, groaning and moaning. From here, the bald spot at the back of his head sparkled in the glow of the oil lamp.

Gasping, Jasmine dropped to her knees beside him. "What the hell's the matter with you?"

"What—quid pro quo doesn't apply here?" I propped my hands on my hips. "He's allowed to push *you* around, but God forbid a woman does the same thing to him?"

Her hard swallow confirmed my suspicion.

Still, she helped him roll over, whispering sweet nothings. Blood dripped from a small scratch on his forehead, no more than an inch long. Must've hit a rock on the way down.

The sight of them had my stomach bubbling and my heart throbbing.

Such a pretty young girl. Sparkling eyes, the right shaped nose, perfect full lips. Though covered in clothing two sizes too big, practically a blanket, her thin body fit perfectly into the beauty standard of our society.

And she kneeled on the ground before a middle-aged, below average, exploitative tyrant. A drug user, and likely a drug dealer.

Beside her, he was nothing. She had a whole life, a whole future, ahead of her. She had time to figure out what she wanted, to make something of herself, and this was why he kept her around, to exploit this youthful energy and effectively suck it out of her.

And yet, this was where she chose to stay.

On her knees for a man who would never deserve her. A man who deserved love from no one but his mother.

"You can do better than this, Jasmine," I said. "This is all a big, screwed up hallucination. Whatever he's told you, whatever you believe is coming, it's not real. This piece of shit is drugging you and feeding you nonsense to keep you under his control—"

Bronwyn pointed a finger at me. "If you don't watch your mouth—"

"I wish you understood, Maddie." Jasmine's eyes filled with tears, and a soft smile curved the edges of her lips. "I wish you could grasp the beauty we cultivate here."

"It's a chemical reaction in the brain, Jasmine," I said. "What you're feeling are the effects of the drug."

"No." Smiling wider, she shook her head. "No, it's so much more than that. I wish you could understand it, but you don't want to. You want to keep your mind and your soul closed off from what could be. We can't help you if you don't want to help yourself."

The words right out of my mouth. The mantra of every drug and rehab counselor in history. You can lead the horse, but you can't make them drink.

This place bastardized every piece of knowledge they had. It was true that someone who didn't want to be helped couldn't be. But I wasn't the one who needed it. They twisted the fact so far that it became fallacy. Willow Grove dramatized, weaponized, then capitalized off of what started as a decent sentiment.

Of course the corporations saved a dollar wherever they could, often resulting in the masses losing nutritional value in their food. Women's bodies were smaller by nature, making us appear the weaker sex. And drugs had a purpose, of course they could be medicine.

But how much better was their homemade sourdough bread if the people baking it were overdosing on some combination of heroin and ecstasy? The ranch dressing didn't have GMOs, but they'd laced it with poisonous mushrooms. Yeah, a flexible work schedule sounded great, until I saw all those zombified people, hunched over the same blanket they had been knitting from sunrise to sunset.

How could they trust anything they had here when so much of it was a lie in the name of profit and power? This was the same abuse of power they'd experienced in corporate America, just in a different font.

But Jasmine was so far gone, she wouldn't listen to any of this rational thinking. Maybe she would listen to one thing though.

"You weren't his first, Jasmine." I gestured to Bronwyn. "He's had other girls. Girlfriends like you. Young, pretty, sweet, smart. And where are they now? Not here. They're gone, and you're wearing your arm in a sling, because it's already started. You've known this man for less than a year, and if he already hits you—"

"Enough!" Bronwyn jolted forward, eyes wide with fury. "Enough. This conversation is over. You're leaving. Both of you. Now. Jasmine, radio Phoenix. Tell him to pack all of Bentley's and Maddie's things. Take them to their cars. Then radio Ivy. Have her bring the ATV up. I don't want them speaking to another person.

I'll sit here with them until she arrives. You head back to the house."

Jasmine's tears dripped over. Her eyes stayed on mine.

"You can leave with us," I said to her. "This doesn't have to be your story."

Still, she held my gaze. Considering. Thinking.

"Now, Jasmine!" Bronwyn's voice deepened.

Clearing her throat, Jasmine planted a kiss on his forehead. She stood, grabbed the lantern, and tugged something from the layer of floor-length skirts. Walking past me, she raised it to her lips. "Phoenix, I need you to..."

Her voice faded as she continued onto the trail.

Bronwyn and I stared into one another's eyes.

"You hate this, don't you?" I asked. "A woman standing over you, knowing she's stronger than you are?"

He scoffed, rolling over to use the ground as leverage to stand. "Go to hell."

"I'll see you there." I sat on a rock beside Tempest and Bentley, never taking my eyes off Bronwyn. "She'll be stronger than you one day too, you know. I haven't lost hope for Ophelia either. Eventually, this whole community is going to get tired of your shit, and—"

He charged toward me.

I yanked my gun from its holster and aimed it at his face.

Tempest went berserk, barking and snarling. She nearly tore Bentley to the ground.

I just smiled at him, the barrel mere centimeters from his forehead. "Go ahead. Take another step. I dare you."

Silence.

Gritting his teeth, he walked backward and sat on a stump.

"Yeah. Not such a big strong man now, are you?"

He looked away, only shaking his head.

I couldn't help but laugh.

* * *

It took half an hour for Ivy to arrive with the ATV. During that time, the sounds of engines and voices grew louder from multiple directions. Bronwyn sat on his stump, checking his watch periodically, that satisfied smile never leaving his face.

When Ivy finally pulled up, fresh mud splattered the ATV's wheels and her clothes. She looked exhausted, dirt smudged across her cheek.

"Sorry for the delay," she said to Bronwyn, not us. "We're working on your order. Jasper has everyone moving fast."

Bronwyn nodded approvingly, then gestured to me, Bentley, and Tempest. "Good. Get them straight to their cars."

She was even younger than Jasmine. I couldn't make out much in the darkness, but the tone of her voice when she said, "Yes, sir," confirmed she couldn't have been more than a teenager.

That wasn't to say I didn't try to get her guard down.

Once Bentley and I loaded into the golf cart style seats, Tempest snuggled closely between us, I said, "Ivy's a pretty name. Did you pick it?"

No response.

"You don't have to stay here, you know," I told her. "If you're scared, or you feel unsafe here—"

She laughed. Otherwise, no response.

"Right. What do I know? I've only been here a day or two," I said. "But this isn't real. This isn't real life. All the drugs that are pumped through this place alter your perception of reality. That's why it seems so good, but it's not. It's not safe."

She didn't so much as look at us. Just kept driving through the rough, mountainous terrain.

Bentley and I didn't speak either.

After seeing that building, knowing that Bronwyn was working with one of Simeon's guys, I had my theories. All the details were still unclear, but I had an idea of what was going on here.

At this point, they thought I was nosy. Too smart, too analytical to be controlled. A nuisance. An inconvenience to Bronwyn's reign.

With me gone, everything would go back to normal. Zombies would sit around making their trinkets, getting high, and Bronwyn wouldn't be questioned.

This place worked because the only questions they were allowed to ask were philosophical.

Questioning the leader himself threatened his rule. If I questioned him, who else could? Who else *would*? Tyrants hated nothing more than freethinking, quizzical people. Especially freethinking, quizzical women.

That's why he wanted us gone.

Not because he knew who I was.

If he realized I was Maddie Castle rather than Maddie Kramer, if he knew of my connections to the police or the FBI, would Ivy still have driven me to my car? Or would she have driven me deeper into the woods to never be seen again?

I had no desire to find out.

When we made it to the car park, Phoenix stood against mine. Smoke trickled from the joint between his fingertips into the air. A small oil lamp sat on my pink, flower-coated hood. All our belongings laid at his feet.

We rocked forward and backward as Ivy shifted the ATV into park. "Get your things and go home."

"Looking forward to it." Bentley jumped out first holding Tempest's leash. She hopped down behind him. "But can I just give you a little bit of advice?"

She turned ahead, not so much as glancing at him.

Still, he said, "I don't know what your life was like before you got here. It must've been bad if this place seems like paradise. And I'm sorry for whatever you went through. But there's more. If you're not an adult yet, you will be soon, and there's a whole world waiting for you whenever you're ready."

Silence.

Heart heavy, I followed Bentley's lead.

Once my feet were on the ground, I expected Ivy to pull away.

That would give me a moment alone with Phoenix, enough time to ask my questions, to see what he knew, to test my theories. But Ivy idled behind us.

"What the hell did you do?" Phoenix scanned me, then Bentley. "Are you okay?"

"We're fine," I said. "Probably wouldn't have been if I didn't nearly break Bronwyn's arm, but—"

"Don't talk to them," Ivy spat. "Bronwyn's orders."

For half a second, Phoenix's jaw tightened. It loosened when he blew out a deep breath.

"Come with us." I stepped closer, keeping my voice low. "You deserve better than this. You all deserve better than this place."

His hunch told me he agreed, but he remained silent.

I had to swallow back my tears, my throat thickening around them. "It's for them, isn't it? For everyone else here. You think they need you. You'll take Bronwyn's brutality so they don't have to, right?"

His eyes glassed over, but no words left his lips.

"I'm going to take that son of the bitch down," I said. "I can't say much else, but—"

Click-clack.

"I'm going to give you until the count of ten. Get your shit and go." Ivy held a shotgun in her lap. I hadn't seen it on the drive. She must have hidden it under her seat. "One."

My heavy sigh formed a cloud before my face.

"Two."

I grabbed mine and Bentley's backpacks off the ground. "You need me to get anything?"

"Three."

"Just you and Tempest in your car." He lifted the tent and his cooler. Heading for his truck, he said, "Meet me on the main road."

"Four."

"I'm leaving, hold your horses," I said, waving a dismissive hand at the girl.

"Five."

I turned to Phoenix, rummaging through my pocket for a crumpled business card I knew was in there somewhere. When I found it, I held it out to him. I hoped that, at the angle, Ivy wouldn't see. "My real name is Maddie Castle. If you need me, call."

"Six."

He took it. "Go, Maddie. She'll shoot."

"Seven."

I opened the rear door, and Tempest hopped in.

"Eight."

"Stay safe," I told Phoenix.

Bentley's car roared to life, and his headlights brightened the lot.

"Nine."

"Go!" Phoenix stepped in front of me, looking at Ivy. "They're leaving. Put the gun down."

I hopped into the driver's seat.

Boom! Boom!

Glass shattered.

Not mine. The back window on one of the cars a few spots down.

Ivy revved the ATV. It rolled deeper down the aisle of the parking lot, giving me room to back out.

My stomach gurgled as I started the car, shifted into reverse, and pulled out behind Bentley.

Chapter 17

Half a dozen times, the glow of Bentley's cell phone shined out his rear window. The red luminance of his taillights and that shining cell phone were the only candor on the pothole-ridden driveway. He kept waving it around, as if to say, *I'm trying to call you.*

We made it roughly a mile onto the winding roadway by the time it finally powered up. As soon as it did, his name flashed across my dashboard. I clicked the green button.

"It just turned on, and it's probably gonna die again if we talk for too long," I said, glancing in my rearview mirror to make sure no one tailed us. Only darkness stared back at me. "So make it quick."

"My tire is losing air," he said. "It only dropped a few PSIs as we were getting out of there, but it's down to twenty now. Should I pull off? Or should we get further away from that place?"

If not for that gun fire as we were leaving, I would've told him to pull over now. But something clenched in my gut. "Go for as long as you can without ruining your rim. Do you have a spare handy?"

"I do—"

The screen turned black.

Grunting, I tossed my phone into the passenger seat.

Bentley gave me a thumbs up out the window. Otherwise confirming he understood what I was saying.

But that clinching in my gut didn't stop. My heart slammed so hard in my chest that my ribs ached. As dark and twisted as Willow Grove had seemed, these deep Appalachian woods weren't much better.

Between my witness testimonies and the photos on my phone, I knew we had enough for a warrant. No matter my theories about the garage, that field of weed was my best bet. Unless they had a license to grow, the amount in that field would send Bronwyn away for a long time.

Enough for a warrant, though, was not necessarily enough for a conviction.

That wasn't all that scared me either.

They sent us out of there, sure. But Ivy hadn't been afraid to use that shotgun. By now, one of them was investigating me. Maybe searching mine or Bentley's cell phone number for our real identity. From there, a Google search would reveal exactly who I was.

If they'd known my real identity before I'd left, I don't know if I would've made it out.

If I had to guess, we were still driving along the property line. The moment we pulled over, someone could come out of those woods with a shotgun. They had enough cars back there. What were two more? Clearly, they had room for our bodies too.

Another mile and a half down the road, though, and we were shit out of luck. Hazard lights flickering, Bentley pulled into the grass on the right side of the road.

I clicked mine on and slid in behind him.

Like lightning, I darted to the passenger side and instructed Bentley to do the same. I opened the rear door and snapped for Tempest. She hopped out, cocking her head left and right. Like she thought I was as crazy as the members of Willow Grove.

Maybe I was. But after that patch of dirt beside the field of pot? I wasn't risking it.

Crouched below his truck, Bentley frowned at me in the brightness of my headlights. "You really think this is necessary?"

"I really don't think it'll hurt." Holding out my hand, I wiggled my fingertips. "Mine's still dead. I've gotta make a call."

His shoulders dropped with a sigh. "My spare's in the bed of the truck, so I'm going to have to stand up at some point."

"The blown tire's on this side of the car, though, right?"

"Front passenger side."

"Then just make it quick."

This time, I got an eye roll. Still crouching down, he made it to the cabin of his truck. As he came back to the rear, he tossed the phone my way, then straightened and fished around in the bed.

I was already dialing and holding the phone to my ear.

On the third ring, a voice came through. "Pennsylvania State Police Department—"

"My name is Maddie Castle," I said. "I need you to patch me through to Derek Ames. Immediately."

"I'm sorry, ma'am, but I'm going to need more than that—"

"Tell him it's an emergency and that it's Maddie Castle." I made no attempt to soften the harshness I had trampled down all weekend. "He's gonna want to hear this."

A few quiet remarks under his breath, followed by, "Hold on a minute."

Elevator music pulsed toward me. I pulled it from my ear, pressed the speaker button, and turned down the volume.

"You could've just called his cell phone." In one hand, Bentley carried the tire, and in the other, he held the jack and tire iron. "I've got it saved."

"It's three in the morning. His wife makes him turn the personal phone off at night." Tempest tugged on the leash to get closer to him. I pulled her back and snapped at the ground. She sat, pulling her ears back. "The station will call his work phone."

"Whatever you say," Bentley murmured, kneeling before the front tire.

The harder he examined that tire, the harder my heart thumped. "Do you think they did it?"

"Could have. I can see the hole back here." He stretched his hand deep into the wheel well. "Could have been a rock on the way in though. Or that shot. Why? What are you thinking?"

"I don't know. Either they really did just want us out of there, or they were waiting for us to get far enough that they could kill us away from the property." I rubbed my hands over the chill that came to my arms. "Also possible that I am still a little wired from last night. Could be making me paranoid."

"After all that, I feel like a little paranoia is justified." He slid the jack beneath the bumper and started pumping. "I just had these tires put on at the shop a month ago. Pretty sure they used an impact gun, so I really hope I can break these bolts. If not, we should just climb in your car and get on the highway. We can come back when we got daylight."

"Yeah, I saw a hotel on my way in," I said. "This ain't over, so no point in going home just yet—"

"This better be good, Mad dog." Derek Ames's sleepy voice came through the speaker. "I was just having a great dream about floating on a cookie boat down a milk river."

I almost laughed. Almost. "I don't know if I'd say it's good, but I'd say I need your help."

"Not good then," he grumbled. "What's going on, kid?"

"I'm not sure. Not exactly, anyway. But a cult. Definitely a cult."

"A cult?"

"No doubt about it, they're a cult."

Oddly enough, at the sound of Derek's voice, the pounding of my heart slowed. As much as I loved Bentley, I'd never seen him as a protector. He was safe, not because he played offense, but because he was my best friend. Derek was the cop I called when my mom was too drunk. He threw her in the drunk tank and gave me candies until she was sober enough to drive the two of us home.

"Like children of the corn or whatever?" He spoke on a yawn. "Or Charles Manson?"

"Honestly can't say." Running my fingers through my hair, I grabbed a fistful at the back. "They operate as a business. Willow Grove. Couple hours north of Pittsburgh, so not sure about the jurisdiction. But I've got decent evidence. Found a big field of pot on the property. Ninety-nine percent sure there's a fresh grave in front of it too. I saw something going on outside a barn garage thing. Maybe they're processing it there? I don't know. I do know one of the girls in the community would've died yesterday if Bentley hadn't narcaned her. But she was on something else too. Molly, I think. Oh, and one of the other girls drugged me via salad dressing."

He snorted. "I'm sorry, what?"

"I really wish I were kidding," I said. "As soon as my phone powers up, I'll get you a video. A couple of videos. They also have this lot of cars. Looks like a junkyard, man. But it's not. They're all people who have been here at the commune. That's where they had me and Bentley park. But there can't be more than fifty people at the commune, and there's way more than fifty cars in the lot. I'm thinking maybe if we can run all the plates and see if anyone's missing, that would be enough to start digging into the place."

"Here?" Panic tinged Derek's voice. "Here, as in, you are there? Right now, you're at a commune?"

"No. Not far from it though." I glanced down the dark road we had just come from. "It was a shit show. They caught me and Bentley taking pictures, and the leader, he got kind of aggressive. He tried to hit me, but I may have broken his wrist. I'm pretty sure he broke his girlfriend's though. So, justice in my book."

"Wait, slow down, Maddie." Something rustled in the background, and he said, "I'm sorry, honey, go back to sleep." A second or two passed, and a door thumped in the background. "Bentley? Bentley's there?"

"He is, yeah." I angled the phone toward him. "Say hi, Bentley."

"Sorry for bothering you, sir." Bentley grunted, struggling with all his might to spin the crowbar. "It's been a wild weekend if you can't tell."

"Since when do you take Bentley on cases?" Derek asked. "No offense, son."

"None taken." Bentley straightened, grasped the side of the truck, and rammed his foot on the tire iron. Still, it didn't budge. "After getting shot at, not sure I want to go on another one."

"They shot at you?"

"When they kicked us out, they shot in our vicinity," I said. "Now Bentley has a flat. He's trying to change it, but if he can't, we're just gonna take my car to a hotel. But that's not the point. The point is, something really weird is going on there. I think they're dealing. We saw a car outside the garage. I recognized it. It's one of Simeon's guys."

Derek huffed. "Then I'm not surprised you think you found a body."

As relieved as I was that he was on the other line, my shoulders still slumped. "Are you saying you're not gonna look into this?"

"I'm saying what we all know. Simeon is untouchable," Derek said. "You know we've been trying to crack those guys for a decade."

"And it's better if you don't," Bentley muttered, probably too quiet for Derek to hear.

Which I didn't disagree with. Not really.

Simeon was a businessman. A careful one. He never let his guys deal to kids. The people who worked for him made decent livings. If you needed a loan for a small business, ninety-nine percent of the time, Simeon would give you one. In high school, he treated his girl-friends well. Went so far as to defend a few from shady guys. His moral compass may have been skewed, but he did have one. After all, he helped me and Bentley find Grace when the Country Killer kidnapped her.

A drug dealer, yes. But a man with integrity.

Bronwyn? The middle-aged weirdo with a harem? One women vanished from?

They weren't the same.

"Then don't go after Simeon," I said. "But somebody has to do something, damn it. They're roping in kids. The girl who overdosed today was a foster care run away. She is skin and bones, Derek. They think the thinner you are, the closer you are to an ethereal form. These people are convinced that you can survive on sunlight and air."

"But she's an adult now?" Derek asked.

"Well, yeah." My heart sank at the point he was making. "But it's bad there. I'm pretty sure the girl who shot at us was a minor. And the girl who OD'd, she was overheating. They didn't want us cutting off her floor-length, turtleneck, long-sleeved dress because she wouldn't be modest enough. All day, she'd been cooking bread in a tiny shed and rolling her balls off. The rest of them, they sit on these little blankets in the grass making hemp bracelets and dream catchers. They're not paid. They don't even have a roof over their head. They sleep in the kind of refugee tents you see in war zones."

"Are they there against their will?"

Pressing my lips together, I shook my head. "Some of them are there willingly. But I think the others are being blackmailed or something. They branded the logo for the place onto one guy's ass as a punishment. I think because he was trying to help one of the girls get out. I don't know if they're brainwashed or if it's force, but I do know drugs are involved. And the picture is evidence of the weed plants. That should be enough to get a warrant, right?"

"It should be, yeah. But tell me more about the shooting. Were you on the property?"

"Yeah, and we were asked to leave." I rubbed my temples. "They were within their rights."

"I'm not just gonna look the other way, kid," Derek said. "I'll do whatever I can. I just don't know how much it'll be. Especially if they figured out who you are. Even if we get a warrant, God only knows how much evidence they're gonna destroy before we get in there. But get me those videos. I'll dig into all of it. Alright?"

Shit. I hadn't even thought about them destroying evidence. But digging into it was as much as he could do, just as it had been the most that I could do when this case began. "Alright."

"But it sounds like you're running on fumes, Mad dog. You too, Bentley," Derek said. "I'm only gonna work on this if you promise me you're going to a hotel to get some sleep."

"Yeah, I'm done messing with this tire." Bentley tossed the crowbar to the ground. "We'll worry with all this tomorrow. Let's go get some vending machine dinner, take a shower, and go to bed."

"That's why you're good for her," Derek said. "She won't slow down until someone makes her."

I harrumphed. "He can't make me do anything. But I hear you. Just please, let me know as soon as you find anything."

"Yeah, yeah. Get some rest."

Chapter 18

THE SKY OUTSIDE THE WINDOW WAS JUST MAKING THAT SLOW switch from deep cerulean to pale blue. The coffee maker spat and sputtered, filling the glass below with

piping hot Java. Another yawn parted Derek's lips.

Stifling it, he filled a mug to its brim. A dash of sugar, a splash of cream from the fridge. Another splash slipped over the edge of the cup when he lifted it from the granite. Slurping at it, floorboards creaked underfoot as he headed for his office off the kitchen.

He sat at his desk, placed his coffee to the right of his mouse, and powered up his computer. The thing was a decade old. It took its sweet time when he clicked that power button.

Derek didn't mind. In the mornings, he preferred a slower pace. Especially when he got to spend his mornings here.

His office used to be on the second floor, right next to his bedroom. Tamra never liked that. Nineteen years ago, their daughter was born. She needed that room. Derek had just been a deputy then, but having a study had always been a dream of his. Losing it to his daughter's birth was the only thing he hadn't liked about becoming a father.

Tamra had suggested turning the sunroom into a study. It didn't get the best ventilation. After all, it had started out as a porch. Derek had swapped each screen for a window, then the storm door for a glass one. In the summer, he popped a wall unit into one of the windows, and in the winter, he used a space heater.

Now that his little girl was off to college, he could move back into her bedroom. But he liked it here now. Sitting in his sunroom office was his favorite part of each day, aside from dinner with Tamra. The fragrance of the coffee on the desk filled his nose. When he turned his gaze out the far-right window, he watched the sun pinken the blue sky. Every spring, a groundhog visited him out the left window.

Today, it was a chipmunk. He crouched down in the bushes in front of the fence, nibbling on a piece of grass. Derek smiled at him and took a sip of his coffee. The chipmunk, unaware of his stalker, came closer. An acorn laid a few feet away from him, closer to Derek. Did chipmunks eat acorns? Derek always thought squirrels were the ones who liked acorns, but—

A squawk.

A bird.

A bird dove into the yard.

Not just any bird. No Robin by any means. Something big enough to snatch up a small dog.

It pounced on the chipmunk.

Squeals. Awful, pain filled squeals.

Derek jolted. Hot coffee spilled down his beard, dousing his chest.

He'd been a cop for many years. Working in a field like that desensitizes you to most things.

But not a hawk snatching up an innocent little chipmunk.

Derek turned away.

His computer dinged to life. Pinching one eye shut, he glanced out the window.

No more hawk. No more chipmunk.

Derek's stomach twisted, knowing the fate of that poor little critter. He shook his head, shimmied his shoulders, and ignored whatever feelings welled in his chest. A job needed doing.

After typing in his password, Derek headed for his email.

From: Maddie Castle

Subject: Video Evidence

He clicked it open and adjusted his bifocals to read the text.

I know the videos are blurry. I had to move quickly. But I think you can get a plate off the car at the barn. As far as the cars in the lot, I know that'll take a lot of time for your guys to go through. I know a guy. I'm gonna put him on it. But if anything stands out to you, let me know.

Alright. Going to sleep now. But call me if anything comes up.

Derek chuckled. That girl was something else.

He tapped on the first video. In heartbeats, it loaded.

Derek created a new case folder in the department's digital evidence system, logging his access at 5:07 AM. Every video Maddie sent would be automatically timestamped and hash-verified. Chain of custody started here. If they found anything, it needed to hold up in court.

The moment he saw the size of the parking lot, a hole formed deep in Derek's stomach. Maddie said there couldn't have been more than fifty people at the commune. But that lot? It was as full as the county fairgrounds in August. At least a couple hundred cars, all lined up in neat rows. Toward the back, a few were wedged in bumper-to-bumper.

Even a New York City native, someone well experienced in tiny, parallel parking spots, wouldn't have been able to get out.

Chills crept over Derek's arms.

That was the video Maddie planned to send to her guy. Derek understood why. If she had a programmer handy, maybe he could run some sort of software that would isolate all the license plates she'd recorded faster than Derek could manually catalog them.

Derek opened the second attachment instead.

Just as Maddie described. A decent plot of land with more marijuana plants than he could count. Whoever put them there did so quite some time ago, judging by their height. They had to have been at least five feet tall.

As for the disturbed soil in front of them? He understood why Maddie believed a body lay beneath. There very well may have been one. They buried something there. But they would need a canine unit trained in human remains for confirmation.

As Maddie had said, though, the weed would be enough to get a warrant. The clock at the top of his desktop read 5:09. It was never a good idea to call a judge before sunrise. Not unless it was an emergency, and this simply wasn't.

Derek clicked over to the next video.

Although the camera quality wasn't ideal, Derek recognized that car. Hard to miss a white Malibu with a purple racing stripe from hood to rear fender.

He leaned back in his seat and looked out the other window and brought the coffee mug back to his lips, relishing the hot sip. Were these people dealing drugs? Possibly. Could he get a judge to care about some hippies on a farm growing pot? Doubtful. Especially if they had the type of money required to operate a business this big.

At seven, when he was sure the judge would be awake, Derek would call. For now? He had another to make.

He dialed the number, held the phone to his ear, and waited. On the fifth ring, a young deputy answered. "Good morning, sir. Everything alright?"

"Something weird's going on, that's for sure." Derek rubbed a hand over his jaw, staring at that vehicle on his screen. "Do me a favor and have everyone keep an eye out for a white Chevy Malibu, early 2000s, with a purple racing stripe. 967 Zebra Yellow X-ray."

"No problem, sir. I'll get the word out," Richardson said. "What are we watching for exactly?"

"I think he's got drugs on him, but it's probably deeper than that. No reason to believe he's armed and dangerous. Honestly, just the tip of an iceberg. I'm after his distributor if I can get enough evidence," Derek said. "Just watch him. With good reason, pull him over. Search the car if you can. But be careful. He works for the Gunns."

"Oh." Derek could practically hear Richardson's hard swallow. "Okay. Sounds good, sir."

* * *

DEPUTY MILLER CLUNKED HIS CRUISER TO A STOP OUTSIDE THE coffee shop. His front end faced the highway, rear aimed at the business. This way, he could sip his coffee and take a few bites of his breakfast sandwich with his eyes on the road.

Peeling apart the paper wrapper, he watched the cars race by. One guy roll-stopped at the stop sign on his left. Miller considered clicking on his lights and chasing after him. Was it worth the effort? Not compared to the savory flavor of cheese mixing with egg and bacon exploding on his tongue.

Minor traffic violations weren't why he'd become a cop. No one was a perfect driver, and everyone broke the law. What mattered to Miller were serious offenses. One day, he hoped to get a position in the city. Pittsburgh, maybe. But he'd always loved Philadelphia.

Maybe that's where he and Liz would go after the wedding. That was right around the bend now. Only three months away.

A reminder of such appeared as a notification on his phone. It floated in the magnetic, hands-free mount on his dashboard. A text from his brother said, *Okay, but how about Atlantic City?*

Miller couldn't help the way his nostrils flared with breath as he read the message. He didn't even understand the point of a bachelor party. He and Liz had been together for three years. Three years ago was the last time he had been a bachelor.

He lay the breakfast sandwich in the wrapper on his lap and texted back, *Not my thing. How about a fishing trip to Virginia Beach?*

Once he shuttered the phone, he leaned back in his seat and took a big gulp of his coffee. Weak. Almost as weak as the coffee at the station. Maybe he should've gotten an extra espresso—

A white car coasted past him. A white car with a purple racing stripe.

Miller leaned forward to get a better view of the plate. 967-ZYX.

Shifting the car into drive, he grabbed his radio from the dashboard. He held it to his lips and said, "I've got eyes on that car you called about earlier, Richardson."

Miller was already pulling out of the parking lot when Richardson came back in. "No shit. They doing anything sketchy?"

"So far, no." They stopped at a red light two blocks ahead. "What's the story with this guy anyway?"

"Ames didn't say. Suspect drugs are in the car, but nothing violent." A keyboard clicked and clacked in the background. "Owner's got a few arrests. Misdemeanor possession. Nothing crazy, but apparently he works with Simeon Gunn. Legal name is Caleb Kennedy. Goes by Ken on the streets."

Miller cocked his head to the side, trying to get a better view of the driver. It was difficult from so far away, but whoever sat behind that wheel had long, dark hair. "What's the guy look like?"

"Six three, blue eyes, bald. Why?"

"You sure?"

"I'm looking at his driver's license photo right now."

"Doesn't look tall enough to be six three to me," Miller muttered. The light turned green, getting him one block closer to the vehicle. "I can't tell from back here but looks like a woman. Could it be his wife or something?"

"I don't see a wife anywhere in his records."

"Huh." Miller took another sip from his coffee, easing through the next green light. "I'll keep tailing them. If he gives me a reason to stop, I will."

"Roger that," Richardson said.

* * *

MILLER FOLLOWED THE VEHICLE FOR ANOTHER FIFTEEN minutes. The driver made a right, then another right, then another. Miller stayed a few vehicles behind, cocking his head left and right, waiting for the driver to make an error. Or to turn into a parking lot. Or to continue on any of the roads they had turned onto.

Instead, they kept making right-hand turns, bringing them back to the same stretch of highway the coffee shop was on.

They were driving in circles. Miller drove in circles behind them.

Five times now, they had made the same circle.

On the sixth lap, they made a right-hand turn onto that same stretch of highway and failed to click on their turn signal. That was his in.

Miller flicked on his lights, popped on his siren, and pressed the gas. The car between him and the white Malibu pulled over. Miller sped past them.

Into his radio, Miller said, "Unit 47 in pursuit of white Malibu, suspect failed to signal, now evading. Speed approximately 55 in a 35 zone. Light traffic. Requesting supervisor approval to continue pursuit."

"What's the nature of the original stop?" Lieutenant Harrison's voice crackled through.

"Surveillance request from Somerset County. Possible drug transport."

A pause. "Approved, but if speed exceeds 70 or enters residential, break off. County safety protocol."

"10-4."

Miller knew the rules—pursuit had to be worth the risk to public safety. Drug transport met the threshold, barely.

Just when he was on the tail, certain now that the driver was a woman from her glance in the rearview, she slammed on the gas.

Miller pressed his pedal to the floor. The speed gauge ticked higher. When he touched fifty-five miles an hour, Miller's heart rate picked up.

The white car sped ahead.

What the hell was this?

"Definitely a woman," Miller said into his radio. "She's screwing with me, man. Made a turn without signaling, I flipped on my lights, and now she's running."

"Do you need backup?" Richardson's voice came through the radio. "We got units nearby."

Miller opened his mouth to respond, but the white Malibu raced through a red light.

A red truck spun from the right of the intersection, pounding on its horn.

Right into Miller's path.

He slammed his brakes. Just in time to avoid an impact.

Traffic on the left and right of the intersection halted.

Miller glanced at the man in the red truck. He looked fine, just stunned. No accidents yet.

"Almost caused a wreck," Miller said into the radio. "Yeah, get me back up," followed by his exact location.

"I've got guys on the way," Richardson said.

Miller's heart pounded as he maneuvered around the red truck. He pressed on the gas again, swiftly reaching sixty. The vehicles on the road parted like the Red Sea. Straight ahead, roughly a mile onto the winding backroad, the white Malibu became clear again. It pivoted to the left, merging onto a larger local highway with less congestion. No shops or businesses, just a long stretch of road. The kind that pressed up against suburbs and neighborhoods.

It didn't take long for him to catch up. The new SUVs had way stronger engines than that little lemon.

Miller said into his radio, "Pull over and stop the car now, ma'am. I don't want to run you off the road, but I will if I have to."

In her rearview mirror, the woman smiled. A dark, twisted smile unlike anything Miller had ever seen.

She accelerated.

Miller did too.

So quickly, he didn't realize he topped seventy-five until a flashing construction sign on the right of the road told him so.

Somewhere off in the distance, between the fire-colored trees, blue and red lights shone. But the road swayed to the left and then to the right. Like all the roads did back here.

Zigzagging side to side ached Miller's neck. He gripped the wheel harder, watching that white car swerve into the left side of the road, and then the right.

Taunting him. She was taunting him.

Why? What was the purpose in this?

No longer was she attempting to evade arrest. She was smiling, swaying onto the opposite side of the two-lane road. If she didn't stop soon, whoever came in the opposite direction would surely collide with her, and then—

Bright red lights.

Her brake lights.

She slammed on her brakes.

Miller pressed his but not fast enough.

His rear end collided with hers. Miller's body slammed forward, just as the airbag deployed. The vehicle slid sideways. The airbag blocked his view. He pounded those brakes. Tires squealed. The smell of burning rubber rushed the cabin.

Bang!

Clunk!

Glass shattered.

Miller's head spun, but he slammed the SUV into park. Out the window on his left, black smoke filled the air. Holding the gun at his hip, he opened the door.

He shrunk down behind it and peered around the edge.

Behind a torn apart guardrail, the white Malibu had wrapped around a tree. Its rear end stayed intact, but the driver's side door must've hit something on its way into the ditch. The metal caved toward the driver.

That driver-side door hadn't opened yet. The driver, no matter her state of mind, could have been hurt. Something wasn't right here, so he didn't loosen his hold on the gun.

But he did this job to help people.

Jogging toward the vehicle, barrel aimed at the driver side door, Miller called, "Open the door and keep your hands where I can see them!"

A sound floated from within the vehicle. Crying? Screaming? Yelling for help?

The window rolled down. Through the black smoke, it was hard to make out much, but the sound became clear.

Laughter. The woman was laughing.

Hands held up in the air, blood trickled from a cut on her forehead. She kept laughing. As Miller approached the driver's side door and flung it open, she just kept laughing.

"Are you hurt?" He glanced her over for a weapon, awaiting a response. All she offered was more laughter. "Ma'am, are you hurt?"

"A little." Giggling, she wiggled her fingertips. "Can I get out? Or are you going to shoot me?"

Miller's face screwed up in confusion. He looked her over again, waiting for a trap. "What the hell were you doing? Why did you make me chase you?"

"What man doesn't like a chase?" She laughed harder, face beat red. "What girl doesn't like to be chased?"

Miller stared at her a few seconds longer, trying to decipher her meaning. "Do you think this is a goddamned game? You almost got people killed back there."

"What else is new." She wiggled her fingers, laughing some more. "Are you going to arrest me or can I put my hands down?"

Blood boiling now, Miller stretched into the vehicle and released her seatbelt. "Hands up as you exit."

Only then, as she stood, did Miller notice the brace around her forearm. He was mindful of that as she spun around with her arms in the air. When he fastened the cuffs from his hip around her wrists, he said, "What's your name, and how did you get the keys to this car?"

Beneath the Grove

Laughing again, all she said was, "Jasmine Armstrong."

Chapter 19

THE SHARP VIBRATION OF MY PHONE ON THE NIGHTSTAND WOKE me. The light of its screen brightened the hotel room. A sliver of sun trickled in from the edge of the closed curtains, informing me it was daytime before the clock on my phone did. 11:32 in the top right corner while Derek's picture lit up the screen.

I slid the green bar and held the phone to my ear. "You got something?"

"We got something, alright." A difficult sound to describe floated from the speaker. A laugh? A scoff? No way to be sure. "When you were at that commune, did you meet a girl named Jasmine? Jasmine Armstrong?"

"She's the reason I have this case." Stifling a yawn, I spoke in a hushed tone. Bentley wouldn't mind if I woke him, but at least I'd gotten a few hours of rest while we were at Willow Grove. He'd only managed five hours of sleep over the last forty-eight. "Why?"

"Well, she was driving Caleb Kennedy's car this morning." As he continued, I shuffled from the bed and headed for the bathroom. "Technically not in my jurisdiction, but I'm working with the sheriff over here in Lawrence County. Either way, Jasmine took one of the younger deputies on a high-speed chase through a suburban area."

Shutting the bathroom door, I blinked hard in disbelief. "Wait, Jasmine was driving the white Malibu with the racing stripe, and she evaded arrest?"

"At first, that's what the deputy thought he was dealing with, but then she started swerving all over the road intentionally. Like she was messing with him. She slammed the brakes, he hit her, and she did doughnuts into a ditch."

My stomach dropped. "Is she okay?"

"Seems to be. Refused to let EMS evaluate her." A slow, shaking breath escaped him. "What kind of drugs did you say they were doing there?"

Knowing she was okay loosened my shoulders. "A little bit of everything, I think. Jasmine was the one who put something in the salad dressing. I don't know if it was acid, or mushrooms, or DMT, but I tripped pretty hard. Another girl overdosed on some combination of opiates and party drugs. Why do you ask?"

"We found something in her trunk," he said. "Looks like a pound of weed and a kilo of something else. White powder. Maybe Coke? Maybe Ecstasy? Doesn't look like dope to me though."

His guess was as good as mine. Chewing my lip, I leaned against the countertop behind me. "She wouldn't say what it is?"

"She won't say a damn thing," Derek said. "We read her rights to her, and she didn't ask for a lawyer. She did say no when the paramedics arrived, but so far, that's all she said. Just 'no,' when they asked to examine her."

Scratching my scalp, I cocked my head to the side. "She's on something, sir. Maybe she'll be more receptive when she comes down."

"Yeah, I'd like to get a piss sample, but she hasn't needed to go yet." A deep breath echoed through the speaker. "You know her though?"

"Wouldn't say we're friends, but we've met," I said. "The whole situation is really screwed up. Either that girl is deeply brainwashed or these people latched on to a mental health disorder she already had.

The others there were weird too, but the way Jasmine clung to that esoteric bullshit was a lot more extreme. Go easy on her. She's damaged, but she's only been there a few months. She's not the root of this."

"I figured something like that. I already talked to the local sheriff here. She wants to know what's going on as much as you do. I told her how I got started on all this, that it was you, and she's actually why I called. She thought maybe you could come in and talk to Jasmine. Maybe you'll have better luck with her than we did."

"Yeah, of course. Thank you for keeping me in the loop." I stifled another yawn. "Text me the address, and I'll head there as soon as I'm done getting dressed."

* * *

THE TOWN WE WERE IN WAS SO SMALL, IT DIDN'T HAVE A NAME. Rather than a city station, the state police had brought Jasmine to the county barracks. Half a dozen cruisers sat out front. Inside, just as many officers sat at cubicles beyond the waiting room. They didn't leave me there long.

Derek led me through to the back and introduced me to the County Sheriff. A woman in her early fifties. Her gleaming gray hair was pulled back in a tight bun. The name tag on her chest read K. Rhodes. She had round, pale cheeks, barely dusted with foundation. Just enough makeup so that she fit the professional image I was sure she had to maintain.

We were lucky in Somerset County to have a sheriff like Derek Ames. He was the first Black sheriff to ever preside over our county, and I was grateful to have witnessed that. We had yet to see a woman in the same position though. It was nice one was in power here.

"It's such a pleasure to meet you, Castle." Rhodes firm grasp closed around mine. "The way everything went down with the Country Killer—I just admire the hell outta you. Thank you for your service."

174

"Thank you for yours too." I shook her hand with just as much strength. "Doubt it's easy wrangling all these boys around here."

Snorting a laugh, she glanced around the room. "Eh. They're pretty well-behaved for the most part."

"When they've got a good leader, I guess they've gotta be."

She chuckled again, gesturing to the hundred-pound German Shepherd at my feet. "And who might this be?"

"Say hi, Tempy." Those big brown eyes turned up to Rhodes, and her tail slapped side to side. "I've always been passionate about handling. One of the guys I knew at the station went down on duty. She had a hard time adjusting, but she's doing a lot better since I took her in."

"Wow, that's so nice to hear." Rhodes only waved at her. "Are you bringing her into the interrogation room with you?"

"Probably better if I don't. I had a not so great interaction with Jasmine's boyfriend while we were at Willow Grove. I'm not sure how Tempest will respond to her." I turned to Derek. "Would you mind keeping an eye on her while I'm in there?"

"Yeah, no problem." He held his hand out for the leash, and I passed it over. "I told Rhodes everything you told me. We think it's best if you go in there alone. Maybe the rapport you two have will give us some insight."

"I'm still trying to get a team together to go search the property anyhow," Rhodes said. "We'd love to have you come along though. If you know the lay of the land at all, maybe that'll help us find some stuff sooner."

"I'm glad you asked, because I was going to beg." I gave a half smile, and Rhodes returned it. "Anyway. Want me to get in there?"

"Yeah, of course." Rhodes turned and gestured over her shoulder for me to follow. "This way."

Sneakers squeaking against the linoleum flooring, Rhodes led me past the cubicles to the rear of the building. A break room on my left, an empty cell on my right. I imagined that cell stayed empty most of the time, given the town's size. Maybe the occasional drunk hillbilly, but not much more.

There was something poetic about that. These places, almost untouched by modern civilization, always seemed so idyllic, so perfect. Just like Willow Grove had, at a glance.

There was beauty in isolation. Peace. Quiet.

Some wanted to live in areas like this for those two reasons. Peace and quiet. Others wanted it to build a kingdom all their own and reign like royalty over whoever entered. Things went on behind closed doors and deep down those gravel driveways in the mountains.

"I brought her in something to eat, but she hasn't touched it." Stopping beside a metal door, Rhodes nodded inside. "If you can get something in her, maybe she'll sober up a little faster."

"Most I can do is try." I raised my shoulders. "Unless she saw you slaughter the protein yourself and pick the produce, I doubt she will."

Rhodes face screwed up in confusion.

"I'll explain more when I'm done in here." I turned the door handle. "Thanks. I'll holler if I need anything."

Jasmine sat at a metal table. Both wrists were cuffed to it, chains long enough for her to reach the tray on the corner. A small cut started at her forehead and extended to the top of her cheekbone. Her eyes stayed fixed on something I couldn't see. They didn't so much as flinch when I walked in.

"Hey, Jasmine." As I lowered myself to the chair, I waited for her to look my way. A laminated card sat on the table between us—the Miranda warning, with a signature line at the bottom. Her shaky signature was already there, along with the timestamp: 11:47 AM.

"You already talked to them?" I nodded at the card.

She glanced at me. That same devilish grin lifted the edges of her lips. She remained silent.

"Smart of you to invoke your rights with them," I said. "But I'm not a cop anymore, remember? This is just you and me talking."

Still, silent.

"You gotta be hungry." I slid the plastic tray toward her. In the center was a sandwich. A fruit cup sat in one corner, a glass of water in the other. "It doesn't look like you got much sleep. You need your energy."

The chains of her cuffs clicked together as she lifted her hands from her lap. I hoped she would take a bite, but she slid the tray toward me instead.

A deep breath lifted my shoulders and escaped my nostrils. "What the hell was that, Jasmine? Why did you get caught on purpose?"

Her smile widened.

Silence.

"Come on. Just explain it to me." The cold metal of the table bit through the fabric of my hoodie when I rested my forearms on it. "Did you realize who I was? That I was going to turn Bronwyn in for dealing? You figured you would take the fall before his arrest could ruin the community?"

A quiet chuckle. Almost a giggle. It reminded me far too much of Ophelia's.

"Clearly, you know you have the right to remain silent." I stayed still, just studying her. "Is that why you're not talking? Or is it something else?"

"We knew you'd come," she said.

"Good. Words. You still know how to make them." My shoulders relaxed, now aware that she hadn't lost all her marbles. "Yeah, I kind of figured you would figure out who I was after I left."

"No." Eyes softening, her smile grew. "We knew you would *come*. Now it can begin."

"You knew I would come to Willow Grove?" I squinted at her. "Is that why you called your mom last week? Because you wanted me to investigate the Grove?"

For half a second, her smile faltered. Her eyes glistened. She blinked quickly, and the twisted smile returned. "We didn't bring you there. We just knew you would come."

So she wanted to play the riddle game. "What—did a prophecy talk about me?"

"Yes."

I propped my chin in my hand. "What did it say?"

"That someone would come to destroy everything we worked so hard to build." Her tone was slower now than it had been. Likely because the drugs she so often took were wearing off. "Then, we would have to fight."

"That's not much of a prophecy, Jasmine." I made sure to soften my tone. "Bronwyn is operating an illegal drug trade. Of course, eventually, someone would catch on and try to stop it."

A shrug. "Maybe."

"No, not maybe." I shook my head. "You're a smart girl. You were in the top ten percent of your high school. You graduated top of your class in college. You have more than basic reasoning skills. You knew that one day, reality was gonna come for that place. So did Bronwyn. That's why he told you it was a prophecy. So that when this day came, the seed was already planted. You would already believe him."

Another shrug. "Maybe."

I wasn't sure if it would be easier to talk to Jasmine or a brick wall.

Running my tongue along my teeth, I leaned back in my seat.

I didn't like the way she looked. She had already been thin and strung out at the Grove. But it had reached a new level, just over a twelve hour period. The dark circles beneath her eyes were one shade away from bruises, pupils pinpricked. Those pretty pink lips from the photos on her Facebook blended into the bleakness of her complexion.

How was it that someone who didn't believe in sunscreen but lived on a farm had remained so pasty at the tail end of summer?

"At least have a drink." I grabbed the Styrofoam cup of water and placed it before her. "You're dehydrated. I can tell just by looking at you."

"Styrofoam takes somewhere between five hundred and a million years to break down." She passed it back to me. "Not only is it ruining our environment, but it is packed with micro plastics that wreak havoc on our microbiomes. When your gut is unhealthy, so is the rest of your body. My back will hurt if I drink that."

Half-truths combined into a cocktail of bullshit. "Your back's gonna hurt in a few hours when that dope wears off. But everything's gonna hurt a lot more if you're dehydrated."

"I don't do *dope*." She spat the word. "Don't talk about us like you understand, Maddie. You don't. You don't understand anything."

"You're right. I don't understand a lot of what you've gone through at Willow Grove." I gestured to her wrist. "I don't understand why you would allow any man to do that to you. Or why you would take the fall for him dealing drugs *after* he did that to you. Or what it is you see in that subpar, middle-age, balding man."

She rolled her eyes and scoffed.

"I don't understand why you would stay with a man who branded his business's logo into your friend's ass as a punishment."

Her eyes snapped toward me.

A swallow bobbed her throat.

She looked away.

"Is that it?" I leaned in, softening my voice some more. "We can protect you from him, Jasmine. We can protect all of you. If you give us what we need, we can keep everyone safe. If you're afraid of him—"

"I love him." Her face pinched with confusion.

"I loved my mom. Doesn't change that I was afraid of her."

"I'm not afraid of him."

"Phoenix is." I kept my voice so gentle, so soft, like I was talking to a toddler. Which wasn't easy for me. But that had worked at the Grove. Maybe it would work on Jasmine out of it. "He didn't say so, but I saw it in his eyes. I saw that the only reason he stays is because he has nowhere else to go and he loves the rest of you too much to leave you behind."

Her glassy eyes avoided mine. She crossed her arms against her chest.

"He was protecting you, wasn't he?" I kept staring at her, hoping that she would meet my gaze again. Hoping she would see the sympathy in my eyes. "That's how he got that brand. Phoenix was trying to get you out."

She wouldn't look at me. She kept her gaze on the cement wall to her right.

"Phoenix has been there since he was a kid," I said. "I understand why it's so hard for him to leave. But you've only been there a few months, Jasmine. We can get you out. We can get everybody out. We can keep you safe from him, but you have to work with us."

"You can't keep anyone safe from anything." Furrowing her brows, she finally looked at me. "You expect me to hate Bronwyn? What about every other man I've met out there?" She gestured vaguely outside. "Willow Grove is a community. We all have each other. We listen to each other, we care about each other. Out here, everyone just shuts their doors. Everybody just ignores the pain everyone else is going through. It's all about the self, the individual, and you expect me to believe this is better? I've lived in both worlds, Maddie. This one is just as dark and twisted as you think the Grove is."

"If you want to have a conversation about individualism in our society, I'll discuss it with you for hours. I understand the good things about that place. I understand you needed to get away from Chase." She flinched at his name. "I don't know what he did to you, but I know it hurt, and I'm sorry. I'm sorry that your mom didn't care. I'm sorry all you had was your brother. I understand how being in that position would've led you to take any other road."

With each word I spoke, her eyes narrowed further. Like she was piecing it all together. "My mom hired you. That's how you found the Grove."

It surprised me she took so long to figure that out. But given how high she was, it shouldn't have. "Yes. And I understand why you would've wanted away from her too. The holier than thou attitude. The lack of compassion she had for your pain. Believe me, I understand. I hate having to pull up my pantleg to show people my scars for them to believe that I'm in pain. It's gotta be a lot worse for you, because your pain is invisible to everyone else."

Her eyes softened a little more. So did her shoulders.

I was getting through to her. This was working.

Maybe that's what they all needed. Everyone who joined the Grove did so because it had open arms. When everyone else shoved you away, of course falling into the warmth of another was appealing.

"And I'm so sorry for that, Jasmine," I said. "I understand, and I'm sorry. But all I want to do is help. Bronwyn is exploiting everyone in the Grove. They're not being paid for their labor. It doesn't feel so bad because even though you guys don't have enough food or adequate housing, you've got drugs that fill the void of both. But Starlight almost died yesterday, Jasmine. Ophelia or Bronwyn or Phoenix could be next. I know you don't want that."

"If the goddess calls us home, then we welcome her embrace."

I couldn't help it. My arms fell flat on the table, head shaking. "What goddess? Who are you even praying to? Because nobody seems to have a consistent belief system there. You all pick and choose bits of different religions and spiritualities. At best, what you're doing there is cultural appropriation, and at worst, it's mass drug-induced psychosis, Jasmine."

"Everyone who was ahead of their time seemed mad while they lived," Jasmine said, voice soft and quiet again. "But in death, they were understood."

"Don't you see what you're doing?" Raising my arms at my sides, I ran over what she said again in my mind. "Everything you say has a little bit of truth in it. But there's so much bullshit, it cancels out everything that isn't."

"Your mind is just too closed off to embrace it all."

"Your mind is so diluted with drugs and conspiracy theories that you can't even hold a coherent conversation."

"I don't do drugs."

"You got caught with a pound of weed and a kilo of Molly—"

"Cannabis is an herb, not a drug. And it wasn't Molly."

"Then what was it?" I snapped. "And why are you so dead set on pretending that the substances you take are any better than the chemicals in this sandwich?"

A half smile paired with a quiet laugh. Slowly, she shook her head. "You just don't understand, Maddie."

"You're right. I don't." I rested my elbows on the table again. "Explain it to me. Make me understand. Explain why whatever you put up your nose is healthier than drinking out of a Styrofoam cup. Tell me why it was okay for that man to brand your friend when he tried to help you. Show me what it is that you see in that misogynistic pig."

"It's bigger than him. It's bigger than Phoenix, or me, or you." She shrugged again, smiling. "It's a revolution like the world has never seen before."

"That's what this is about?" I did my best to remain soft, to keep my tone gentle, but my confusion must have been evident. "Politics?"

"Who said anything about politics?"

"Revolutions are generally politically motivated."

"No, no, no." Frowning, she shook her head. "This is a spiritual revolution."

"What the hell does that mean?"

She laughed. "You'll see."

"Just show me. Make it make sense. I want to level with you. I want to see things through the lens that you do, Jasmine. You just haven't given me enough to do so."

"Because you choose to keep your eyes closed."

"My eyes are wide open." I waved at the side of my head. "I'm listening. Help me understand."

Another laugh. This one louder, more playful. Teasing, almost. Her shoulders shook, and her face turned beet red. It didn't have that same devilish tinge to it. It was the kind of laughter that trembled her shoulders, that would've had her slapping her knee if she could reach.

"What?" I looked her over. "What's so funny?"

She laughed and laughed some more. I waited. Almost an entire minute passed before she stopped.

"My ears are still as open as my eyes," I said.

"You want me to show you?" That devilish grin returned. "I'll show you."

Jasmine stuck out her tongue. She pressed her teeth down on top of it, still grinning ear to ear.

She slammed her chin on the table.

Crimson sprayed across the room.

It doused my face, the table, even the walls.

Like a garden hose, it sprayed and sprayed. It even sounded like a garden hose. Maybe like a burst pipe.

Over it though, louder, her gurgling laughs bounced off the walls.

I rushed around the table, screaming, "Help! We need help in here!"

Chapter 20

For the first time in my career, I froze at the sight of blood.

Deputies, Rhodes, even Derek stormed the door. As they shoved cloths into Jasmine's gurgling, cackling mouth to stop the bleeding, Rhodes barked orders: "Mitchell, photograph everything before EMS moves her. Every blood spatter, every surface. Wilson, bag that tray—it might have DNA from before. Someone preserve the video recording from this room."

I stood frozen, watching them work with the efficiency of a trauma team. Even in the chaos, they maintained the scene's integrity. Deputy Mitchell circled us with a camera, the flash popping every few seconds.

"Castle, I need you to step back," Rhodes said firmly but kindly. "You're evidence now too. Mitchell, get photos of her clothing."

Only then did I realize I was covered in blood spatter. My clothes were part of the crime scene.

In heartbeats, paramedics flooded the room. Apparently, they were already outside the barracks. Made sense, since the station was next door.

Blood was everywhere. All over me, the table, the walls, even the floor. Throughout all those first aid trainings I'd received, no one had specified what to do with a severed tongue. While they worked on her, they hooked up her IV, loaded her onto a gurney, all I did was stand there and stare.

Rhodes turned to Deputy Mitchell. "You're riding with her. She's still in custody, even in medical. Get me a medical clearance form as soon as the doctors allow visitors. We'll need to maintain security at the hospital. She's a flight and self-harm risk."

"Should we cuff her to the bed?" Mitchell asked.

"Soft restraints only, and only if medical approves. We document every mark on her body from here out. This is a custody death investigation now, even though she's alive. By the book, people."

I appreciated Rhodes' attention to detail, her regard for protocol. But all I could do was watch in horror as that girl faded out of consciousness. What was she so committed to? Why did she take the fall for the drugs? What was the purpose of this?

Sure, a poetic way to inform me she was done talking. But why? Why give up her voice for the rest of her life?

One of the paramedics informed me that wasn't necessarily the case. Since it happened so close to the hospital, and they had her triaged less than fifteen minutes from the incident, there was a chance she would be able to talk again. But she had done this to herself. Even if they repaired it, what would keep her from doing it again?

Rhodes offered me a spare outfit from a bag in her office. Just a pair of jeans and a T-shirt. She showed me to the locker room in the firehouse next door. There, I rinsed off the blood from my skin and put on the clean clothes.

When I finished, Rhodes told me she had a team ready to go to Willow Grove. They were heading out to serve the warrant. Was I sure I still wanted to come?

As ominous as this all had been, no way in hell was I walking away from this case now.

Tempest and I followed her and the other dozen officers to

Willow Grove. It was an hour's drive from the small town. Throughout it, I kept replaying those final moments in my mind. Loyalty so profound, she severed a significant part of her own body. The way she laughed about it, smiling as crimson showered us both, as though she were a sacrificial lamb for her cause.

What mattered more to her than her own voice?

No amount of money would convince me to bite off my own tongue. No religion could justify it.

Why had Jasmine? And what the hell was I going to tell her mom?

We arrived at the Grove at 1:15.

Bronwyn and Ophelia stood at the bottom of the stairs, like they had been waiting. Anticipating.

No one sat around on blankets assembling beaded bracelets and weaving baskets. All the tents were gone. As if they'd never existed there at all.

Rhodes stepped from her vehicle first. As I shifted the car into park and stepped out, Rhodes passed Bronwyn a sheet of paper. They exchanged a few words, none of which I caught at the distance, and Rhodes came back our way.

While she instructed her guys on where to search, I locked my gaze with Bronwyn's. His arm hung in a sling. I tried not to smirk at that.

But he gave me one instead. His eyes were narrowed, his smiling lips pursed.

My stomach sank.

It was past poetic.

He'd hurt Jasmine. I'd left him in the same pain.

That couldn't be. A leader like Bronwyn couldn't walk around this camp in front of all his people appearing weak. Not without retaliation.

Bronwyn couldn't reach me. But Jasmine was his pawn to do with as he wished.

I still couldn't fathom why she'd fallen for his bullshit. What I did know was that Bronwyn saw me extend a hand to her as she dangled off a cliff. He might not have known the details yet, but he knew I wanted to help that girl. He knew to hurt me, all he had to do was hurt her.

That gun on my hip burned, aching to aim in his direction.

"We've got those coordinates you gave us," Rhodes said, drawing my attention her way. "A couple of my guys are coming up in four-wheelers. I'm thinking you come with me to check out the field of cannabis, then we'll hit that garage."

I propped open the rear door for Tempest. As she jumped out and I took her leash, I turned to Rhodes. "Yeah, that sounds good."

"But while we're waiting." She wedged her thumbs beneath her bulletproof vest, scanning our surroundings. "Anything else I should know about this place?"

I gestured over the lawn. "There were at least a dozen tents set up here yesterday. None of them were real tents, just sheets thrown over pieces of wood to make a teepee. And just as many people. Maybe more. I didn't count, but I'd say fifty?"

A stray cat bolted from the farmhouse to the field. Rhodes's eyes followed it. "Any idea where they could've gone?"

"There's a solarium about a mile that way." I pointed past the Weeping Willow. "They treat it like a cafeteria. That's the only place I can think of. I didn't get to stay here long, so I don't know as much as I'd like."

"We've got the okay to search all five hundred acres of this place." She nodded past the willow. "Judge Martinez wasn't happy about signing such a broad warrant at 7 AM, but your photos of the marijuana field, plus Jasmine's arrest with the drugs, plus the overdose you witnessed gave us exigent circumstances. She said, and I quote, 'If there's evidence of drug manufacturing and potential graves on that property, you search every damn inch.'"

"Helps that it's all one property under one owner," I said.

"Exactly. No multiple warrants needed. Bronwyn's insistence on keeping everything in his name just bit him in the ass."

* * *

As we walked, I gave Rhodes the entire story. Didn't spare a single detail. Everything from the emaciated cats and dogs to the emaciated people. What I'd gathered of their belief system. Starlight's overdose, and Ophelia's reaction. Raven's reaction. Their explanation for it—the drug they called glow.

Rhodes suspected that's what Jasmine had in the trunk. She had rushed the forensics team to get an answer on what the drug was, but she suspected some cocktail of uppers and downers. So long as we found a connection between the drugs in Jasmine's car to this place, even eyewitness testimony would be enough to make an arrest.

"The best chance we've got at that is Phoenix." Holding a tree branch aside for her, the solarium came into view. "If we find him, I might be able to convince him to talk."

"The kid who acted as your tour guide?" Rhodes swatted a fly away. "If he didn't leave last night, what makes you think he will now?"

"Jasmine." I lowered my voice now that the solarium was within hearing distance. Figures moved behind the glass, confirming my suspicion. "They were friends. He tried to convince her to leave. Maybe once he knows this, it'll be enough to get him out of here."

"We can hope." Rhodes studied the solarium, likely trying to make out the people behind the glass. "You don't think these folks are dangerous, do you?"

"I don't. They're addicts, but they're decent people."

Rhodes gave a nod. She took a few steps forward, careful to avoid tripping over Tempest's leash. "Why do you think he brought them here?"

"If I had to guess, he's covering his ass. I doubt township codes allow people to live in tents. Especially children. There are a few of them here."

The color trickled from her cheeks. "Remind me to make a call to

CPS on our way out. If they do a surprise welfare check down the line, that might be enough right there to shut this place down."

That pinched something deep in my chest.

Were these conditions ideal for children? No. Of course not.

Was forcing someone like Raven back into foster care a better option? From my experience in the system, I couldn't say it was. Especially if it meant separating a child from their sibling.

But maybe it would force the people here to get help. If Raven and Starlight had to choose between their daughter and niece or drugs, I prayed they would choose that little girl. I didn't know for certain that they would.

Sure would be nice if parents chose to sober up for their kids. Most of the time, they didn't. People only got clean when they wanted to. They did it for themselves and no one else, the same way they got addicted to begin with. There was no altruism in addiction. All that mattered to an addict was the high. Until they decided the high wasn't worth it anymore.

Time and time again, my mom had chosen drugs over me. I prayed Raven would be different.

Her daughter was under a year old, white, and pretty. As screwed up as it was, she had a better chance in the foster care system than her mother and aunt had.

Clearing my throat, I stopped walking. "I'm sorry, ma'am. Could I ask you something before we head in there?"

Rhodes looked at me over her shoulder, propping her hands on her hips. "Ask away."

"Can you go easy on them?" I nodded toward the solarium. "Especially the parents? I know how all this looks. I know this isn't a good place for kids to grow up. But I know the system is worse. I lived in it. And these women, they're addicts, but they love those babies. They love each other. That's why this place works. They have Ophelia as the figurehead, and at her core, I think she's a decent, kindhearted woman. Bronwyn—I mean Calvin. Calvin's abusing these people, and her, and he's using her. She's the mother they look to and try to emulate, and I'm—I guess I'm just trying to say that these people are victims. Jasmine, what she did this morning, she did because she's been brainwashed. They may not realize it, but they're all victims, and I don't want to hurt them any more than they've already been hurt."

Rhodes pressed her frowning lips together and gave a nod. "I respect you, Castle. If you think that's the right call, we'll work up a plan together. One that doesn't demonize the people being harmed here."

I managed a smile. "Thank you, ma'am."

She gave one back, then gestured to the solarium. "You should be the one to knock."

I did.

Beyond the foggy glass, a figure approached. It didn't shock me when Phoenix opened the door. Lined up against the walls, sitting at the tables set with pancakes and bacon, were all the others. At least as many as I'd seen at the fire on Friday night. Not to mention Dude, who lay by the table at the far end of the solarium. Bronwyn's table.

"Hey," I said.

He glanced at Rhodes, then turned back to me. "That was illegal, wasn't it?"

"I'm sorry?"

"What you did." Crossing his arms against his chest, he leaned against the doorframe. "Pretending to be a civilian to get in here. Lying to us all about who you are. Isn't it illegal for a cop to do that?"

No, lying wasn't illegal. Any cop could've used a fake name and accepted the invitation to spend the weekend here. But I wasn't here to argue semantics. "I'm not a cop. I'm a private investigator, and I was hired by—"

His laugh cut me off. "Oh, so that just makes it okay? It's totally fine that you lied to me, lied to Ophelia, lied to everybody, because you're *not* a cop?"

Should've known that was coming. "Jasmine's mom wanted to know what the hell happened to her daughter."

Phoenix's tight jaw released. Only for a second or two. Then he was all but gritting his teeth. "Maybe if she gave a damn about her kid, she wouldn't have wound up here."

"Maybe," I agreed. "Maybe if Jasmine would've left on her own, she wouldn't be lying in a hospital bed right now."

The already quiet room behind him broke to utter silence.

"What?" Phoenix's forehead scrunched down in confusion. His mouth opened, then shut. He shook his head quickly. "No. I just saw her a few hours ago. She was up at the house with Ophelia and Bronwyn. She was fine."

"She took one of my officers on a high-speed chase early this morning," Rhodes said. "Wound up with the front end wrapped around a tree. There were a good deal of drugs in the trunk."

His always ghastly face paled a few more shades. "Is she okay?"

"That's not what put her in the hospital." I glanced behind him at all the people listening, including children who sat in their mothers' laps and lay in their arms. "The details are probably something I should tell you in private."

A quick look over his shoulder. His fingers trembled, and he gave the slightest shake of his head. As if to remind me that they all were listening, that they would tell Bronwyn he spoke to me alone.

"Just one minute." Rhodes reached past him for the door handle, evidently coming to the same conclusion I had.

"I'll fill you all in." Phoenix stepped forward, arms up at his sides. Like he could cite this to his leader as the reason for speaking to us in private. They would all agree that he was forced to do so. Even though the three of us knew otherwise.

When the door clicked shut behind him, he lowered his voice. "What the hell are you talking about? What put her in the hospital?"

"They brought her in for questioning, and she wouldn't talk to anyone but me." It was hard to hold his gaze, knowing how this would hurt him, but I shook off my discomfort. He needed to know. "It was the same vague shit for a while. Spewing stuff about enlightenment and a better way of life and the dangers of microplastics. And then I thought I was getting through to her. I thought we were making some progress. That she was realizing how twisted and nonsensical all this is." My throat swelled, and I swallowed to soothe it. "But I guess she didn't want to talk anymore, because she... she bit her tongue off."

His brows stayed furrowed, but his eyes widened. His mouth dropped open, and when enough time passed, he lifted his hand to cover it. Face a sickly shade of green, he shook his head in disbelief. "You're not serious."

"I wish I weren't," I murmured. "She's in surgery now. If all goes well, she might eventually be able to talk. But if she decides to do it again—"

He held up his hand to stop me. Shutting his eyes, he turned toward the ground. "Holy shit."

"Yeah," Rhodes said. "It was pretty bad."

"I think she was playing some sort of game with us," I said. "Bronwyn probably told her to do the rest. I don't know about the tongue thing, but I think he wanted to get caught. Or to play with us. Jasmine said this was prophecy, so I think he used that to further convince her of his beliefs."

Eyes on the ground, Phoenix nodded. "Yeah. Probably."

"Have you heard about that?" Rhodes asked. "The prophecy?"

Phoenix rolled his eyes. "There are a thousand prophecies. Everyone thinks they're a prophet. That particular prophecy just says that eventually Bronwyn would get caught."

"Get caught for what, exactly?" Rhodes asked. "Drug dealing?"

"No. No, it's more complicated than that." Phoenix rubbed his eyes between his thumb and forefinger. "They don't even look at the stuff here as drugs. They think of them as spiritual guides. Nobody here trusts the government. Some think you're in cahoots with lizard people. Others think you're working for the devil." Massaging his temples, he shook his head. "They think Willow Grove is one step away from another realm. A higher energy. An ethereal plane of existence. The prophecy says some shit about how evil forces will keep us from reaching that higher vibration."

Apparently, I was the evil force. But the way he said that piqued my interest. "*They* think that? But you don't?"

Shoulders slumping, he trailed his tongue along his teeth. "I don't know what I believe in, Maddie. But my parents liked to party. They said a lot of crazy shit when they were messed up. Just like everybody here does."

So I'd been right from the beginning. Phoenix didn't believe in all this. He was just a desperate kid who'd found family here that he didn't want to lose. "So you don't believe in the enlightenment revolution that Jasmine was talking about?"

The edges of his lips turned downward. "I don't know anything about it. Probably by design. If not for Ophelia, Bronwyn would've kicked me out by now. Or worse. Certain people, he lets in on his mission. Jasmine's one of them. Ophelia is not. Most of us aren't."

"His mission," Rhodes repeated. "That's what he calls it?"

Phoenix nodded. "And whatever it is, he's not gonna let you guys get in the way of it. He's not like everybody else here. Everyone else believes in weird shit, sure, but they do it for good reasons. The same reason most people choose religion. To find some greater meaning, to make their life worthwhile. I don't think Bronwyn believes in anything. He just uses spirituality as a weapon. It's his way of controlling everyone. Especially Ophelia and his girls."

"Do you have a list of them?" Rhodes grabbed her notepad and pen from her breast pocket. Clicking it, she said, "Those other women who stood in Jasmine's place. The ones who vanished."

Phoenix shook his head. "No one uses their real names here."

Which was the answer I expected him to give. But it wasn't my last question. "If you don't think Bronwyn is doing this for spiritual reasons, what could his mission really be?"

Scoffing, Phoenix gestured around. "What rules the world, Maddie? Why do you think we don't get paid? It's not a coincidence that he preaches about stoicism and leaving earthly possessions behind while we all sleep on the dirt and he lives in a remodeled, five-bedroom, three-bath house."

My suspicion from the beginning. "To him, this place is about money."

"I think so, yeah." Phoenix shrugged. "Money and power. He's invincible here, and he knows it. Whatever you think you have on him, you don't. Whatever you're searching for, you're not gonna find. As soon as you left last night, he woke everybody up, and he made us stay in here. Around sunrise, I heard trucks and people yelling, like they were moving things. It's gone. Whatever you were looking for is gone."

Not pleasant news to hear, but what I'd prepared for. "It doesn't mean it's over. And without all of you, that guy's nothing. If you leave, if you convince everybody else to leave—"

"Jasmine was here for a few months, Maddie." Barely above a whisper, but still so fierce in his tone, Phoenix leaned closer. With each word he spoke, spit flew. "Not even a year, and she bit off her own tongue for that son of a bitch. Imagine how committed the people who've been here since they were fourteen are. The only hope they have is you getting rid of him and Ophelia running this place. That's the only way things get better here."

I hated that he was right. But it was the truth. Cults only fell apart when their leader was gone.

"We're at the location, ma'am." A voice came through Rhodes's radio. "But there aren't any plants up here. Just a burned field. Smells like it was pot, but all that's left are ashes."

Lifting his arms at his sides, Phoenix harrumphed. "See? I told you."

Rhodes took a few steps away, speaking into her radio. "Do you have the hounds up there yet?"

"If you think you're gonna find a body, I promise you won't." Phoenix glanced at Rhodes, still shaking his head. "There probably are a few out there. Lots of people who question Bronwyn vanish the next day. But he knew you were coming. You're not going to find anything."

"We're still going to try," I said. "And you're right. Today might not be the win. But it's not over, Phoenix. I'm not giving up until that bastard is behind bars or in a body bag."

His eyes grew hopeful, but his jaw stayed tight. "I hope *you're* right."

"Pretty rare that I'm wrong." I forced a smile. "But you're wrong about something."

"And what's that?"

"This place won't be better if Ophelia's in charge. She's kind, and she's got a good heart, but she's not a leader. All it would take is one more shady man to step into Bronwyn's shoes, and you'd be right back in the same position you're in now. But if you were in charge? Maybe this place would have a shot."

Phoenix studied me for a long moment. Then, so quietly I almost missed it, he said, "Starlight's been asking questions since yesterday. So has Raven. About the drugs. About what's really going on here."

"And?"

"And I've been answering them." His jaw tightened. "Truthfully. For the first time in

years, I'm telling people the truth about this place. Maybe that's how it starts. Not with cops and raids, but with people finally opening their eyes."

Rhodes called for me again, but Phoenix grabbed my wrist. "That number you gave me. I memorized it. When enough of us are ready to leave, when we need somewhere to go..."

"You call me," I finished. "Day or night."

"They're gonna start digging up there, Maddie," Rhodes said. "We better get on one of the four-wheelers and check it out."

"Give me one second," I said, turning back to Phoenix. "Come with us. Right now. Get in my car and leave. You can help with the investigation, testify about what you know. We'll protect you."

Phoenix's eyes darted to the solarium windows where dozens of faces watched. Among them, I spotted Starlight, still pale from yesterday's overdose. Raven holding her baby. A couple of teenagers who couldn't have been older than Phoenix was when he arrived.

"You know I can't," he said softly. "Not yet. But I've been paying attention. I know things. Things that can help." He glanced at Rhodes again, lowering his voice. "Things that incriminate him."

My pulse quickened. "Tell me—"

"Not now. But when the time's right, when I can get some of the others out safely first, I'll contact you. I'll tell you everything." He pulled out a scrap of paper and pencil, scribbled something down. "This is Starlight's real name. And Raven's. Start there. Find their old friends, or any family they've got left. Maybe if they have somewhere to go..."

He pressed the paper into my hand and walked away before I could respond.

Chapter 21

It didn't add up.

Rhodes and I drove up the mountain on the back of a four-wheeler, Tempest sandwiched between us, and arrived at the same spot I'd found the field of pot last night. Like the deputy informed Rhodes, there wasn't much left behind.

That four-by-six square of recently tilled soil was at least a few inches higher than it had been. Tempest, Bentley, and I had walked this trail only a few hours ago. Then, I'd referred to it as a deer trail. That's what it had been. No more than three feet wide, overgrown in spots. I'd even made a comment about needing a machete.

Not anymore. Now, it was as wide as the main path we'd followed Jasmine and Bronwyn down. Someone had put a machete to use. Bushes and limbs on my left and right were hacked, leaving a clean, easy trail to venture down.

What greeted us when we arrived at the pot field was devastating in its thoroughness. And its sloppiness.

Half the plants were gone, stalks cut hastily at different heights. Scorched earth showed where fires had been lit and either burned out or been abandoned. Boot prints and tire tracks crisscrossed everywhere. In their haste, they'd left a chainsaw behind, still warm to the touch. Drag marks led off into the woods in three different directions.

Rhodes lifted a wooden stake from the ground. "Fire drill," she read from a laminated tag. "Sector 7."

My stomach turned. That's what Phoenix meant when he made that snarky remark at dinner. The fire drills were them practicing this. Destroying evidence, clearing the grounds of anything they'd go to jail for.

One of the hounds lay down atop the grave, signaling that there was, in fact, a body there.

Rhodes gave them the go-ahead to start digging. Getting the tractor up here would take time. She suggested we go check out the garage in the meantime.

We got back on the main trail, followed it to the pine tree I'd climbed in the darkness, and continued the path downhill. The garage still stood tall. But the large sliding door was wide open. Inside?

Nothing.

It wasn't that there was nothing notable. There was *nothing*.

The cement floor. Metal walls and metal roof. A few support beams throughout.

In the ceiling, light peeked through a few ventilation holes—the same ones that last night had chugged smoke into the atmosphere. Now? No chimney. No stove. No wood burner.

But they'd made mistakes in their hustle. Outside, tire tracks from multiple heavy vehicles carved deep grooves in the dirt. They led in various directions. A coordinated dispersal.

Oil stains on the concrete showed where equipment had been. Scuff marks indicated heavy objects dragged toward the door. In the corner, forgotten in the rush, a single glass beaker lay on its side.

Rhodes picked it up with a gloved hand. "Still has some residue. Maybe enough for testing."

She was right. The dots were connecting. If Bronwyn had called in favors from his drug connections—Ken's associates, maybe others—

he could have had thirty or forty people working through the night. Enough to create this scorched-earth devastation in ten hours.

"They had help," I said. "This wasn't just the commune members. They brought in a crew."

Spinning around slowly, Rhodes exhaled slow and deep. "They cleared the place."

"A dog still lay down." I propped my hands on my hips. "There's something in that grave."

Trailing her tongue across her mouth, Rhodes spun in another slow circle. "Didn't you say it was a beaten path last night?"

A deep breath sank my shoulders. "I did."

"Soil looked disturbed. They made room for us to get a tractor to that spot." She slumped. "I don't think we're gonna find anything."

I nibbled on my bottom lip. "No. Probably not. But we still have those drugs. If we can connect them to this place, that's something."

"True. But that still leaves the question of *if*. Seems like these guys know how to cover their tracks."

"I think that once Jasmine sobers up and comes to, we can flip her." Hope tinged the edge of my voice. "She's very delusional right now, but eventually, I think she'll come around. And when she does, if she testifies that he gave her the drugs, that would be enough for an arrest."

"Yeah, but again, the question is still if." Rhodes shook her head. "And if we can get a judge and jury to agree. There's a good chance that girl has some serious mental health issues, whether it's schizophrenia or mania. Those don't discredit her in my opinion, but a prosecutor might not even let her take the stand."

It took everything in me not to stomp my feet and shake my fists. Not because she was wrong. Just because this wasn't right, damn it.

"Ma'am, you're not gonna believe this," came from Rhodes's radio. "We just finished digging. You better get up here."

She jogged for the door, and I was right behind her. She replied, "Do you have a body?"

"A couple actually. But not in the way you're thinking."

They sure as hell were not the bodies we were looking for.

We raced back up the mountain, down that beaten trail, and jumped from the four-wheelers. I stayed close at Rhodes's flank as she pushed her dozen guys aside, getting us close to the grave.

And I couldn't help it this time. I stomped and slammed my fists down at my sides like a toddler throwing a tantrum.

"Jesus," Rhodes said, surveying the destruction. "How many people did this take?"

Beside that grave, half a dozen bodies lay atop white sheets on the soil in varying degrees of decomposition. One, a skeleton. Couldn't say for sure, but judging by the size and shape, I had to guess a dog. Five small critters, likely cats. Maybe even possums or raccoons.

"Son of a bitch," I grunted.

"It doesn't even make sense." Rhodes gestured over them, shaking her head. "A dog trained in human remains wouldn't have lain down for dead animals. Right, Maddie?"

"No, he shouldn't have." I took a few steps closer to the hole. Had to be at least seven feet deep. "Make sure to sift the soil. There could be something in it. Maybe a finger or blood-drenched cloth. Something. A hound wouldn't have signaled for a dead animal."

"What if there *was* a body here?" Rhodes crossed her arms against her chest. "What if they moved it? Would a dog still signal?"

"If they left something behind, yeah," I said.

"What if we don't find anything when we sift the soil?"

"I'm not a forensic expert." I squatted to give Tempest a pat on the head. "So don't quote me. But if there was a body here, say five hours ago, I'd think the decomposition affected the soil. Moving a decomposing corpse isn't easy either. Not if it's recent and there're any liquids to deal with. In which case, they could've spilled into the soil, gotten absorbed, but the smell remained. That would explain why the dog signaled. But good luck proving it."

"I want soil samples," Rhodes said, turning back to her guys. My phone buzzed in my pocket, and I took a few steps aside. "Hundreds of them, if you have to. I want to test everything that dog could have signaled for."

Debbie Armstrong's name lit up the screen.

This wasn't going to be easy.

Swiping the green bar, I snapped for Tempest to join me. "Maddie Castle."

"What the hell is going on?!" Not just a yell, but an ear-piercing screech. "What happened to my daughter?"

Closing my eyes to maintain my composure, I apologized. Then I explained. I didn't tell her everything I found at the Grove. I didn't go into every single detail. But I relayed what I knew as I walked back down the trail. Jasmine had taken an officer on a high-speed chase, ran off the road, and bit her tongue off while being questioned.

"Oh my God," Debbie cried. "Oh my *God*."

"I'm so sorry, ma'am." Truly, from the bottom of my heart, I was. "I haven't gotten an update yet from the hospital, but one of the paramedics said it's possible she'll be able to talk again. The other possibility is that she could do it again, in which case—"

"No the hell she won't." Keys rattled in the background. "I'm getting her on a psychiatric hold. I don't care how much money I have to pay, how many lawyers I have to hire. It doesn't matter. She's out of that place, and she's gonna stay sedated until her body heals. Then, and only then, she will be admitted into psychiatric care for as long as necessary. I don't care how many of her rights I have to strip away, she doesn't get them anymore. Not after this."

Mainstream psychiatric care sucked. It just did. But if money wasn't an obstacle? If Debbie was willing to pay as much as it took to get her into a good facility? That was the best chance she had at recovering from this place. "I'd get started on that soon. There are a lot of laws when it comes to psychiatric care, and they're there for a reason. But given the circumstances, I think you can prove that Jasmine is a danger to herself and others."

"You're damn right I can. I'm heading to the hospital now." A shaking breath echoed through the speaker. "Given the circumstances, I'm assuming the investigation you've opened with the state police will be ongoing for some time. But to get a judge to sign off on the kind of treatment I want Jasmine in, I think I'll need everything you've got. If the—" Pausing, she went silent for a few heartbeats. "If the incident was recorded, as I imagine it was if conducted at a police station, the video of it would be very helpful."

"I'm sure we can arrange that," I said. "The police understand that Jasmine is a victim in all this. She's not who anyone is after. Whatever you need, I'm sure the sheriff is willing to help."

A long moment of silence, followed by a whimper. "Thank you."

"Don't thank me." Chest tight, heart hurting, I kept my eyes on the soil as I walked. "Just get to that hospital and sit with your little girl. She may not realize it, but she's gonna need you."

"Yeah." She spoke the word on a strangled breath, likely choking back tears. "And I'm gonna be there. But I really would like the whole story. Not the shortened one. Could you meet me at the hospital?"

"Of course. I can't guarantee what time, but I'll go straight there when I finish up here."

"Just let me know when you're on your way."

As I finished up the formalities, Rhodes's voice boomed behind me. "You're not gonna believe this damn shit, Castle."

Her cheeks were blood red, teeth pressed so tightly together, I was surprised they didn't shatter.

I ended the call and slid the phone into my back pocket. "What? What's going on now?"

"Even if we found the drugs, we couldn't charge them." Rhodes scoffed her annoyance. A rock lay on the trail, and she slammed her foot through it. When it landed in the woods, she said, "They're designer. Research chemicals. The drugs are manufactured by a street chemist. They're not even illegal."

Slowly, my jaw dropped. "What do you mean?"

"It's a legal loophole." She threw her arms in the air. "Products like these can be sold as bath salts or soil fertilizer. The intended use is actually to get high, but because they don't match the chemical makeup of opiates and MDMA, these bastards get away with it. They have that shit up on their website, Maddie. It's buried deep in their body care section, but that's how they're selling it. As an herbal bath supplement. This shit is no different than meth made in a shed, but because it's not technically illegal, even if Jasmine testifies, we can't take him down. We're up shit creek, and I don't see a damn paddle."

Chapter 22

We kept searching, and we kept coming back with nothing.

No drugs. No bodies. No paraphernalia.

Nothing.

By sundown, I was exhausted. I still needed to visit Jasmine and Debbie. Over the last few days, I'd hardly eaten a thing. Bentley had texted a few times, worrying about me. Dylan got back to me, saying it would take him some time to isolate all the license plates and run searches, but he was working on it.

There wasn't much more I could do at this point.

And after the results on those drugs came in...

Suffice it to say, I needed a break and fresh eyes.

I stopped for some gas on my way out of Willow Grove and went to the hospital. The sickly smell of cleaning agents and the flickering fluorescent lights weren't my idea of a good time, but when I made it to Jasmine's room, hope warmed my chest.

She lay unconscious in the hospital bed. A small plastic tube protruded from her throat. Matt sat beside her, holding his sister's hand. Debbie stood over her with a washcloth. She dabbed Jasmine's face, combed hair behind her ears, and touched her daughter with gentle, loving hands.

No longer did she wear an apron. The room smelled of bleach and rubbing alcohol. No fresh-baked pastries laid on the rolling table.

Stained sweatpants lined her legs. A Columbia University sweatshirt hung loosely, messily, over Debbie's shoulders. She looked as anyone should in a moment like this.

The first time I'd met her, Debbie had seemed so perfect. That performance led her daughter to where she was.

It may not have looked like a hopeful sight, but after questioning Jasmine this morning, I understood her. I understood just how sick she was.

She needed this.

Jasmine had a long road ahead of her. But maybe, if her mother extended the kindness that the Grove had, she'd come out the other end in one piece.

That was why I came. To check on Jasmine, sure. But more than anything, to speak with her mother.

Knocking softly on the doorframe, I managed a smile.

Matt couldn't give me that much. Just a curt nod.

Teary-eyed, Debbie waved me into the room. "Thank you so much for coming."

"Thank you for asking me." Stepping closer, I stowed my hands into my hoodie pocket. "I wish it were under better circumstances."

"Think that goes without saying." Matt cleared his throat as he stood. "I'm gonna go hit a vending machine. Anyone need anything?"

"Just a water please, honey."

I shook my head but muttered thanks.

Once he was out of sight, Debbie sat in the chair her son had been in and gestured for me to take the one next to it. I did.

"No dog today?" Debbie swatted at the wetness under her eyes. "Or are they not allowed in the hospital?"

"She's out in the car. The best part about fall and winter." I leaned forward on the stiff leather seat to get a better view of Jasmine. "How's she doing?"

"Not great." Taking her daughter's hand, she lowered her voice. "Given the location of the incident, they felt it best to trach her. It's not what I would've liked. Her recovery will be much more difficult because of it. But I suppose that's inevitable. They were able to reattach it, so, in theory, she could make a full recovery. It just—you know, it could be worse. It could be much worse. They're having to give her large doses of morphine to keep her asleep. I didn't understand why at first, but Matt made it clear that I was wrong. I've been wrong all along. Drugs are a large component here." Debbie pressed her lips into a thin line and sniffled. "She has an exponentially high tolerance to opioids."

"That's not necessarily a bad thing." I rubbed a hand up my goosebump-covered arm. "It'll take some time to leave her system, but it helps you know this isn't all in her head. It's much easier to treat drug-induced psychosis than it is to treat a lifelong mental health condition."

"Addiction *is* a lifelong mental health condition." She wiped another tear away. "I don't even know how this is possible. No one in our family are addicts. I didn't raise her this way. I really didn't, Maddie." Debbie's lip quivered, and she held her daughter's hand tighter. "I don't understand how she could go from who she was to who she is now so quickly. Not even a year ago, she was completely normal. We just had Christmas together, and she was entirely herself. She was holding Chase's hand, and they were laughing together by the fire, and now she's... now she's here."

No one had to tell me twice that addiction was a lifelong condition. Addiction ran in my family, but that wasn't how I'd gotten addicted. An injury had been. "Pain, Debbie. Chronic, debilitating pain. That's how she wound up here."

Debbie huffed, sparing me a glance before turning back to Jasmine. "We all have pain. We don't all wind up here."

"No, we don't. But some of us do, because these things don't exist in a vacuum. You're a doctor. You know that. Two people can have the exact same injury and feel the pain on entirely different levels."

Facts soothed Debbie. That was why she'd spent over a decade in college. No one who hated knowledge became a doctor. And the loosening of her shoulders proved it. "Yes, I'm aware of that."

"Listen, ma'am, I'm not here to pass any judgment." I propped my elbows on my knees, softening my voice. "But I spent some time with Jasmine this weekend. There were a lot of components that led to this. If you want to talk about them, we can, but you have to listen with open ears. Or, when she does get better, she'll end up back where she was again."

Either that, or she'd never get better.

It took a few long moments of silence. Eventually, on a calming breath, Debbie turned my way. "I'll do my best to hear you out and remain neutral."

I nodded. "When I got to Willow Grove, I didn't see what people liked about it. I couldn't understand why they stayed. But by the second night, it started to make sense." I gestured to Jasmine. "The leader is manufacturing research chemicals. His particular brand is something they call glow. It seems to be a cross between an opiate and MDMA. So it has pain-relieving, sedating effects, but also tickles all the happy spots in the brain. I think everyone there is taking it. If not everyone, at least all the girls.

"That also seems intentional. Bronwyn, the man who founded the Grove, believes a woman's place is catering to men. When they're high, they're easier to control. But none of the people there think they're taking drugs. They think that because they make it themselves, it's safe and natural. At first, I thought the drugs were all for fun, but now I see the larger picture. After the evidence came out today, I realized why Jasmine did this to herself."

Gesturing to the young girl lying on the hospital bed, I made sure to keep my voice calm. "This drug they're taking, they see it as a portal to another dimension. A greater vibration. A way to connect spiritually with the earth and some esoteric deity. In the interview,

Jasmine mentioned a spiritual revolution. She wants everyone to feel as connected as she does when she's high. Of course, she doesn't really understand that she's high, because she's been manipulated by the leader.

"Everyone there is on a quest to better the world, to better each other, to care for one another. But Bronwyn is out to make money. By any means necessary. Unfortunately, he's a very smooth talker, and there was something in Jasmine that he liked. She was likely desperate for someone to listen, for someone to care about what she thought and had to say. This made her an easy puppet for him. I don't know exactly how it happened, but the two of them became romantically intertwined, so we're not just dealing with drug-induced psychosis.

"Jasmine doesn't realize it yet, and she probably won't admit it for a long time, but she's been his victim of domestic violence. When she does recover, she'll likely have severe PTSD. This man was your age or older, and he had her wrapped around his finger. But soon, a new young girl will take Jasmine's place. When that day comes, she'll face complete exile from Willow Grove. Which is good for her, in a lot of ways, but it could be devastating too. Especially if she's still unstable when that happens."

The whole time I spoke, Debbie just listened, staring at her daughter. But I'd been going on for a while, and I wasn't sure what else she wanted to hear at this point. I imagined that was difficult to accept. It was a lot to take in.

Eventually, hardly above a whisper, Debbie said, "What would you recommend I do?"

"Don't lock her up here." I glanced around the four white walls, the white ceiling, the white linoleum. "In some capacity, I think Jasmine was held against her will. She may deny it at first, but at the very least, she was coerced into staying. A place like this is a prison cell to her. She needs to recover, but this isn't the place for it."

"Again." Teeth gritted, eyes watering, Debbie shot me a look. "What would you recommend I do?"

"Once her physical recovery is done?" I shrugged. "Get her into one of those intensive mental health retreats celebrities go to. The hippie-dippy, spa-like retreats. One where she can be outside, because she loves that. Someplace with yoga would be nice. But, most of all, make sure these people aren't going to tell her everything she thinks and believes makes her crazy. A lot of it does, and a lot of that will fall off the longer she's away from the drugs. What she needs more than anything is someone to validate her pain, because after this, she's gonna have a hell of a lot more."

Debbie stroked her fingers over the back of her daughter's hand. After a long moment of silence, she said, "I think that's a good idea."

"And don't let Chase anywhere near her."

Debbie's face screwed up in confusion. "He's worried. He wants to see her."

"She doesn't want to see him." I shook my head. "I don't know what happened between them, ma'am, but I know there's damage done. He's hurt her. Deeply. Women who experience domestic violence, whether physical, verbal, or emotional, tend to experience it on a carousel. Bronwyn wasn't the first man to take advantage of her, but you can do everything in your power to make sure he's the last. Getting her into the right treatment, surrounded by the right people, will help her tremendously. I know that's what you want. For your daughter to be healthy again."

Ever so slightly, Debbie's expression softened. Squeezing her daughter's hand, she nodded. "That's all I want."

"I'm sure she will be." I gave Debbie a gentle pat on the back. "If you have any other questions, feel free to text me or give me a call. I really do need to get going now. It's been a long weekend, and my dog can't be in the car alone too much longer."

"Right. Sure, of course." Debbie did her best to smile, but it wasn't quite right. She pointed to the windowsill. "Your check is over there. I did some quick math and jotted it down. If it's not right, give me a call. But thank you for everything, Miss Castle."

I stood, grabbed the envelope, and gave Jasmine one last look over.

Hope still radiated in my chest. This girl's story wasn't over yet.

"Just don't give up on her, alright?" I adjusted the blanket over Jasmine's legs, ironing out the ends that hung off the edge. "You might not like me right now, but I think one day, you're gonna be glad I showed up at that place."

Chapter 23

ON MY WAY HOME FROM THE HOSPITAL, I CALLED BENTLEY. AAA had helped him with the flat. He was on his way home as well, about an hour ahead of me. Tomorrow, he'd take his car to a local shop to get the doughnut off and a new tire on. Tonight, though, he was making dinner for his girls. Stuttering, he asked if I wanted a plate.

I chuckled and said yes.

I wasn't sure why he double-checked. Because he was a good ally and didn't want suggest ownership by lumping me in with "his girls"? Or because he still wasn't sure where we stood?

Without doubt, I knew.

The last month of anger with him was not squandered. Not because I believed he needed punishment, but because my frustration was valid. While I recognized why Bentley did what he had, he needed to understand why it hurt.

Now that he did, and now that I'd come to terms with what exactly hurt me, we could move past it.

I was half an hour from home when I got another call.

Sam lit up the screen.

Chest heavy, I pressed the green button. "Hey."

"Oh, hey." Surprise riddled his voice. As if he weren't the one who placed the call. "Hey, sorry. I didn't think you were gonna pick up."

But he'd kept calling. Even when he thought I'd ignore him, he kept calling, because he wanted a relationship with his daughter as badly as I wanted a relationship with my father. Just knowing so scratched some rejection itch I doubted would ever completely heal. "Well, I did."

"Yeah. Yeah, I see that." Clearing his throat, something rustled in the background. "I'm sorry. I shouldn't be caught off guard right now. But I—well, that doesn't matter. It does matter that you answered though. How are you?"

"Tired." At the word, a yawn parted my lips. The strobing streetlights that brightened the car only to darken it half a second later didn't help in that department. Just the yellow lines ahead, the headlights passing on the left, and those streetlights were enough to dull my senses to sleep. "Hungry. Annoyed that my case didn't work out how I wanted it to, but otherwise okay. How about you?"

"Damn, really? What happened?" Sam asked. "I'm hanging in there. But I don't want to talk about me. I want to talk about you. I've missed you, kid."

Those four words shouldn't have made my heart flutter the way they did. "I don't know if I really want to talk about the case right now either. Kinda just need to forget about it for a little while and come back with fresh eyes. But I've missed you too, Dad."

Another moment of silence. I could count on one hand how many times I'd called him Dad. Usually, he was Sam. It just wasn't easy to transition from calling a man you hardly remembered as a small child to the father you'd always wanted.

But it mattered to him. That was why I said it. I didn't know if I was ready to talk about what he'd done and all the implications of it. All I knew for certain was that too much of our lives had gone on without each other. I couldn't get those years back, but I could make the most of what we had left.

"Uh, I talked to Bentley." Another sharp clear of his throat. "Which I know is how we got to this mess in the first place, so I'm sorry about that. But on Friday, he told me you were working on a case, and then today that you were coming home. Since you're so tired and everything, maybe we could get together tomorrow at some point? Dinner or something?"

"I'm more tired of being on the road than anything. I'm sure once I'm out of this car, I'll wake right up." Now it was me pausing to search for the words. "Bentley's making dinner. Daisy's only been home for a couple days, but she was eager to see me. Obviously she doesn't have all the context, but she'd probably like to meet you too. Maybe you could meet me there?"

An audible breath of relief. "Yeah, of course. That sounds great. Where are you at now?"

A road sign said *Pittsburgh 5 miles*. "About half an hour out. Maybe forty-five minutes, traffic depending, but the roads look empty. If you leave in a few, we'll get there at the same time."

"That's perfect. I'll change out of my work clothes and be on my way."

"I'll see you there."

* * *

OUTSIDE BENTLEY'S TRAILER, A SMALL FIRE PIT DID ITS BEST TO contain orange and yellow flames that stretched and throbbed for the cerulean sky. A few fold-up chairs sat around, waiting for someone to plant themselves in them. Bentley stood beside it with a big stick in one hand and a baby in the other. Rather than on his hip, he held her belly down like a football tucked into the crook of his elbow. Her chubby fingers stretched toward the flames, babbling something incoherent.

As I stepped from the car, we shared a smile. The kind that said more than words ever could.

"You better be careful with her." I opened the rear door for

Tempest and took hold of her leash as she hopped out. "She really wants to play with that."

"Maybe she'll be a firefighter one day." Tossing his stick aside, he grabbed her up with both hands and hoisted her over his head. Then he dropped her. My heart stopped for the second it took for him to catch her a few inches lower. She giggled and laughed as he lifted her to his chest. "Or a skydiver."

"God, I hope not." I walked that way, smiled and waved at the little girl, and stretched onto the tips of my toes to give Bentley a kiss.

"Ew," Grace said, prancing down the steps with a tray. "Gross. But good, I guess. Good that you made up, I mean."

"Nice to see you too." Propping my hands on my hips, I nodded to the plate in her arms. "Need any help?"

"I think we've got it." Behind Grace, Daisy came down the steps with a bag over each arm and a tray of her own. "You like burgers, right?"

"I would literally kill for a burger right now," I said.

"Or you can just put one together." Grace laid her tray on the table by the door, then took the other from Daisy. "Assemble yourself with your own condiments and everything. But you better like it, because I worked hard on these. Normally, I just put the seasonings on top, but I watched this video online, and—never mind. Just eat it and tell me if they're better than usual."

I raised a brow at Bentley. "I thought you were cooking tonight."

"That was the plan. They put me on baby duty instead." He pressed a kiss to Bella's forehead, and she giggled some more. "I'm not complaining though."

"Cooking is so much easier than handling an infant." Daisy gestured to the table. "Seriously, eat. Everybody eat so we don't have to put away leftovers."

That, I wouldn't argue with.

I clipped Tempest to the line Bentley had put in for her a while back and headed for the foldout table. More than a dozen burgers were piled up on a glass plate. Beside it, a plate of tomatoes, another for onions, and a last one for lettuce. Daisy was still unpacking the bag of condiments and buns beside me. "This looks really great. Thank you."

"Me? Nah, thank her." She gestured to Grace, now standing by the fire. From another bag, she laid chocolate bars and graham crackers and marshmallows onto the end table. "I don't hate cooking, but I bet you money, that girl's gonna be the next Gordon Ramsay."

"I bet you're right." Laughing, I peeled apart a bun and set a patty on top. "Thank you, Grace!"

Grace waved me off. "Just leave some for Sam. Dad said he's on his way."

"Yeah, he's your dad, right?" Daisy asked, cocking her head to the side.

"He is, yep." With my burger on the paper plate, I started for the chair beside Bentley. He still had Bella in his lap, bouncing her up and down, singing a silly nursery rhyme that kept her giggling. "May as well be Bentley's too, considering how close they are."

He gave me a narrow-eyed smile. "Is that a problem?"

I returned his expression. "Only sometimes."

"So you knew him when you were growing up then, right?" Daisy sat beside me. "Because you guys all lived here?"

A breathy laugh escaped me. Oh, the intricacies of my life story.

But Bentley just said, "When we were little, yeah. Sam wasn't in the picture for a while, but he always wanted to be. Always liked him better than my own dad though."

"Yeah?" Daisy asked. "Why is that?"

Just as she finished that sentence, headlights shone around the bend, and Sam's truck rolled to a stop outside the driveway. Bentley said, "His timing has always been impeccable." He stood. "Where's that playpen? If I don't sit her down, she's gonna toss my burger over there for Tempest."

"In the hallway closet by the back bathroom." Holding a stick with a marshmallow on its end, Grace sat in the chair beside her dad's. "Can't miss it."

"Come on, little one." He dropped Bella again into a football hold. "Let's get you all set up."

As he ventured up the steps, Daisy squinted at him. She lowered her voice so he wouldn't hear. "He doesn't talk much about his dad."

"Didn't talk much about him when he was alive either." I shrugged. "Some things are better left unsaid."

Tempest barked a time or two as Sam approached, wagging her tail like a whip. Sam greeted her first. Crouched on his knees, he gave her pets all over, voice too quiet to hear from here. When he straightened back up, our eyes met, and his grew as dopey as the puppy's he'd just given so much loving.

But I smiled.

That worry in his gaze dissipated, and he smiled back. He, too, carried a bag over his arm. Approaching, he held it out to Grace. "I made those snickerdoodles we were talking about. You were right, needed more cream of tartar."

"Ooh, snickerdoodle s'mores." She gasped, snatched the bag from his arm, and returned to the table she'd laid all the other fixings on. As for the marshmallow she was roasting? Straight into the fire. "These are going to be amazing. Daisy, don't tell anyone until I've got a snickerdoodle s'more prepared for us all."

"Don't tell anyone what?" I asked.

"Yeah." Juggling the baby and the pack-and-play, Bentley descended the steps. "Tell us what?"

Daisy slumped her shoulders and rolled her eyes. "I wasn't going to tell anyone anything yet, you little shit."

"Oh boy," Sam muttered, lowering himself to a chair on the other side of the fire. "What did I just walk into?"

"Nothing bad." Grace grinned and began a circle around the fire, handing out sticks with marshmallows on them. "Good news, actually. Really good news."

"Is that right?" I accepted the marshmallow stick she offered.

"Well, you gotta tell us now." In one fluid motion, with skill and precision I'd never seen before, Bentley popped open the playpen.

He sat Bella inside and looked between his girls. "We all know I don't like secrets."

"It's not a secret. I was just waiting to have time to tell you." Daisy waved at his seat. "Come on. Make your snickerdoodle s'more so I can get into it."

"Seriously?" Bentley took the stick Grace handed him. "We've gotta have the s'more before the burger?"

"For cinematic purposes, yes." She returned to her seat and passed the Tupperware full of cookies to the left. "This is a big moment, and we all need to help set the tone."

Bentley let out a long, exasperated sigh as he took a few cookies and passed them my way. "Get on with it then."

I took a few cookies as well, then handed them to Daisy, who handed them on to Sam.

Holding her marshmallow to the fire, Daisy raised her shoulders. "I know I haven't been back long. And as grateful as I am for everything you're doing, Bentley, and everything you've done my whole life, at some point, I need to get on my own two feet. If not for anything else, for my daughter."

Daisy smiled and waved at the little girl cooing in the playpen. "So when I got that deal with the publishers, and all those funds started coming in from the things Grace organized, I knew that the first thing I had to do was look for a place to live. And it didn't take long to find the perfect spot. It's only a couple miles from here. Just an old farmhouse on a ton of land, and I loved it. Grace and I went to see it yesterday while you were out of town."

"Oh my God, it's gorgeous," Grace said. "There's this little pond with a dock and fish. So many fish. Then we went back at night, and there's, like, no light pollution. You can see every star in the sky."

"I think that's great," Bentley began. "But you haven't been out long, and I don't know if you're ready—"

"I'm ready." Smiling sadly, Daisy shook her head. "I'm ready for a good, normal, stable life. That's all I've wanted for as long as I can remember. My daughter deserves that. But I don't want to do it alone.

Not really. That's why I was looking for a spot with land. Grace told me that was your plan when you moved here. Buy the trailer, pay it off, and move it onto a piece of land you could stay at forever. And I know you're gonna tell me that you're not comfortable with that, that it's too much money, and I don't want to hear it. You gave up so much for me, and it's the least I can do. Plus, it's what I want. Bella needs a grandpa. Next door would be ideal. Especially for babysitting purposes. So it's actually kinda selfish."

A half laugh escaped Bentley.

I wanted to join in, but suddenly, my chest was a little tight.

In that hallucinogenic-induced dream, I'd thought about how much it meant to come full circle. How grateful I was that life brought Bentley and me back to the trailer park at the same time. That he and I got to be neighbors again.

I wasn't prepared to no longer be his neighbor.

"And, like I said, the land is huge. Something like a hundred and fifty acres?" Smiling at me, Daisy shrugged. "The place is gonna need a lot of work, so I already talked to a developer. They said it'd cost some money to hook up water and electric and all that, but not too much. And you saved my life, Maddie. You saved my daughter's. You mean everything and more to my dad, and now, everything and more to our whole family. If you're down, we've got plenty of room for your trailer too."

To be Continued

Beneath the Grove

Maddie Castle's story continues in *Disappearing Act*.
Click here to grab your copy now!
https://a.co/d/iYXMi8V

Want a free copy of the Maddie Castle prequel novella? Sign up for
my newsletter and download a copy today:
https://liquidmind.media/maddie-castle-newsletter-signup-1/

The Maddie Castle Series

The Handler

Tracking Justice

Hunting Grounds

Vanished Trails

Smoldering Lies

Field of Bones

Beneath the Grove

Disappearing Act

Want a free copy of the Maddie Castle prequel novella? Sign up for my newsletter and download a copy today:

https://liquidmind.media/maddie-castle-newsletter-signup-1/

Also by L.T. Ryan

Find All of L.T. Ryan's Books on Amazon Today!

Noble Judgment

Never Cry Mercy

Deadline

End Game

Noble Ultimatum

Noble Legend

Noble Revenge

Never Look Back

Bear Logan Series

Ripple Effect

Blowback

Take Down

Deep State

Bear & Mandy Logan Series

Close to Home

Under the Surface

The Last Stop

Over the Edge

Between the Lies

Caught in the Web

The Marked Daughter (Coming Soon)

Rachel Hatch Series

Drift

Downburst

Fever Burn

Smoke Signal

Firewalk

Whitewater

Aftershock

Whirlwind

Tsunami

Fastrope

Sidewinder

Redaction

Mirage

Faultline (Coming Soon)

Mitch Tanner Series

The Depth of Darkness

Into The Darkness

Deliver Us From Darkness

Cassie Quinn Series

Path of Bones

Whisper of Bones

Symphony of Bones

Etched in Shadow

Concealed in Shadow

Betrayed in Shadow

Born from Ashes

Return to Ashes

Risen from Ashes (Coming Soon)

Blake Brier Series

Unmasked

Unleashed

Uncharted

Drawpoint

Contrail

Detachment

Clear

Quarry

Dalton Savage Series

Savage Grounds

Scorched Earth

Cold Sky

The Frost Killer

Crimson Moon

Dust Devil (Coming Soon)

Maddie Castle Series

The Handler

Tracking Justice

Hunting Grounds

Vanished Trails

Smoldering Lies

Field of Bones

Beneath the Grove

Affliction Z Series

Affliction Z: Patient Zero

Affliction Z: Abandoned Hope

Affliction Z: Descended in Blood

Affliction Z : Fractured Part 1

Affliction Z: Fractured Part 2 (Coming Soon)

Alex Hayes Series

Trial By Fire (Prequel)

Fractured Verdict

11th Hour Witness

Buried Testimony

The Bishop's Recusal (Coming Soon)

Stella LaRosa Series

Black Rose

Red Ink

Black Gold

White Lies

Avril Dahl Series

Cold Reckoning

Cold Legacy

Cold Mercy (Coming Soon)

Savannah Shadows Series

Echoes of Guilt

The Silence Before

Dead Air (Coming Soon)

* * *

Receive a free copy of The Recruit. Visit:

https://ltryan.com/jack-noble-newsletter-signup-1

About the Authors

L.T. RYAN is a *Wall Street Journal* and *USA Today* bestselling author, renowned for crafting pulse-pounding thrillers that keep readers on the edge of their seats. Known for creating gripping, character-driven stories, Ryan is the author of the *Jack Noble* series, the *Rachel Hatch* series, and more. With a knack for blending action, intrigue, and emotional depth, Ryan's books have captivated millions of fans worldwide.

Whether it's the shadowy world of covert operatives or the relentless pursuit of justice, Ryan's stories feature unforgettable characters and high-stakes plots that resonate with fans of Lee Child, Robert Ludlum, and Michael Connelly.

When not writing, Ryan enjoys crafting new ideas with coauthors, running a thriving publishing company, and connecting with readers. Discover the next story that will keep you turning pages late into the night.

Connect with L.T. Ryan
Sign up for his newsletter to hear the latest goings on and receive some free content
➜ https://ltryan.com/jack-noble-newsletter-signup-1

Join the private readers' group
➜ https://www.facebook.com/groups/1727449564174357

Instagram ➜ @ltryanauthor
Visit the website ➜ https://ltryan.com
Send an email ➜ contact@ltryan.com

* * *

C.R. GRAY goes by a lot of names, but the most know her as Charlie, a fantasy romance author who's finally diving into the genre she's always wanted to write in - mystery and thriller. She's from a small town outside of Pittsburgh and hopes she does her city justice in the books she works on!

If she isn't writing, she's chasing after her three adorable, but incredibly stubborn, puppers - who may or may not have some of the same bad behaviors as Tempest in the Maddie Castle series. When she isn't writing, she's watching Criminal Minds or binge reading a Kathy Reichs or Kelley Armstrong novel for the millionth time. (They never get old!)

Made in the USA
Middletown, DE
18 July 2025

10830088R00130